Kiss and Part

Kiss and Part

Short stories by

JO BAKER

JOAN BAKEWELL

JILL DAWSON

LUCY DURNEEN

CATHERINE FOX

MAGGIE GEE

MARIA McCANN

ELIZABETH SPELLER

SALLEY VICKERS

MARINA WARNER

Introduction by MARGARET DRABBLE

CANTERBURY
PRESS
Norwich

First published in 2019 by the Canterbury Press Norwich
Editorial office
3rd Floor, Invicta House
108–114 Golden Lane
London EC1Y OTG, UK
www.canterburypress.co.uk

Canterbury Press is an imprint of Hymns Ancient & Modern Ltd
(a registered charity)

Hymns Ancient & Modern® is a registered trademark of
Hymns Ancient & Modern Ltd
13A Hellesdon Park Road, Norwich,
Norfolk NR6 5DR, UK

Acknowledgement is made for permission to use extracts from
T. S. Eliot, 'Little Gidding', in Four Quartets, Faber & Faber, 1941.

Page xii portrait: British School, Michael Drayton, 1628, oil on
canvas, 54.5 × 41.0cm, DPG 430, Dulwich Picture Gallery, London.
Used by permission.

British Library Cataloguing in Publication data

A catalogue record for this book is available
from the British Library

978 1 78622 192 6

Typeset by Regent Typesetting
Printed and bound in Great Britain by
CPI Group (UK) Ltd

Contents

The Writers   vii

Preface   x

'Kiss and Part' by Michael Drayton   xiii

Introduction by Margaret Drabble   xv

Buck Moon   *Marina Warner*   1

'A Merrie Meeting'   *Salley Vickers*   17

The Incumbent   *Elizabeth Speller*   41

'Colossal Wreck'   *Maria McCann*   75

The Visitation   *Maggie Gee*   107

And the River Flows On   *Joan Bakewell*   117

The Creature   *Jill Dawson*   137

The Turn   *Catherine Fox*   153

The Fabric of Things   *Jo Baker*   187

'Place of Dreams'   *Lucy Durneen*   205

Afterword by Sarah Hosking   225

Acknowledgements of Photographs   229

The Writers

Dame Margaret Drabble (Lady Holroyd) is a novelist, biographer and critic. She has published nineteen novels, biographies and stories and a personal memoir. Her non-fiction includes *A Writer's Britain: Landscape and Literature* and the *Oxford Companion to English Literature*. Among many awards and honours, in 2011 she was awarded the Golden PEN Award by English PEN for 'A Lifetime's Distinguished Service to Literature'.

Marina Warner is Professor of English and Creative Writing at Birkbeck College, London. She is a writer of fiction and cultural history, especially on myths and fairy tales. Her books include *Stranger Magic: Charmed States and the Arabian Nights* (2012) and *Forms of Enchantment: Writing on Art and Artists* (2018). She gave the Reith Lectures in 1994, was made a DBE and awarded the Holberg Prize in 2015, and is president of the Royal Society of Literature. She has been a patron of Hosking Houses Trust since 2006.

Salley Vickers' début novel was *Miss Garnet's Angel* (2000). She has since written many other acclaimed novels including her latest, the *Sunday Times* best-seller *The Librarian* (2018). A well-known critic and reviewer and frequent guest of the BBC, she lectures widely on the connections between literature, psychology and religion. She was formerly a university teacher of English and a psychoanalyst. She now writes full-time.

Elizabeth Speller is a poet and writer of fiction and non-fiction. Her first novel *The Return of Captain Emmet* was published by Virago and was Orange Book of the Month in 2009. She is currently completing her fourth novel for Virago and, as a poet, was short-listed for the Forward Prize. Her non-fiction includes *Following Hadrian* and a family memoir. She teaches creative writing at Cambridge University Institute of Continuing Education.

Maria McCann is a historical novelist and short story writer based in Somerset. Her first book *As Meat Loves Salt* was published in 2001 and was an *Economist* Book of the Year; her second, *The Wilding*, was long-listed for the Orange Prize in 2010. Her most recent novel is *Ace, King, Knave* (2014).

Professor Maggie Gee OBE has published fifteen books including a collection of short stories, *The Blue*, and a writer's memoir, *My Animal Life*. Her novel *The White Family* was short-listed for two global prizes and she is translated into fourteen languages. In 2012 the University of St Andrews held an international conference about her work. Her thirteenth novel, a black comedy, *Blood* was one of the *Sunday Times'* Best Literary Novels of 2019.

Dame Joan Bakewell (Baroness Bakewell, a Labour peer) presented the ground-breaking television discussions *Late Night Line-Up* and *Heart of the Matter* in the 1960/1970s, and has worked consistently as a gifted broadcaster, author and journalist ever since. Most recently, she has presented seven television series of Sky Arts *Artist of the Year* and a BBC Radio 4 programme *We Need to Talk about Death*.

Jill Dawson is a novelist and poet who won the British Council Writing Fellowship at Amherst College in 1997. She has published over ten novels and edited several anthologies. She has been short-listed for both the Whitbread and

Orange prizes, won three Arts Council England awards, and won the East Anglian Book of the Year in 2016 for *The Crime Writer*.

Dr Catherine Fox is a senior lecturer in Creative Writing in the Department of English at Manchester Metropolitan University. She is the author of seven novels that explore the themes of the spiritual and the physical with insight and humour, as well as a memoir about her quest to become a judo black belt. Her novels include the Lindchester Chronicles: *Acts and Omissions*, *Unseen Things Above* and *Realms of Glory*.

Jo Baker is the author of seven novels, of which *A Country Road, A Tree* (2017) was short-listed for the James Tait Black and Walter Scott awards, and was a Guardian Book of the Year. Her novel *Longbourn* (2013) is in development as a feature film and her most recent novel is *The Body Lies* (2019). She has written short stories for Radio 4 and reviews for the *New York Times Book Review*.

Lucy Durneen is a newly established writer of fiction, non-fiction and poetry. Her first short story collection *Wild Gestures* was published in 2017 and won Best Short Story Collection at the Saboteur Awards that year. Her non-fiction has been adapted for broadcast on Radio 4, and her work was included in *Best American Essays 2017*. She teaches at Cambridge University Institute of Continuing Education.

Sarah Hosking is the founder/secretary of Hosking Houses Trust, and commissioned *Kiss and Part*. Her background is in the visual arts (art college in the 1960s), and she worked for some years in government arts subsidy. She then worked for the NHS as an interior and garden designer, and co-authored *Healing the Hospital Environment* (1999), which dealt with non-clinical aspects of in-patient care. She founded HHT on her retirement in 2000.

Preface

The Hosking Houses Trust is a small charity that exists to give older women writers of merit personal time, privacy and money with which to start, continue or complete innovative work on any subject whatsoever. It was inspired by Virginia Woolf's 1928 polemic *A Room of One's Own*, in which she famously said: 'A woman needs money and a room of her own if she is to write fiction.' To this we have added: 'if she is to write anything at all', and we have been operative since 2002.

We are based in Clifford Chambers, a village two miles from Stratford-upon-Avon with its theatres, libraries and cultural enterprises. We own the tiny eighteenth-century Church Cottage, which is adjacent to the church and its burial yard, and near the River Stour. This is where our incumbent writers stay, and to date we have hosted one hundred residents, including poets and performance artists, novelists and musicologists, historians of film and gardens, medicine and markets, social historians and journalists, playwrights and hat-makers. We are currently seeking to expand and welcome women artists who work with words and letters, and composers involved with sound and words.

We exist entirely on money raised by the charity and, over the years, have made over 3,000 applications and appeals resulting in many failures but enough successes on which to operate. Our constitution includes the sentence:

Trustees may do all such lawful things as are necessary for the achievement of their objects. This facilitation encouraged us in 2013 to commission and publish a study of our immediate area, the church and river and accumulation of humble houses and utilised land, including accounts of the two artists associated with the village, Tibor Reich the twentieth-century designer and Michael Drayton the Tudor poet. The resulting book *Round the Square and Up the Tower: Clifford Chambers, Warwickshire* was sufficiently successful for us then to commission this anthology of stories, once again centred in this small part of our village and again involving these two creative people, for no other reason than we want to echo

'I like this place, and willingly could waste my time in it.'
William Shakespeare, Celia, *As You Like It*, 2.6.93–4

Commissioned and conducted by the Hosking Houses Trust and edited by George Miller

Trustees of the Hosking Houses Trust
www.hoskinghouses.co.uk

Any similarity between the characters in the stories and people in the village of Clifford Chambers is entirely co-incidental.

This anthology has been supported by the Skoyles Bursaries Fund, donated by the Foyle Foundation.

British School, *Michael Drayton*, 1628, oil on canvas,
54.5 × 41.0cm, DPG 430, Dulwich Picture Gallery,
London.

Kiss and Part

Michael Drayton

Since there's no help, come let us kiss and part,
Nay, I have done: you get no more of me,
And I am glad, yea glad with all my heart,
That thus so cleanly, I myself can free.
Shake hands for ever, cancel all our vows;
And when we meet at any time again,
Be it not seen in either of our brows,
That we one jot of former love retain.
Now at the last gasp of love's latest breath,
When, his pulse failing, passion speechless lies,
When faith is kneeling by his bed of death,
And innocence is closing up his eyes,
Now, if thou would'st, when all have given him over,
From death to life, thou mightest him yet recover.

The 61st poem in a sonnet sequence entitled *Idea's Mirror*,
published in 1594.

Introduction

by Margaret Drabble

The Hosking Houses Trust and this ancillary volume of stories are both the creations of Sarah Hosking, who lives in a little house in a little village near the River Stour, surrounded by cats, dogs and hens and books and paintings and a garden. The Trust is a visionary project which offers older women a writing space, with financial support from bursaries. Hosking has taken literally Virginia Woolf's declaration: 'A woman must have money and a room of her own if she is to write fiction', and made it one of her missions. And she has not rested there. She has devoted more than two decades, and much energy, to fund-raising and administration. She has turned Clifford Chambers into a unique creative centre, welcoming women from all over the country. Many of them have found the experience of staying in Church Cottage inspirational, as these stories show.

Two years ago, Hosking conceived the idea of commissioning ten women writers, some of whom had spent residencies in Church Cottage and some of whom were especially selected, and asked each of them to write a short story prompted by Michael Drayton's celebrated sonnet 'Since there's no help, come let us kiss and part'.

Drayton's connection to the neighbourhood is explored in several of these tales, sometimes playfully – Salley Vickers in 'A Merrie Meeting' paints a lively and sardonic picture of Drayton's jealousy of his contemporary Shakespeare (ragbag plays, contempt for the poetics, theft of ideas and story lines, and a ridiculously successful Bohemian bear) and his one-sided relationship with his ageing muse, Lady Anne Rainsford of Clifford Manor, who no longer fits comfortably into her farthingale and avoids the low neckline of her cerise gown in favour of the more flattering sea-green. Maggie Gee chooses a contemporary setting (with an accompaniment of heavy and threatening traffic) for her ambitious rendering in sonnet form of a story of unrequited love, 'The Visitation', but plays close attention to Drayton's sonnet, weaving it skilfully into her own verse narrative. Shakespeare, Drayton and Ben Jonson hover behind most of these texts, occasionally interjecting comments in their own words.

Other artistic spirits inform the volume. Tibor Reich, the Hungarian-born textile designer who settled in Clifford Mill on the Stour in 1945 in flight from the Nazis, also provides a strong linking presence. One of Hosking's achievements has been to bring a whole neighbourhood, historical and actual, to new life, through community research and local initiatives, including her beautifully illustrated and eclectic 2013 volume *Around the Square and Up the Tower: Clifford Chambers, Warwickshire*, which tells the story of the church, the square and the village. She has given her commissioned novelists a good deal of suggestive recovered material to work with, and they have made good use of it. The narrator of Marina Warner's ecological ghost story about a wounded fawn, 'Buck Moon', is a scholar interested in modern design and Tibor Reich, whose vision, she says, 'defined the look of the Festival of Britain and other proud breakthroughs of happier times', and she evokes in some detail his workplace at the mill, his craft and his attachment to the river. Reich's mill and his 'daydreams' also appear in Jo Baker's 'The Fabric of Things', an erotic adventure of wakening sexuality featuring two very different young women, who swim, scandalously, naked in the river: 'Soup, your mother says; filthy, full of germs; but no, it's misted, fresh, cleaner than a bath.'

It's not surprising that several of these tales are ghost stories. Church Cottage adjoins the graveyard of St Helen's church, and for some of the fictitious writers-in-residence the graves are a little too close for comfort. The protagonist of Maria McCann's very funny 'Colossal Wreck' is a successful romantic novelist, the unfortunately named Jane Doe, who is in retreat and suffering from writer's block: inconveniently, she has a vivid horror of tombstones, cadavers, tumbling bones and death itself, and the peace and privacy of the cottage (into which Miss Hosking in person ushers her) prove a very mixed blessing. The cast of Elizabeth Speller's 'The Incumbent', with its satiric survey of the contemporary village life of B&B and Airbnb, includes a prosaic local resident, Margaret, the organiser of the village reading group, who does not like to think of 'the rows of skeletons that lie, albeit neatly, just beneath the surface'. Margaret, who is keen on neatness, finds the incumbent herself (tall, barefoot, androgynous and beautiful) unsettling; she is a mysterious figure, shape-shifting and miracle-performing. Jill Dawson's 'The Creature' offers a vivid portrait of a cottage interior with its log fire and red tiles and flowered curtains and comfortable couch, and a poignant evocation of the 'ramshackle churchyard' beyond. The recluse here is not a writer in Church Cottage, but a woman cat-sitting for a friend's Devil Cat, Georgio: into this quiet refuge comes another creature from beyond, a girl tapping on the door and window like the ghost of Catherine in *Wuthering Heights*, asking to be let in to tell her tales of woe.

Catherine Fox's spirited 'The Turn', although precisely located in June 2018 in St Helen's Church, Clifford Chambers, turns the tables on all the other narratives by providing us with a protagonist who, far from being a woman poet or woman novelist, is a camp and theatrical male middle-aged vicar called Christy, seized by career doubts and worrying memories, but well informed about Michael Drayton and the Royal Shakespeare Company; his stream of consciousness is a flow of intertextual reference. Fox has turned the cottage from writers' retreat into a bolthole visited by priests, bishops and their hangers-on, and gives an up-to-the-minute view of contemporary faith, doubt and church-going, washed down by champagne.

Lucy Durneen, in 'Place of Dreams', launches us far into the future, but this too is a kind of ghost story, in which Miranda, aka R578, on her research ship in space, seeks echoes from the distant past. The background texts here are *The Tempest*, *Romeo and Juliet*, and Drayton's sonnet, as Miranda tries to understand the lost human concepts of poetry, of metaphor, of irony, of happiness, of sadness, of love itself. Her vision of Drayton is more benign than that of Salley Vickers, and she sees him sitting at a desk in the Manor, writing Anne, over and over. 'Anne, *Anne*.' He is 'quieter, will be spoken of less' than Shakespeare, and he is 'unaware that he can be seen from a research ship orbiting above him in another dimension'.

Joan Bakewell's 'And the River Flows On' is a bravura account of the funeral at St Helen's Church of a celebrated actor, seen largely through the eyes of Liza, his long-divorced ex-wife. The congregation is packed with extended family and worthies from the RSC and the National Theatre, and the service embraces *Jerusalem*, T. S. Eliot, and The Kinks. It is a celebration of Englishness and rural England and lost remembered love. The river here plays its part too, running like a thread as it does through so many of the stories, and the mood is of reconciliation. Liza is revisiting the scenes of former happiness, and of a parting recalled with valediction and without bitterness.

These ten stories, all by gifted writers, add up to more than the sum of their parts. Together, different though they are in tone and treatment, they summon up the spirit of place, the spirit that Sarah Hosking has done so much to foster. This diverse anthology springs directly from a very particular place, from one tiny village in middle England, from which the ripples spread outwards to reach us all. It is a unique enterprise, with some of the magic of a mid-summer night's dream. The stories speak eloquently for her vision and are a tribute to the success of her imaginative, brave and original twenty-year-old enterprise.

Margaret Drabble
September 2018

Buck Moon

by Marina Warner

'I've been working in Planning here for more than thirty years now and there hasn't been any let-up for a single moment since I started. You might think a place like this – Stratford-upon-Avon, no less – has no need for yet more drama but I'm telling you, you couldn't be more wrong. There might've once been the need to wall-in deer forests against poachers – our own Will was caught red-handed – and the Reformers might've come along and wiped the gorgeous medieval stories painted on the walls of the Guild Church (the father of our local hero was closely involved, remember, his signature is on the invoice for the white-wash and brushes that did the deed), but troubles still come not single spies. The theatre keeps being remodelled and breaking out into new venues, all strenuously contested by the good burghers of our town, who want their peace and quiet and don't appreciate cars and coaches revving up at 11 p.m. after a performance of some blood-soaked Jacobean revenge tragedy.'

You could tell that Gill Plover, Chief of Planning, had been a stage-struck child, a lifelong regular in last-minute seats, with her deep voice and her ironic flourishes: there was more than a touch of the Judi Dench about her.

I tried to bring her back to the reason for our meeting: 'And Two Token Beat?'

But on she went: 'They far prefer crowds who spend, spend, spend on ice creams and souvenirs, who wander about watching the swans on the river and go home early. In my time, I've seen fires and floods, if not famine, and the wild schemes that follow, backed up by even wilder insurance claims. Applications to convert a medieval barn where Anne Hathaway's third cousins once farmed into an aromatherapy clinic – we approved it. I've had petitions landing on my desk – or rather sailing onto my screen – for children's zoos of animals mentioned by the Bard … Hyrcanian tigers … a wilderness of monkeys … marmosets … venom toads, newts and fillets of a fenny snake or two. You couldn't count on the fingers of both hands the numbers of proposals that land here for Shakespeare theme parks – storm-tossed rides on ships and thunderstorms on blasted heaths, Doll Tearsheet's molly house and haunted Glamis Castle – you get the picture.

'Feelings run very high, you know, on all sides. In my job, you have to listen and listen some more and then decide. It isn't easy. I think they could use some of us in Brussels, as we've had years of practice at subtle adjudication and balancing negotiations. Not like that lot. Now here's the thing …'

I was now frowning at her, mildly, in an attempt to speed the spate towards the subject I was hoping to write about. The editors of a collection of essays on Place and Belonging were aiming to raise funds for an NGO of ecological activists working with and for refugees, and we contributors had been asked to explore ways you could come to feel at home somewhere different from the place where you were born or grew up. I'd always been curious about Tibor Reich. A Hungarian textile designer who'd settled in the heart of the Cotswolds and run his company from a disused mill on the Stour near Stratford and then become a great British success, he seemed a promising subject for the book. Born in 1916, he'd got out of Hungary in the thirties, just in time. The family were already in textiles in Budapest and they'd been able to come to this country without too many objections. That was the way it was, then, with refugees from Europe.

Modern design is an interest of mine (I collected G-plan furniture till it became too pricey). But I didn't have much hope that such a book would sell. You never know, though, maybe someone would notice, and opinions might ... well, change.

Very soon, when Reich was still only in his thirties, he was pulling in commissions from all sides: the new Elizabethan age had its sights on progress, modernity, the future, and his fabrics changed the national environment. He brought with him that revolutionary Russian, Eastern European aesthetic sense for line and colour, abstraction and geometry: a Bauhaus approach to good vernacular design for the people. His vision defined the look of the Festival of Britain and other proud breakthroughs of happier times, when the QE2 was launched and Concorde built by the French and British working in partnership. His shapes had dash and élan; allusions to anything figurative were uncompromisingly condensed and abstracted. He cut all ties with the fusty, musty past, aspidistras and antimacassar interiors, chintz florals, brocade and braid, tassels and bows, lace and net. You couldn't even think of making a pelmet from a Tibor Reich fabric or upholstering a button-back Victorian armchair. Tibor Ltd was filled with optimism of the will: its creator even brought out a collection called 'Atomic'. In fourteen colourways, it exulted in the structure of the atom: moiré and shimmery, like reflections of moving water on a ceiling – magenta, sky, lime. The designs radiated a dark halo, as clouds do when backlit in a thundery sky under a bright moon.

I tried to coax the planning officer back to my purpose. 'And the Two Token Beat case?' I repeated. 'I hear it was unusual.'

'Yes, indeed it was. Quite the weirdest thing I have ever known,' she replied, with a theatrical slowing of her speech. 'The application was for a model steam railway through the meadows along the Stour, a loop that would rake in the moolah from day trippers. The council rather favoured it. Such an attraction would keep earning in winter, always a slack time. It'd be picturesque – authentic heritage, the puff-puffs, the whistle. The River Dart has one, and it's a reliable money-spinner.' She shook her head and chuckled. 'But the development plans were stopped, as you know. And the manner of it! Greater crested newts would have been less of a surprise.'

She tapped a box file on her desk. 'You can have a look. It's all here.'

* * *

Two Tokens Beat is the fishermen's name for a third-of-a-mile stretch of the River Stour that runs along the northern edge of a hamlet, Clifford Chambers; a hidden, languid stream of brown satin-dark water, shallow and, where a sunbeam strikes through it, translucent like maple syrup or those cakes of soap – what was their name? Pear's, that's it. I had been out on the river in a small boat, to reconnoitre the site of Tibor Ltd, and was surprised by the pastoral, unearthly seclusion of that Warwickshire back-water: the current pulses along past muddy paddling places and crooked moorings for small craft like the one I'd been lent, and I had to manoeuvre round flood-splintered trunks sprouting new shoots and push through low-hanging alder and willow. Shaggy gardens ran down to the banks from scattered houses, which are safely set back in case of floods: the river can swell all of a sudden. It was late August, and there were lily pads in flower: their big gold cups smell of old wine, so locals call them 'brandy bottles'. Spikes of water parsnip and thistly rushes caught at the boat, and the meadows on both sides were fringed with undisturbed clumps of mint and loosestrife and Herb Robert.

Though the water was molasses brown, I could see through it to the muddy bottom, where lots of fish hung like ornaments: the Beat's a favourite with anglers. It's no wonder Shakespeare, that Warwickshire lad, had such an ear for English music in the words for flora and fauna: his county's a natural nature reserve. Chub, roach, gudgeon, pike, perch, minnow, tench, barbel, bream, dace, stone loach, bullhead, bleak and rudd: the stream teems with fish which sound like a strong charm Puck might have made up.

The website of the Environment Agency reported – and this turned out to be a crucial part of the story I was to discover – that a recent survey showed a thriving population of rabbits, voles and shrews, stoats and weasels, some snakes, various species of newts, and a few badgers, many escaped mink (a pest). But no longer any otters, or beavers. Also, several species of deer had been sighted – the littlest ones are dainty muntjacs, the largest those candelabra-antlered roebuck, who begin to grow their racks again when the fullest of the full harvest moons sails up the pale night sky in July.

As the afternoon drew on and I started rowing back, a mist began to roll in softly over the water meadows; the light turned eerie.

Tibor Reich used to work on the first floor of the mill, by the window overlooking the cascade foaming into the race below; the water, forced through a narrow gap, loses all its silky calm as it hurtles down and boils up again below.

When he moved in, he found the big wooden wheel was still in working order; the machinery a marvel of early industrial engineering, but Reich stuck some logs into the spokes to hold it fast, as the noise was overpowering. He set up his work table by the window, in a room over the loft where the grain was stored; it was a small enclave, next to the darkroom where he developed the studies he made towards his designs. This studio space was set apart from the main office where the design team worked open-plan, itself a pioneering concept in the fifties. The family lived in the other wing on the first floor, as far away as possible from the rush and roar of the weir.

Living as it were over the shop, Tibor would often stay at his table drawing and painting into the small hours. On most days in the studio, even in winter, the light bouncing off the water played on the low ceiling in blobs and loops; on the brightest summer days, these liquid refractions danced on the drawing paper under his hand. He was inspired by the patterns the water made – this was nature drawing of her own accord, he would say. He set up mirror panels here and there to enhance the effect, for the play of light revealed to him the structure of the universe, he maintained, the inner dynamics of phenomena, and made it possible to grasp something of their wonder. Hence the Atomic series: atoms were visible if you knew how to look.

He would take his Leica and walk to the river above the weir, where he kept a boat – an old wooden tub – and he'd go out at different times of day with a local lad, Robin Farrell, who helped in the studio and would row him upstream while Tibor took photographs of the dance of light on the water and the foliage. With that make of camera and its precision lens, he could capture nature's drawings, he'd say, in the weeds and wild flowers and grasses in the meadows and on the banks, in the blades of the reeds, the woolly bolsters of the bulrushes, the cow parsley umbels and the knubbled ears of escaped barley and wheat. Later, with Robin's help, he'd begin developing the film and printing out the images, and in the baths of developing fluid, the forms and patterns materialised.

It so happened that in one or two of the pictures, a pair of eyes could be seen shining from the thatch of grasses and wild flowers: Tibor's human eyes had not picked up a dormouse hiding in the undergrowth or a vole peeping out from a runnel in the soft muddy riverbank, but the lens on his camera had. 'My work serves the white heat of technology, absolutely,' he would say, 'but my handbook is nature herself.'

***

The file I opened included a document written by hand, neat and clear, on headed paper from Tibor Ltd, The Old Mill, Clifford Chambers. The heading was underlined: 'TR, May 14, 1964: A private memoir. Not to be read until 20 years after my death.'

Reich died on 3 February 1996 so, I realised with a start, the file had only recently been made available.

The planning officer's eyes widened with glee and nodded me towards the document. 'There you have it. Enjoy!'

I began reading:

For a long while I would contemplate the reflections of the water on my ceiling and on my drawing board and lose myself in the images beamed from the mirrors I had set up at angles in my studio to catch the life of the river in their depths. I'd recently also built a rostrum camera to make images of the kinetic parade flung on to my walls by the river below. When I joined Robin in the darkroom to wait for the pictures to emerge from the chemicals, he would often look rapt, as if in a dream, and his state communicated itself to me and I would fancy I could hear a voice, or sometimes voices, stirring in the patterns the light made, something like the mewing of a kitten or the more liquid song of a blackbird. I would look closer, my nostrils pricking at the smell of the solvents, and I would glimpse, but so fleetingly I couldn't be sure I had seen anything at all, a shadow of a tangle of thick brown hair over the rest of the face, a face I couldn't make out, not exactly.

Robin was jubilant when he found creatures emerging in the pictures. Look, he would say, Look, sir, at that shadow – that's one of them deer. She – it's a doe – was there almost beside you, concealed in that clump, could have heard her breathing. Look closely and you can see where the fur blends with the flicker of light in that tangle of growth.

When Robin first came and asked if he could help around Tibor Ltd, he was a skinny lad with a shock of curls and freckles; his left eye had a fleck in the hazel iris where he'd pierced it on a branch one day, and this gave him a mismatched look; impish when he smiled, dreamy when he was still. He had the touch: he could heal any hurt thing and could have charmed his own kind if he'd wanted, I'm sure, but he seemed happier with animals than with people. Or at least than with any of the girls. There were many who hoped to catch his attention, but he seemed not to notice.

I took him on. He gave us all a sense of depths stirring, and I was pleased how he could turn his hand to anything he tried, especially working in the dark room. Robin exulted in the visitations, as he called them, when he'd find a creature in the mottling of weeds and water, and he'd take the prints and blow up details of the photographs far larger than I asked, to show me what he'd spotted with that sixth sense of his. The countryside around and the banks of the rivers were his hunting grounds, though hunting isn't the *mot juste*, since Robin raged against the sport in every form. If he saw a pair of antlers as a trophy in a pub, he'd not go in. He was one of those people who, ever since their infancy, love rescuing creatures; he would bring back to his bedroom an unfortunate animal from a poacher's trap, a fallen nestling, a swallow that had hurtled into a glass pane and dropped, one wing broken, and he would nurse the creature back to life with twig or matchstick splints, and drip-feed it from his old school fountain pen plunger. He once realised, from distant scuffling high up inside a chimney in a neighbours' house, that a nest had been dislodged and fallen halfway down, and he clambered up – he was a lithe nipper – and came back down cradling against his chest a soft ball of fluff with two huge golden eyes. They renamed their house Owlet in honour of his rescue and, in my case, I called a collection – 'Baker's Daughter'. I should add (though I do not wish to boast), it is considered one of *the* classics of postwar design and was used when the Stratford Memorial Theatre was renovated in the 1950s.

This was a time when I realised many of my most seminal works: the Colotomic fabrics within the Atomic series, for example. Ideas poured out of me. I felt plugged in to the mystery of things, that I was passing through the skin of the visible world of manifest matter into its essence. This is what I have endeavoured again and again to capture in my designs: the true qualities of organic phenomena.

Robin urged me on in these efforts, and there was something uncanny about him; we all felt he was tuned to something beyond our pitch of hearing. But the first time we had forewarning of what was to happen was when, one afternoon, he leapt up all of a sudden, shot down the steps and flew out of the back door of the mill towards the river. One or two of the team rose to follow him, and when they reached him, found him dazed, staring into the foam at the bottom of the weir. He only said, composing himself, I thought I saw…

What? What did you see? we asked him. He looked so startled, we were concerned for him.

He hesitated, then said, Maybe a trick of the light. An otter? Maybe a beaver?

The lads laughed. They said, no beavers here, not since a long while. Nor otters neither.

Yes, Robin answered. Of course not. When I reached the spot, I … he stopped. There was nothing there.

His senses really were preternaturally acute, as we were to find out all too clearly.

It was a hot summer. July baked the fields and the huge moon drifted so close to earth that at midnight you could see clear as day. It was during that time that Robin began talking to me, confiding. I fear I was a bit impatient as I wanted him to get on with his work – and to let me be so I could get on with mine.

I regret now that I did not listen more carefully, since what was to take place was so mysterious and ultimately so grave.

He told me: I'd been hearing cries from the meadows along the river for ever so long, they'd been growing more and more intense, calling to me. I'd ask the others on the benches, Can you hear that? They never could. But it sounds as if it's calling me, I'd tell them, and they'd just laugh, Yes, likely to be a mating call. They'd roll their eyes at him saucily, Robin told me, looking puzzled with those different coloured eyes of his.

One night, he went on, the yelps and mewings he thought must be coming from inside his head became even closer and louder and he couldn't let it go, so he followed them to the river once again, and on this occasion, there was a doe on the rim of weir just upstream from the mill.

He told me, when she saw me, she didn't bound away, which was really strange. She kept there, stood on the dam, making that sound of weeping, dipping her head and stamping. As I got near – to my amazement not putting her to flight – I saw that a scrap of a fawn was fallen in the race: her child, who'd been swept downstream and through the gap in the weir into a thick messy reef of last winter's weeds and leaves, broken branches, mud and stones. As he struggled to get free (I was soon to find out it was a male, Robin explained), the little creature was getting his fragile legs ever more caught up in the tangle of debris where the water churned below the cascade, and the mother's moans became more and more piercing, for she couldn't reach him. The fawn was floundering, round eyes starting out of his head, and I could see his small reserves of strength were giving out. From the upper stream, it's not easy to reach the lower stretch, as you know (Robin said to me), but I jumped down the bank and waded in and swam over – the water was very cold and the churn heavy – but I managed to free the delicate creature's limbs one by one from the tangle of brush and felt the trembling, barely warm body against mine as I got us both to the shallow water away from the current and waded out. The doe came leaping to us. One of her child's legs hung useless, but I held him to nuzzle his mother and drink. Then I set him down and he faltered, but then stood shakily on his three good legs, and she led us away into the woods, and it seemed to me she was turning her head to check not only that the little one was still at her flank, for she could sense him limping beside her, but that I was still there.

Deep in the woods, she stopped in a small clearing, well hidden from anyone but the most determined hunter, and I did what I could to mend the leg of her child – the twig-like left foreleg had snapped just above the tiny hoof, which was pointed and cloven like a reed pen, as delicate as porcelain. I made a splint and tied it with a piece of fabric I tore from my shirt.

It is hard to explain, said Robin, how much love I felt for the pair of them, from that moment.

He also told me, we could communicate as if we spoke each other's language, I swear it. I still heard her cries in my head as I had before, when her voice sounded in the visitations I found in your photographs. Those trysts I kept with her were very sweet. Her boy grew strong, though he listed to one side a little, the left foreleg retaining some memory of its break. The long summer evenings that year gave us extraordinary moments together, when she would seem to me to be a real woman. I feared that my arms might close on air, but no, she was firm and warm and as if vitally charged, electric. We made a pledge ... I would never speak of her or reveal her existence to anyone as that could place her in jeopardy from ... those who'd violate her ... shoot her, as her mate had been hunted down and shot, his magnificent rack taken for a trophy for some townie consortium's fancy home ... Robin's queer unmatched eyes flamed with rage as he was telling me all this.

She was my own white hind, he said, my very own enchanted princess.

Another time he said, it hurts me to see how much she wants to remain in her world and for me to stay in hers. She's afraid that our ... love ... will part her from her own kind. I try to reassure her that her secret – this double life of ours – is safe with me, that I'll always care for her and for her fawn. But she won't be comforted. She knows – and here Robin was very grave – and I know what she fears is true, that we must kiss and part.

This is why I am telling you (said Robin). I've become afraid. If we don't, don't part, I know I'll soon be disappearing from this world. I'll be taken to live with her in hers for ever.

Tibor's account continued:

I was very disturbed, naturally. In many ways. But I told Robin that I had heard about such things and knew the danger of walking between worlds, as my nurse used to call it when I was a child, and she remembered stories from our country traditions. I made him promise to accept the inevitable: he must break with this fantasy.

She has promised me, said Robin. If you are ever in need, call on me, and I'll rally my friends around and move all our combined powers to help you.

One fateful evening, she was coming down to the water with her fawn, and a local farmer out on the river with his lad to catch something for his family supper caught sight of her. When the bullet from his shotgun grazed her flank, Robin heard her cry and flung himself out of the mill once again to find her.

Doubtless, with his healing gift, he tended the wound, and then found himself on the other side again.

If you are ever in need, call on me: that is what she promised, he told me. I will rally my friends around and move all our combined powers to help you.

When Robin took off for the meadows, we waited a while for him to come back. But when no news came, we had to call the police. The search went on for days. A team dragged the river, we all volunteered and fanned out across the meadows. Not a trace. His body was never found.

In the mill and in the village, we always hoped he had upped sticks and quit for a new life somewhere else. But in my heart of hearts, I know what happened. To this day I sometimes think I hear his voice by the meadows or even in the play of light and shade in the images I make.

And there, Tibor's story stopped abruptly.

* * *

The folder contained several more documents. A number of villagers had submitted that Two Token Beat was so called because an ancient piece of local lore held that the riverbank was haunted in the long summer twilights by a wailing figure who would be placated only if you threw two silver coins in the stream. 'I don't believe in such things,' one witness wrote, 'but plenty do, you know.' Another simply declared, 'The place is jinxed, everyone knows it.'

The last document in the folder about the planning application for the model steam train was a CD, labelled 'Infrared photographs, May 2012–September 2014'. I slotted it into my laptop and opened the files: twenty-four images that chronicled the sightings of beavers building a dam in a bend of the stream below the weir, the muck of branches and stones caught there providing them with a perfect footing for their own construction.

The last known beaver in the archipelago of the British Isles was shot in Scotland in 1526, and this couple, which had appeared and made their home in Clifford Chambers, were the first to appear in the river system of the county of Warwickshire for four hundred years.

The CD included some notes, reporting that naturalists from the University of Exeter had begun reintroducing beavers into the mainland of the British Isles in 2011; the first pair was released into the River Otter in Devon, and began quickly to build a lodge and hollow out a labyrinthine system in the banks, damming the stream to trap food and keep out predators. The species had been travelling eastwards and had reached the Avon, and two of them were now busily damming the Stour as it flows past Clifford Chambers, where there was plenty of woodland to glean for their work.

Ecological activists were ecstatic. Instagram went wild with photos taken by nature lovers equipped with infrared cameras, and in short order the dam and their architects had to be secured behind electric defences against ... animal paparazzi, pirates and poachers.

Coincidentally, the arrival of the beavers dealt a clean blow to any speculator's plan to develop the river and its banks. New housing, model railways on the Stour? Not a chance, on the stretch of water where the wonderful creatures had appeared and taken up occupancy, from the weir and the mill where Tibor Reich's headquarters stood to the other, eastern end and the beginning of the woods.

When I returned the folder to the planning officer, she looked at me intently: 'Well, what do you reckon?'

'Stroke of luck, I'd say, those beavers turning up.' I didn't feel like saying more. I needed time to think about what I'd found.

'Yes,' she said, 'and would you know, there are still sightings in these parts of a stag ... a magnificent great buck. Surprising, you see. And here's the thing. He still has quite a limp.'

Kiss and Part

'A Merrie Meeting'

by Salley Vickers

'Shakespear Drayton and Ben Jhonson (sic) had a merrie meeting and it seems drank too hard for Shakespear died of a feavour there contracted.'

> *Entry in the diary of John Ward, vicar of*
> *Stratford-upon-Avon, 1662–81*

One early spring evening two men sat talking over tankards of ale in a Stratford inn called the King's House.

'As I see it,' the graver-looking of the two remarked, 'the true poetics is dead and gone. Those of us who really know how to scan a line are considered old hat, all washed up, past it.' He sipped his beer with the gloomy pleasure of one who enjoys a prophetic gift for bad news.

His companion, shorter, dumpier and with a merry, rosy countenance, altogether less romantic than his comrade's pallid complexion, evidently possessed a more sanguine nature.

'You know, Michael, I doubt that,' he reassured. 'It stands to reason that new talent will always be coming along and threatening to shove us old hands aside. But you and I can still hold a reader, or in my case capture an audience, well enough.'

'You, maybe,' his fellow drinker said. 'But all of that, ah –' He waved a parchment-coloured, long-nailed hand contemptuously in the direction of the other drinkers in the inn, 'that crowd-pleasing matters less to you now. You are already a made man with your plays. But we poets ...'

The sentence petered out with the unspoken suggestion that a poet's was altogether a finer sensibility than that of a humdrum dramatist and therefore more susceptible to the fickle fads of an undiscerning public.

His companion was not by nature touchy. Indeed, an analyst of human nature might have surmised that this trait – his unwillingness to take offence – was an ingredient in his unusual professional success. He was aware that although his companion's work was admired by a small, select coterie, it had failed where he had most sought to find success, the very area where he himself had made it. Impossible for the poet not to resent this and very probable, too, that he comforted himself with a conviction that his more fortunate colleague's popularity was undeserved.

The rosy-faced dramatist sighed inwardly. His several vociferous critics were of much the same opinion as the poet. There were days when he himself was not at all sure that his reputation was merited, which did not mean that he did not greatly relish it.

Hoping to soothe a ragged nerve, he enquired, 'What are you engaged on at present, Michael?'

This was a mistake. Accustomed to writing plays at a pace to fit a tight commercial schedule, he had overlooked his friend's more leisurely habits of composition.

The poet frowned. 'I am still working on my long pastoral piece.'

The other nodded. 'Yes, I read it when you brought out part a few years back. Most –' He hunted for a word that would flatter and not stray too far from the truth, which was that he found the other's lengthy pastoral discourse frankly tedious. 'Accomplished,' he finally settled on. The other inclined his head slightly in acknowledgement. 'It's a style I could never manage myself,' the dramatist continued. Seeing too late an ambiguity in this compliment, he swiftly added, 'Anything else in the pipeline?'

His companion uneasily shifted his lean buttocks on the wooden bench. 'I have a sonnet brewing, but one cannot rush the muse.'

His fellow artist who, as well as several best-selling narrative poems, had knocked off over a hundred sonnets in his day alongside his plays, nodded agreement. 'The usual theme, I suppose?'

This too was a mistake. 'When you say "usual"? I hope I always present my subjects in an original light.'

His companion again nodded equably. 'But of course. Love has as many lights as the play of sun.' And as many shades and shadows, he thought. Seeking to shift the conversation from the fraught subject of their respective careers, he gestured, 'Fine painting that is.'

The tall poet, who was a little short-sighted, squinted at some figures depicted on the wall opposite. 'Who is it?'

'Old Tobit and his wife.' Then answering a passing look of puzzlement, 'the Biblical book, you know. The angel's that one there.' He pointed at a shadowy shape lurking behind a drape in another section of the painting. 'Tobias and the Angel. A pretty yarn. You know, I haven't done an angel – fairies, ghosts, goddesses, even a god or two off stage, but no angels. It's a gap I might fill some day.'

His companion compressed his full, somewhat feminine lips. He was familiar with this magpie habit of his fellow writer. 'A snapper-up of unconsidered trifles,' Ben Jonson had called him once, as an insult and to his face. But, by Our Lady, rather than taking offence the man had only gone and put the very phrase, word for word, in one of his tinsel romances. A particularly annoying fantasy in which a bear had appeared on stage for no better reason than that rascal Burbage had got hold of a tame bear cheap and had bet his dramatist, over a pint, that he couldn't write it into the next production. The kind of ridiculous jape that those two enjoyed and which only confirmed their lack of the true artistic sensibility. And as if that were not enough, adding insult to injury, the rag-bag of a play had made a nonsense of the poetics. Vast gaps of time were breezed over with no apology and such an ignorant grasp of basic geography, giving Bohemia a coastline, that both he and Jonson had expected the nonsense to be howled off stage.

And yet it was these very gimcrack tricks that had seemed to feed the play's popularity and fuelled its author's already roaring success. The bear, far from making the company a laughing stock, was considered a triumph.

'Are you likely to be staying here long?' Drayton asked, hoping to hear that this was just another flying visit.

'That depends,' his colleague replied. 'I can afford to take a break and I have a mind to reacquaint myself with the countryside of my childhood.'

* * *

Michael Drayton, inwardly cursing, crossed the Avon by the bridge at Lucy's Mill. The spring evenings were lightening and the sky above still held out a Madonna blue against which the newly arrived swallows made graceful ellipses. He stood on the bridge as a pair of the scimitar-winged birds swept the face of the water in pursuit of flies. A dabchick paddled into view and pecked voraciously at some floating weed. Nature is ruthless, Drayton thought to himself. Unguardedly so, without any milk-and-water Christian apology.

The return of Will Shakespeare had rekindled an anger that had never been snuffed out. They were of an age, give or take a couple of years, and came from similar backgrounds.

Modest country backgrounds. He was if anything the more cultivated of the two, for hadn't he served as page in Sir Henry Goodier's household where he had met his beloved Anne? There had been no reason to suppose that their careers would not match, or at least march side by side. But where the Stratford boy had gone from obscurity to renown, his own progress had been – what would he say? – confined. It was not that he had not attempted to bring his talents to greater public notice. For a time had had high hopes of a career as a dramatist. But the Children of the King's Revels, the company at Whitehall that he had joined in an attempt to eclipse or at least rival Burbage's crew, had failed, and dismally. He had grown to dislike the drama with its crude display of mincing boys in female attire, its rollicking madcap clowns and its vainglorious, trumpeting, puffed-up heroes.

Above his head a canopy of knotted willows swayed slightly, the fine, spear-like leaves making dancing patterns on the sluggish water. A vision of that wretched girl rose unbidden to his inner eye. God's bodikins, he himself had told Shakespeare of the love-sick chit who had been found pregnant and floating half-submerged, waterweed entangled in her hair, by the bridge in this very spot. Even as he recounted the sad tale of the wench, he had witnessed a fiendish light kindle in those mild-seeming hazel eyes and had recognised, too late, that this piece of local gossip was destined to appear in one of the owner of the eyes' melodramas. And so it had, to sickening acclaim, in that mishmash of the old chestnut *Amleth*, a tale that had already been done to death, surely, by Kidd. The man was never original; another reason to despise his work. What was it in the fellow that enabled him to spin cast-off snippets and oddments into seeming gold?

And now, God's teeth, he had come back to Stratford,

where, although he had claimed some five years back he had wanted to settle he had in fact seldom ventured, to his vulgar new house and his malt investments, to gloat over his assets made through his favour with the king. The king – here an observer might have wondered if Drayton were perhaps grinding his teeth – who had scorned his own efforts at preferment and chosen his rival's company at the Globe to bear the royal imprimatur. The King's Men had performed God knows how many times at his majesty's behest, and at Whitehall too.

Granted the fellow was a Stratford native-born; but his presence felt to Drayton like a rude intrusion. He had become accustomed to 'recreating' himself – as he liked poetically to put it – with his annual visits to the Rainsfords, living in great elegance while absorbing the healing air of the countryside (and a full belly of delicious food besides). He had come to look upon Stratford and its environs as his own rightful domain.

Drayton walked back through the water meadows to the outlying hamlet where he was staying. Still brooding darkly, he was oblivious to the way that his fine new leather boots, a present from his hostess, were getting thoroughly drenched. Sir Henry and Lady Anne lived in the Manor House at Clifford, where for years he had been their honoured guest. They were, Lady Anne especially, tact itself, but his own sensitivity made it impossible to forget his position. Unlike Shakespeare, who had made a tidy fortune and had invested richly in land and property, Drayton was a poor man, supported by the Rainsfords' patronage. They would expect him to acquaint them with the famous playwright once they got wind of the fact that he was back in town.

Clifford Manor, a fine, roomy, timbered building, and its extensive gardens, lay within a bend of the River Stour, a livelier river than the stately Avon. Close by stood the mill, which served the manor and its tenants. Approaching the little humpbacked bridge by the mill, Drayton saw a figure. Old Joan, Clifford's so-called 'wise woman', who lived hugger-mugger with her sisters, two other crones, in a tumbledown hovel nearby.

Drayton was fastidious and the woman with her scrawny limbs and balding, scurvy scalp was repellent to him. He would have passed on, but she hailed him.

'Master Poet!' Her face with its bristled chin was lifted obnoxiously close to his own.

'Mother?' The hag appeared to be toothless and her breath was vile.

'You have come from the town.'

It was a statement rather than a question. 'What is that to you, Mother?'

'You're out of temper, Master Poet.' Her breath stank foully and her rasping voice offended Drayton's sensitive ear. He made to step past her pulling aside his cloak as if to avoid contagion. 'Well, well, go your way to your fine friends. You may have need of Old Joan yet.'

Something in her tone delayed him. 'I doubt that, Mother. What need in the wide world would I have of you?'

'With your precious Lady Anne to nurse your fine fancies, you mean? Ah, but can your pretty pet look into the seeds of time as Old Joan can?'

Drayton shrugged and walked off. Really, he couldn't think why the Rainsfords didn't turn the disgusting old body out of her hovel. The tenants were required to keep their properties in order and the reed roof of the shack in which she and her sisters lived was almost as bare as Old Joan's scalp. The place must be fit for nothing but frogs and –

As this thought crystallised in his mind, a large toad flopped out of the grassy bank landing full in his path. It stared at him with two gleaming and, to Drayton's mind, malice-laden eyes.

Drayton had a horror of all such creatures, and besides was superstitious. The strange conjunction of the subject of his rumination and the toad's appearance made him uneasy. He would have liked to crush the toad but the thought of the crunching little bones and toad slime beneath the sole of his boot sickened him. He stepped over the creature and quickened his pace towards the manor house.

Entering the great hall, he was met by the soothing scent of lavender and clove from the bowls of dried flowers and spices with which Anne filled the house. They mingled with the savoury smells of the evening meal cooking. He sniffed. Roasted pork. His favourite.

A shaft of evening sunlight through the latticed window illuminated the richly patterned carpet, brought by some Rainsford ancestor from Persia. Drayton felt the tension in his body relax; if it was not his house it was where he was at home. He was safe here, with his Anne.

* * *

Lady Anne Rainsford was being dressed by her maid for dinner. It had been a dull day, and promised to be a dull evening. Her husband Henry was away seeing to some business and there was only the parson, who was turning senile and whose conversation tended to lapse into pig Latin, and a dull local couple to dilute the presence of Michael that evening.

She sighed as her maid, Susan, fastened her into her farthingale.

'Am I pinching, my Lady?'

'The whalebone must have shrunk.'

'I shall see what adjustments can be made, my Lady.'

Susan clamped tight the fastenings, so that Lady Anne's belly bulged over the low waist of the boned farthingale, and strapped on the stomacher. The truth is the old bag had grown stout and was too vain to admit it. 'Your peach silk for this evening, my Lady?'

'Not the peach, Susan, the sea-green with the slashed sleeves.'

'Very good, my Lady. The colour brings out the grey of your eyes.'

She must have noticed, Susan speculated, how these days the cerise showed off too much of her scraggy neckline. With luck it would be passed on to her with a typical pretence of generosity. Susan fitted on the heavy silk gown, cut in the French fashion, adjusted the girdle to cover what the stomacher failed to hide and began to dress her mistress's hair.

Lady Anne had for some time dyed her once fair hair yellow with a concoction of cumin, saffron and celandine. But it was thinning badly and these days she favoured a snood, well padded out with hair bought from one of the many young women who sold their own plentiful locks to those who, through age or disease, were losing theirs.

Once the hair was suitably dressed, Susan powdered her mistress's face and neck with the white ceruse which produced the fashionable pallor set by the example of the late Queen. Then she eased her mistress's feet into the velvet slippers she had lately taken to wearing for greater comfort.

'These are tight. It is too bad, Susan. You must send them back to John shoemaker.'

'Very good, my lady.' It was only that her feet had swelled with age. A good chance she would get the cast-off slippers too.

* * *

Picking a stray flea from her cheek, the Lady Anne descended the great stairs to the oak-panelled dining hall where the poet, Sir Nathaniel the parson and Sir James and Lady Margaret Stanford awaited her. The dementing Sir Nathaniel, tedious Sir James and swarthy, gossipy Lady Margaret were far from ideal company but they would at least save her from an evening's tête-à-tête with Michael.

'Oh dear,' she thought. 'Michael. What *am* I to do with him?'

Not for the first time she was regretting the youthful impulse – soon after her marriage to Sir Henry and to compensate for it – to invite her admirer to stay at the manor, an invitation that she had never found a polite way to rescind. Her mind rarely reverted to her younger days, when the poet had been her tutor and she had looked up to him and admired his seeming sophistication and his romantic poeticising. An occasion when she had spotted a stray button fall from his doublet and had slyly slipped it into the recess of her wide sleeve returned unbidden. For all her imagined furtiveness, he had observed this; and had taken the opportunity to place a long cool hand fondly against her young cheek. She had blushed deeply at the time and the recollection almost made her blush again in embarrassment at the thought of the green girl she had been.

The parson was nodding in his chair, a drip of saliva untended at the corner of his flaccid lower lip. Sir James, who had cleaned his platter, was wiping grease from his chin with a lace cuff encrusted with the remains of old food. Lady Anne observed these sights with distaste.

'Sir Nathaniel!' She addressed the parson sharply so that he woke and cried out in a voice like the screech of a peacock, '*Attende Domine*, have mercy on us, for all are sinners!' before nodding off again.

'More pork for Sir James,' she ordered.

'Most succulent, most succulent, very,' Sir James said, tucking in.

'And for Lady Margaret?'

'Just a morsel. It is excellently done.'

Really, those two lived for eating.

As if reading her hostess's mind, Lady Margaret pulled herself together and addressed the other guest. 'Your stay with us will be long, I trust, Master Drayton?'

'As long as my dear Lady Anne will extend her kind hospitality.'

Lady Anne wiped her lips delicately on her napkin to hide a grimace. As she feared, he had no plans to leave soon. 'Any news from the town, Michael? You were there earlier this evening, I think?'

Drayton considered. This might be a trap. No doubt she had been told who he had drunk with at the inn and, if not, she would be sure to find out. She was sharp; too sharp he sometimes reflected. 'I met our local playwright. An amusing fellow. He and I go back a way.'

Lady Anne smiled. Not too widely for she was missing a front tooth. 'Master Shakespeare? How fortunate. I have long longed to meet him. We must invite him here when Sir Henry comes home.'

* * *

The evening had not gone well for Drayton. To his intense annoyance, Lady Anne had been as good as her word and invited his Stratford rival to dinner. The meal, he could not fail to notice, was superior – both in the richness of the dishes and the number of courses – to the repasts he customarily shared at the Rainsford table. Lady Anne had worn a brand-new gown, embroidered with seed pearls, and her pearl earrings that followed the fashion of the late Queen, along with a gold-filigree, pearl-encrusted snood. She had placed Shakespeare on her right hand and spent most of the meal flirting ostentatiously with him, while Michael had been put next to Dame Alice Page, stout, poorly dressed and given to belching, with her pock-marked, spinster daughter on his other side.

Shakespeare, as was his way with any social event, had come alone. Although he habitually expressed affection, even admiration, for his wife they were never seen in public together. Lady Anne enquired courteously after her.

'She has a quinsy,' Shakespeare explained. 'She is of the phlegmatic humour that makes her a martyr to them and begs my Lady to forgive her absence.'

He had smiled, a smugly contented smile, and Lady Anne had almost simpered back – hypocritically, in Michael's view, given the attentions she was paying to Mistress Shakespeare's unaccompanied husband – 'I am most sorry to hear this'.

'Has she been bled by Hall?' Sir Henry enquired. Doctor John Hall was the local physician and married to Susannah, Shakespeare's elder daughter. 'I set great store by Hall. He bled me half to death when I had a quinsy here.'

Sir Henry smacked his large rump loudly, farted and laughed heartily. Dame Alice's daughter tittered – a sound, Drayton thought to himself, like rats skittering over an attic. Her mother leaned across him, to slap her daughter's hand. Her breath was almost as foul as Old Joan's.

* * *

Amid the laughter Shakespeare was heard to say that he was happy to report that his son-in-law afforded his wife every attention and had prescribed a cleansing draft of sage and sweet marjoram, thought most efficacious.

'A poultice of wormwood,' Lady Anne interceded. 'Our local wise woman swears by wormwood for the quinsy.'

Dame Alice saw fit to throw in her penny's worth. 'I swear by garlic. Garlic and a boiled root of cow parsley.'

'No, no, wormwood,' her hostess insisted.

Wormwood might well have described Drayton's mood by the time the dinner guests came to depart. Lady Anne's hand lingered in Shakespeare's and he had raised it to his lips and kissed it unctuously and then donned his cap and walked off whistling, the vain fellow.

Lady Anne had been cool with Drayton too, offering only a bare 'good night' as he left to go up to his chamber. He had slept fitfully, plagued by dreams in which he was asked by Royal Command to compose a sonnet, only to find himself poised to read it with nothing on the page but a lot of meaningless jabber. He woke exhausted, his nightshirt wrung with sweat, as the dawn light was seeping through the latticed glass.

Drayton clambered from the high bed, stubbed his toe, swore and hobbled to the window. The chamber overlooked the Stour and across the way on the farthest bank he spied a figure, one of the local women, no doubt collecting herbs or simples for some potion. As he watched, the woman unbent and seemed to look across in his direction. Not quite knowing why, for as a rule he was a dilatory riser, Drayton dressed and went outside.

The manor garden was fresh with dew and still cool in the early April sun. He strolled along a box-lined gravelled path towards the trellised parterre. Beyond that, an avenue of pleached fruit trees led to an Italianate marble fountain.

Ay me, thought Michael Drayton. How often had he sat with Lady Anne by this fountain, listening to the tinkling fall of scattered water and the coo of doves from the red-brick dove house in the warm balm of a scented summer evening? It was on just such an occasion that he had read her his great sonnet, the sonnet for which surely he would be forever famed, in which he declared that his love was so passionate, so intense and all-consuming, that the only help for it was for them to part.

Except that they had both known – and did those last lines not confirm this? – that he would never surrender what had become a life-line. The affair had woven itself so inextricably into their lives that to finish it would threaten the whole fabric of their being. His being, anyway. For Lady Anne, he was all too aware, was quite content with her married lot, the grand manor house and its estates and her generous and frequently absent husband.

She had, however, played the role of muse and ideal mistress faithfully for many years. How far Sir Henry was in on the act he had never been sure. He had occasionally caught glances, even once or twice a wink, between the couple when he had produced some more than usually sugared compliment to his beloved. But Anne was clever and tactful; the signs of conspiracy with her wedded lord might well be her way of keeping any uxorious suspicion at bay.

But latterly, he had detected signs of weariness, even irritation, in his living muse. He had even overheard a conversation in which she was pleading with her husband, off on another business jaunt, not to leave her 'to be bored witless with you-know-who'. He had tried, not wholly successfully, to dispel the disturbing thought that the unnamed bore might be himself. But he could not fail to mark that it was some time since he and Lady Anne had sat together by the fountain while he read aloud his latest composition to her virtues. She had even found excuses, sometimes hurtfully trivial ones, not to hear his latest offering when he had proposed it.

Alack, thought Michael Drayton, wandering down a path towards the river. It is a cruel business playing the part of a faithful lover.

By the riverbank he startled a heron into clumsy flight and was visited by another bitter recollection. As a young man, he had once described to Shakespeare how Anne's father, who had a passion for hawking, had spoken of a certain quality of light in which you couldn't 'tell a hawk from a hansa', a local term for the grey heron, intending it as a piece of jocular gossip to demonstrate how fixated the old man was on his blessed hawks. And Shakespeare had filched the phrase and jammed that too into his vile corruption of *Amleth*, a play that offended the new faith to boot – for was not purgatory now outlawed? And where did that damned ghost come from if it wasn't purgatory? And yet the play had gone uncensored.

Jonson, he knew, had thought of dropping a discreet letter pointing the heresy out to the Lord Chamberlain; he must have thought better of it. For it was true that Ben had had to be prudent and keep a low profile since he was charged with that unholy murder. Recalling this, Drayton shuddered delicately. At least there was nothing so dangerously untoward in his own past.

'Master Poet? You are up betimes!' The reedy voice startled him. Old Joan was staring boldly from the opposite bank. At her voice, a ragged company of rooks rose cawing from a nearby elm.

Drayton gathered his wits. 'I am composing and in need of solitude.'

The hag laughed. 'How was Master Shakespeare? He'll be composing too, I'll be bound. Making a pretty tapestry of the words dropped from your Lady's lips.'

The remark was too close to the bone for Drayton to take the better part and keep mum. 'What do you know of Master Shakespeare?'

The creature laughed again. 'What does Old Joan *not* know, Master Poet? What does she not …?'

Later that same day, Drayton met Lady Anne in the hall. She was booted and dressed for riding and seemed anxious not to be delayed.

'Michael, Sir Henry rides to Coventry today and will not be back until tomorrow. And I have some business in Stratford that may detain me, so it may be that you dine alone tonight.'

She bustled out and Drayton was left with the unhappy foreboding that he knew where, or rather to whom, she was hurrying.

Drayton spent the rest of the day and half the night composing a sonnet. It did not come out well. Anger may serve as a spur for many forms of artistic endeavour but it is not the best prompt for a verse designed to win back a lady's favour.

Nonetheless, the following day, Drayton attempted to read his new composition. 'My Lady, I spent the empty hours yesterday with the intangible muse for my own was sadly gone from my purview. But her spirit afforded me some few lines which I dare to suggest –'

With a look of palpable irritation, Lady Anne interrupted. 'I am very glad of it.' She made to hurry away. But he stopped her.

'Anne?'

Her maid Susan was passing and Lady Anne frowned. 'Not here, Michael.'

'You would not once have said so.'

Lady Anne almost stamped her foot. 'Once is long since. I have an appointment in town and must go.'

'Who is it you are meeting?' Rage made him indiscreet.

She stared at him with cold grey eyes. 'I am meeting Master Shakespeare. He and I,' – she played with a glove – 'let us say we have our plans.'

Drayton spent a wretched day in his own company. Passing Lady Anne's room on his way to bed that evening he heard peals of laughter. Something was amusing her Ladyship. He stopped and pressed an ear to the door. The solid oak door rendered the conversation within indistinct, but a word he heard repeated amid more peals. 'Bed.' He was sure of it. And then 'Will'. By God's teeth, his own true love – who had spent half a lifetime resisting his advances on the grounds of her much-declared virtue – was boasting to her maid of being bedded by that spotted villain, that viper-in-the-grass, Will Shakespeare.

***

'Good day, Master Poet,' Old Joan said, screwing up her bleary eyes against the sun. 'We were expecting you.'

She was sitting outside smoking a pipe when Drayton arrived at the tumbledown cottage by the mill. It had taken a while to screw his courage to the sticking point; but frankly he was desperate. If he were to lose his berth at the manor, where would he go? Such a prospect he would once have deemed inconceivable. God's teeth, but he was not prepared to lose his muse by whose patronage he had so long set his poetic course.

'Mother, a question for you.'

'Come in, Master Poet. Come with Old Joan inside.'

***

When Drayton had gone, Joan's sister Audrey asked, 'Will he keep his side of the bargain?'

'He's an honourable man, our Poet. An *honourable* man,' Joan repeated, and her other sister, Marion, gave a fox-bark of laughter. 'Besides, he'd be too frit not to. I've told him what will happen if he don't come through.'

'Now fair is fair and foul is foul, Master Poet, and you play foul with Joan and it's as a toad you'll see out your days, mind.'

She had enjoyed scaring the cream-faced loon. But not as much as she would enjoy paying back that Master Shakespeare. Taking her name in vain, 'Greasy Joan' indeed. And if he thought he could escape her noticing how he had played her and her sisters with those three damn witches he'd another think coming. She kept her ear to the ground. She had her informants. She'd given the Poet a dose to put in the Playwright's drink strong enough to clean empty his bowels and make him so sick he'd never want to see Stratford again as long as he lived. And in return, the Poet had promised to persuade his Lady Love to rethatch their cottage, or failing that to find the means to pay for it himself. It was a fair bargain.

* * *

'Well met,' Shakespeare said when he saw Drayton entering the King's House. 'By good fortune Ben's in town. We shall make an evening of it.'

Drayton smiled nervously. He fingered the powder he had wrapped in a kerchief in his pocket. What was it Old Joan had said it was? Wolfsbane? Foxglove? He felt suddenly apprehensive and confused.

'By Christ's bones and it's time that we three met again,' Ben Jonson declared when he joined them. '*When shall we three meet again?* Eh, Will! One of your finest, I always said so. And by God, didn't the king, save his soul, lap it up?'

His colleague bowed his head modestly. He well remembered how Jonson had predicted that he was bound sure as hell to lose his head over that particular play; 'it is a most horrid nightmare of phantasms and bound to greatly displease his majesty, who has sworn blind to rid the country of witches and their noisome craft,' he had been reliably informed by more than one source Jonson had said of it.

The three writers passed a merry evening. Shakespeare was the merriest of the three. A moderate drinker as a rule, he was putting it away that evening. It was not difficult for Drayton to find a moment, when Shakespeare and Ben had gone together to piss, to slip Old Joan's powder from his kerchief into his rival's ale. He had intended a mere pinch but at the last moment Ben had returned and he had shaken in the lot and wiped his forehead with the kerchief, feeling strangely disconnected from his own being as he did so; as if another man were performing the action. But it would do no lasting damage, Drayton assured himself. Only give the man, Joan had promised him, a particularly nasty turn of the bowels.

Towards the end of the evening, Shakespeare clapped his fellow drinkers on the shoulder. 'Between you and me, friends,' he said. 'I'm celebrating. I'm off out of here tomorrow. I believed I'd come back for good but I find I can't settle and it seems I have the funds for a new playhouse.'

Jonson looked intrigued. 'Will you rebuild the Globe?'

'Another site, I'm thinking. And we'll do your plays again, Ben, it goes without saying, so put on your thinking cap. You, too, Michael, if your fancy turns to playwriting. Fletcher will want to join us. And if Fletcher comes in, Beaumont won't be far behind, you may be sure. They hunt in pairs, those two and the more the merrier, I say.' He beamed affably at his fellow artists.

'Won't the wife cut up rough?' Jonson asked.

His friend laughed. It was a pleasing laugh, gentle, ironical. 'You know what? I supposed she'd be glad to have me back, but the truth is she has managed so long without me that she finds I get under her feet. And then there's this play that Michael here suggested. I have been thinking that I might have a go at it and I can't write a line here. Too quiet!'

'What pearl have you gone and dropped into his ear now, Michael?' Jonson asked.

Drayton, whom this sudden turn-up had frankly horrified, hardly heard and it was the other who answered.

'The "pearl" painted on that wall opposite. Tobias and the Angel. I'll muck it around a bit, of course – move the time period probably, no one's much interested in Ancient Assyria, cut out the old couple, but an angel disguised as a serving man and a mad maid with a womb full of devils, that's good copy. All thanks to Michael here – I'd never have thought of it myself.' He thumped Drayton hard between his bony shoulder blades.

'I'll be off, then.' He banged down his tankard and stood up. 'I've a wife to take leave of as will be waiting up for me. She's not a bad wife at that – a beagle, I call her when I'm in her good books – shrewd, can be shrewish but we settled all that a time back, and she understands an artist's needs, if you take my meaning.'

Drayton all but winded sat speechless, and Jonson, who if he had ever had a wife had long ago lost sight of her, simply nodded.

'I'll see you, Ben, back in London,' their colleague continued. 'And Michael, thank Lady Anne for her kind suggestion, but tell her London's the place for our enterprise. Stratford hasn't the audience for a playhouse yet. Good luck with the sonnet.'

Still Drayton sat dumbly while Jonson, who was not perceptive, polished off the dregs of Shakespeare's ale. After a while Drayton found words. 'Did he say he was leaving?'

'Tomorrow. I came to entice him back to London, as it happens. Never thought I'd say it, but by God I found I missed the old magician – missed the rivalry. It sharpens one's wits to have a keen blade to strike one's own against.'

* * *

Drayton did not attend Will Shakespeare's funeral. He sent the Shakespeare family his condolences and regretted he was indisposed. Jonson too was somewhat indisposed with a bowel disorder, but made it, pale and shaky, to the service in the church. Later, he wrote a heartfelt poem on the occasion of England's great loss and, sometime later, Drayton wrote a sonnet on the same subject. A somewhat lacklustre one.

But the year following Shakespeare's sudden death, he sent another sonnet addressed to Lady Anne, together with a note saying that most unfortunately he was unable to join her and Sir Henry for his customary retreat at the manor.

Lady Anne read the sonnet aloud to her husband when he visited her one evening in her chamber, where the bed she had been left in Shakespeare's will had been installed.

'Comfortable, very,' Sir Henry remarked. 'You say it was his best bed? Damned decent of him.'

'It was for the money I promised for his new theatre. The Queen's beds have greatly fallen in value. She gave away so many in her declining years, God rest her soul, that they are two a penny – no prestige in them any more. But the bed of our leading playwright preferred by the King,' Lady

Anne smiled like the proverbial cat that has got the cream, 'that you must admit is unique. There'll be no new theatre now, of course. But his wife gets the money, so she's quite satisfied.'

'You're a clever weasel, Nan.' Her husband patted her bare bottom fondly. 'Now, read me the latest ditty from your departed swain. You know, I shall miss him. It gave me much mirth watching him make eyes at you.'

He lay back on the plump feather pillows as his wife read:

If in time's toils some future living fire
Could set ablaze thy fickle faithless heart,
Or, if not thou, where once I did aspire
To live, that we might never be apart;
Then I could rest beneath the pleasant loam
And my vexed self could be for ever free.
Until that's done, why then I'm doomed to roam
A shadow shadowing vast eternity,
A soul in torment, lost to heaven above
Until released by flame from thy cold love.

'I'm no judge,' Sir Henry declared, scratching his scrotum, 'but it sounds to my ear as if your poet has gone off the boil. It's not a patch on that other one you were so fond of.'

Lady Anne thought so too. But out of regard for the long acquaintance, and maybe out of relief for its timely ending, she did see to the reroofing of the cottage where Old Joan and her sisters lived, which poor Michael had so strangely taken it into his head to fret about.

Note: the meeting described in the entry in John Ward's journal is very likely a fiction. But given his own methods I feel that Shakespeare would forgive my taking licence with it. The old Tudor Manor at Clifford (now called Clifford

Chambers), where the poet Michael Drayton was known to have stayed with Sir Henry and Lady Anne, was destroyed by fire in 1918. In 1927, during renovation work on the White Swan in Stratford-upon-Avon, workmen found evidence of surviving wall-paintings concealed behind panelling. The building itself dates back to the mid-fifteenth century, and by 1560 was known as the King's House or Hall. The paintings of the Apocryphal story of Tobias and the Angel have been dated to around 1555–65, so would have been fairly new in Shakespeare's time. The paintings are visible today.

The Incumbent

by Elizabeth Speller

The first signs appeared in late April, around Easter. It was good timing, of course, because several locals were on holiday and others were caught up in the Easter pageant or had holiday jobs in nearby Stratford. On fine days the annual tourists wandered into the village, choosing their usual bizarre places to picnic or photograph. That was despite the suggestions on politely jokey notices, each with a little cartoon of Shakespeare scratching his head or shaking a fist: No Parking on the Verge.

Some said, later, that it should be easy to work out who had started the trouble – or miracles, the village was split on this – simply by checking who was where that week, but it wasn't a small village and included a pub with rooms, two houses offering B&B, and one young couple who had an Airbnb – Rory and Donna. There were visitors coming and going there. All sorts. There seemed to be no system, no rosettes to distinguish them as approved by somebody somewhere. Nobody was free to interrogate the neighbours or commit themselves to the time needed to extract information through casual conversation. Virginia had tried this as a way of finding out if the young couple paid tax on their intermittent income. Nothing but the consolation that Rory was a handsome chap, a bit like Alan Bates, in his youth.

Nobody knew what his job was but by day, except when it was raining, Donna was a living statue outside the theatre.

Virginia's home was the smart B&B. Arden House (three rosettes and an entry in the *Gazette*) had four guest bedrooms. They were initially named after characters from the Bard's own work: Juliet, Ophelia, Desdemona and Lavinia. Virginia had been tempted by Cleopatra; she had seen some fine lotus-patterned wallpaper, lightly metallic, in Stratford. But in the end she rejected Cleopatra as a bit exotic, despite already having shelled out for Egyptian cotton bed sheets. It didn't carry with it the sense of the pastoral that this jewel of Middle England merited. Nothing of the Forest, nothing of the Avon and the Stour. Her husband, Simon, said Portia sounded like a car and Hermia, which she had her own doubts about, made him raise an eyebrow in that way he had perfected from watching Dirk Bogarde films on Sunday afternoons. Virginia's cleaner, Sue, seemed similarly affected by Titania.

The second couple to book in were connected with the theatre itself, which Virginia had been delighted about, at first. Not actors but in lighting or special effects. Although the couple, who turned out to be friends – they were two men – seemed to have a sense of humour which existed entirely between each other. When the older one asked if they were in the suicide, drowning, strangling or tongue-severing room, while his younger companion smiled at the floor, she was glad she'd had the nous to turn her back on Cleopatra and that asp.

After that the rooms were renamed: 'A Midsummer Night's Dream', with a wallpaper of butterflies and honey-suckle; 'As You like It', much of it green with tiny Laura Ashley leaves; 'The Merry Wives of Windsor', which had magnolia walls but cheerful cushions and curtains in bright red and royal blue chevrons; and, at the end of the corridor,

'A Winter's Tale'. She had wondered about that, but hoped it might attract low-season custom. It had an ornamental Victorian fireplace, no chimney but a grate of russet dried flowers, and padded green velvet love seat. The bed was shrouded with snow-flaked net draped from a gilt coronet. It was wrong, probably, to have favourites – not really professional – but for Virginia the room had become her retreat. When no one had booked it, Virginia would lie on the bed and wonder if there was more.

Glass shelves held Virginia's childhood collection of snow globes. She suspected that those two men had stolen one when the room was still Lavinia. It was a statue by Michelangelo. It hadn't been her favourite and she would have let them have it if they'd asked. Three books lay, and were dusted daily, on an occasional table by the seat. The top one was by a local man. *Shakespeare's Animals*. He had signed it.

Her cleaner, Sue, still seemed amused by the room called 'As You Like It' and if there'd been anyone else in the village who would have cleaned so well, Virginia might well have sacked her. But the balance of power was not clear. Sue was connected; she was related to half the village (not the better half, Virginia would sometimes think but never say, except to Simon) and she was the conduit for information in all directions.

The other B&B was Mrs Hicks' at Number 25. Mrs Hicks was Sue the cleaner's aunt by marriage. She had just two rooms for visitors and a shared bathroom for the whole household. The bedrooms had once been one so, although divided now, offered quite an intimate experience to residents. The lemon sheets were cheerful polyester. The late Mr Hicks had been a martyr to DIY. Almost literally, as he had been electrocuted (and worse, it was rumoured) when he fell in the ornamental pond while hedge-trimming.

Virginia was pretty sure that Sue sometimes put Mrs Hicks' easy-care sheets in the Arden House tumble dryer. Sue, and through her, Mrs Hicks, thought that Virginia's white 400-thread cotton sheets were all very well, but it was she, Sue, who had to iron them.

Nobody knew what was in the Airbnb. In fact, most of the village were unsure how to pronounce it (*airbernerb* was in general usage, thought, by Rolf, to be of German origin). Nor did they know what it was, except that it occasionally brought partying strangers to the village. But most of the people who came seemed happy and quiet. Retired couples who enjoyed the Green Man, serious walkers with kit, Americans watching RSC performances night after night. John at the pub sometimes asked visitors who popped in for a pint and some local colour what the *airbernerb* was like. 'Oh, nice,' they invariably said. 'Lovely.'

Strangely, Rory and Donna disappeared to stay with friends when the visitors came. Both Mrs Hicks and Virginia thought this an extraordinarily amateur oversight. More than the odd snow globe would vanish sooner or later, Virginia thought, while Mrs Hicks would never have been deprived of the insights into human behaviour that she passed along on Friday nights to feed the village maw: 'Married? Oh yes. They were *married* all right. But who knows who to.'

'Stains, well, one gets hardened. Stains are part of the trade. But drop a ciggie and they melt a whole patch of carpet.'

'Breakfast in bed? The Full English? With my back? No, I thought, NO, Mrs H. But that Scottish lad, he had a bit of a twinkle, so I said if he wanted to come down and take a tray up, Sue would fix it.'

Then there was the Problem. The Incumbent.

The village was rare in being a cul de sac; the road stopped dead at the big house and then a narrow lane curled down to the river, a waterfall, pretty bridge and beyond that paths across fields to Stratford and Shakespeare's bones. The Drayton Trust's medieval cottage was one of a short and ancient cluster of timbered dwellings built into St Fiacre's churchyard wall or, possibly, in one of the village plagues bodies had been piled up against it in the Dark Ages.

The trust had been set up in the nineteenth century by the then-village heiress, a woman disappointed in love and in art. Her ideals in both had been shaped by the spirit of the Renaissance poet, Michael Drayton, who had once, possibly, been to the village and had mentioned it in a poem, ensuring its faint posterity. Were it not for the cottage, not one of the villagers would have heard of the sixteenth-century poet, but a respected local historian suggested that he might conceivably have met the Bard on that visit. The same historian stated that the heiress had indeed been disappointed in love, but it was forty-five years of marriage to a livestock auctioneer and butcher (the certificate was in the county archives) that had crushed her girlish dreams.

The legacy had only three stipulations: that the female beneficiaries of the trust were creative, and had kissed and parted. The women could be installation artists or instrument makers, singers, performance poets, writers of novellas or weighty academic histories; they could have been abandoned, abruptly widowed or have summarily dumped their other half by text. It was the parting that mattered. And the earlier kissing, of course. There had to be passion, melancholy, a longing for solitude. And Art. On one interior wall was a mural painted by the first incumbent, a creative typographer. The letters looped up to the beams and collapsed across the red floor tiles. *'Ich verge-heimnisse die Materie, indem ich sie entkleide.'* A translation was scrawled in biro on an old envelope, Blu-tacked to the capital M, apparently by the following incumbent: 'I undress to reveal things', and then, in brackets, 'what utter bollocks!'

A later resident had attempted a *trompe-l'oeil*: a doorway on the churchyard-facing aspect of the downstairs room. It was garlanded with ivy, berries, small creatures of the night, and, in Gothic letters, *Resurgam*. The corner of the fridge slightly impeded the effect of weathered timbered doors, drawn just slightly ajar, exposing painted gravestones and bats, but it was a wonder, all the same. Few had seen all this, but in a village it only takes one.

The poets mostly, bar one famous writer of concrete poetry, wept, as did the memoirists. The musicians were, inevitably, noisy. The artists drank and the fiction writers took in men. Or sometimes women. Or both. A couple of years earlier a celebrity novelist arrived following a very public break-up reported in the press. The faint lustre of notoriety was enough to ensure a tolerance for the recent short residence of a little-known player of the ondes Martenot.

The current one was a mystery. She was tall, androgynous and, some said, beautiful.

'If you like that kind of thing,' said Mrs Hicks cheerfully.

No one quite knew when she had arrived. There was no music, which was quite a relief. No letters received, the postie said. She seemed to spend much of her time outside, walking by the river. Judy and Beryl Parsons, the twin sisters who lived in the Old Bakery, had decided she must be a poet. There was a problem in that nobody had quite grasped her name. 'Anna,' said Donna. 'Cecily,' said Doug in the post office. 'Nice name. Old-fashioned. Nice lady. Smiles.' The Incumbent smiled but kept herself to herself. Always a bad sign. 'An anchorite,' said the vicar. As if anyone knew what that was.

'You throw her in the river to keep your boat from getting carried away,' said Simon after the vicar had walked on, and gave a laugh that indicated that it was not just a joke but a double entendre.

Next door to Drayton's Cottage, across an ancient, rather damp ginnel, which ran up to the church wall, with no conceivable purpose other than separating the cottages in the row, Margaret, the organiser of the reading group, is wondering whether, should an Incumbent throw herself in the river, the whole trust might be brought to an end. One Latvian composer had needed to be taken to the mental hospital twenty miles away, although her subsequent song cycle, *The River of Endless Tears*, was performed at the Proms. A stained-glass window maker had been easier than generally expected until she held a local exhibition where the highly eroticised version of various biblical scenes caused a boycott by various church members. As a result of a piece in the *Gazette*, the exhibition was a tremendous critical success and had to be moved to Birmingham Museum of Art, where her technique, hazy veils of jewel-like colours and a delicacy of etching, gained her a review in the *Sunday Times* and a major prize. In gratitude she donated £2,000 and a small roundel of St Fiacre digging a trench in the nude to the village church.

A textile designer, inspired by a Hungarian artist who had also been associated with the village, but less famously than the Bard, had needed to be told that heavy metal was not acceptable flaring from open windows on a summer's night, nor was it possible for her to park her motorbike in the small square. That was for the exclusive use of permanent residents. The residents had made that up, but it had come to assume the status of truth in their minds. It felt right.

The situation is worse than care in the community, Margaret thinks; it was in some ways worse than the half-way hostel she had managed to get closed down in her former home. In that small town at least there had been authority to appeal to. Processes that could be followed. She had been happy there. But since she arrived seventeen months and two weeks ago, oblivious then to the status of her new neighbours, she had been unable to settle. Even when silent this relentless stream of women, man-less, their pasts unknown, and all in the clutch of neurosis and creative inspiration, unsettled her; it was neither healthy nor safe. Only the side ginnel, over which one window, which she never opened, projected slightly, distanced her from all this, which gave her, she felt, some right of proximity to object. Objecting, with charm, was what she was good at, she thought; it was part of a responsibility to the neighbourhood. Mrs Probert lived at the same distance on the far side but tended to keep herself to herself, making dried flower bookmarks and greeting cards for craft shops and village fêtes, and was increasingly vague when asked for a view.

Margaret had introduced herself, of course. It was only neighbourly; although by the time she arrived home from her two weeks in Portugal with Martin, having left only old Phil, the decorator, in charge, it felt as if the Incumbent was the resident and she the visitor. They bumped into each other just outside and the stranger asked Margaret if she lived here. Margaret had a headache from the smell of fresh paint but she exchanged the usual pleasantries, made the usual jokes and somehow failed to get her neighbour's name. Nor had her hand been shaken, though Martin, who was standing directly behind her, where she could sense him gurning like a fool, seemed to be the recipient of a smile that went way beyond a greeting. The woman – it was hard to estimate her age – was barefoot. Bare-ankled, too, under her muslin skirt. What fine bones she had, Margaret thought, looking at a dirty mark or perhaps small bruise on her foot. She was too thin; her skin was almost translucent, not a trace of make-up, her short hair an improbable shade of red. Her mouth was small but full-lipped.

Martin refused, when they got home, to remember how thin, how probably anorexic, the Incumbent was. It was not dirt or a bruise, he said, but a compass tattooed on her foot. Her toes pointed west. Virginia, socially one notch up from Margaret, agreed on the thinness. Margaret kept an internal diagram of the social structure in the village in which her own standing was clear. She was happy with this. Virginia – as she was in the reading group, she tolerated the diminutive Ginny from Margaret – said she sometimes wondered who was in control of the Incumbents. 'I mean there must be a committee or something. The trust must have a headquarters.'

'Well, presumably somebody pays the council tax.' Margaret was genuinely perplexed.

'The land registry' – she had looked months ago – 'only has the trust as owner. I got Martin to look on his computer, but he couldn't find anything about the trust itself or who the trustees are. Nothing on the Charities' site. It's hard because the trust started so long before any of us came.'

They both thought this through, minutely nodding their heads in agreement with themselves, as if it was the first time they'd discussed it.

'One day,' Margaret said, 'one of them will do something. Mark my words.'

'I had a visitor once,' said Ginny, reflecting back. 'October weekend. My third guest. Perfectly pleasant. But he drank. He went up to the Green Man. Rolf from the new houses brought him home and he was sick, not tidily, in the bathroom. I ask for a little deposit now.'

When Margaret got home, Martin had, to give him credit, flung open all the windows and rearranged all the furniture in the two rooms they'd had decorated while they were

49

away. And the smell of paint that had made her nauseous was drifting away.

'Why've you moved the bed?' she said. The head was now up against the wall to the ginnel. He had even prised open the tiny window with its lozenges of distorted glass.

'Plugs. It's the only place with two sockets, what with the light, the electric blanket, my Kindle and charging the mobiles. Times are changing, my old duck, like your waistline.'

He took a squeeze of flesh between finger and thumb and she pushed his hand away.

'For God's sake, Martin, you're not exactly Mr Universe yourself.'

'Only teasing. I like a bit of flesh on my women. And with the bed moved you get the nice view of the churchyard.'

She looked round to the main window. For once he was right. And thank heavens she was not all bones like the Incumbent. She wasn't sure about his use of the plural of 'women', but decided to overlook it.

The next day it was hot. Behind her house Margaret has a narrow strip of neat grass and beyond that only graves, but the wide bed outside her front door is an orderly grid of French marigolds, salvia, begonia and stone mushrooms. To her surprise, despite her absence, the beds are damp, recently watered. The hanging baskets, too, are thriving, with symmetrical curtains of fuchsia and lobelia. She reaches up; her finger sinks into damp earth. Old Phil has never watered so thoroughly.

Later she asks Ginny, who had recently turned her own garden into a sort of Elizabethan parterre, or so she called it: box hedges and rose trees, none of which was thriving.

'Nope. Not me. If you'd asked, I would have. Like a shot.'

She asks Rolf's wife, Sonia, an earnest woman who worked for the Ministry of Agriculture, but she clearly doesn't even understand what Margaret is talking about.

The *airbernerb* had an unkempt wilderness for a garden; you could see it from the bedroom of the house behind it, so she'd counted Donna out as a possibility.

It was evening when the Incumbent wandered up the path from the river, her hem green and clinging, her bare feet slimy with smears of mud. Margaret snipping leaves off a pot of mint, nods and the woman smiled in response to Margaret's minimal greeting, and stops. 'Aren't you lucky to live here?' she says. 'So much peace'. And then, while Margaret thinks what to answer: 'Oh, I hope you don't mind. I gave your plants a bit of water. Such a hot week and they looked a bit sorry for themselves.' Inexplicably, Margaret feels criticised, but she forces some warmth into her voice. 'Very kind,' she says. 'You didn't have to.' She looks downwards to the compass feet. 'Did you fall in?'

She is met by another smile that would have worked wonders on Martin. 'No. Just paddling. So cool and clear in the shallows.'

'Don't you worry about catching things? Diseases? Or leeches?'

The next smile says, 'So, you live just yards from a small river and you've never even put a foot in it.'

Margaret can read smiles. Smiles are easy. But she just says 'there's a swimming pool in town. But I'm not a great one for swimming.' She pulls her floppy hat down over her wiry, brown hair, aware that her face is red in the heat and she thinks she'll get Martin to look up Lyme disease. But when she gets in, she lies on her sofa eating Rose's chocolates out of the box and thinking that she'd never considered whether she was lucky to live in this village. You just lived where you lived. She can't even remember why they'd chosen the cottage in the first place. Martin, no doubt. She never wanted to move. They could probably have lived in a new house in Stratford, one with a garden.

That night Martin is suddenly up for it in a big way. A way he hadn't been on holiday or, indeed, for months. A year maybe. He doesn't even pick up his Kindle, but once the lights are out, sinks his hands into her plumpness and pushes her nightie up to her armpits. She finds it all faintly distasteful. They know each other better than this. Fortunately he doesn't mess about too long; he's evidently built up a head of steam and although his few vigorous thrusts are enough to make the bed bang into the brand-new wallpaper – and tomorrow she knows she's going to feel really peeved, because she let herself be patronised by Ginny into paying far too much for it – it is soon done, albeit noisily. He clambers off. He snores. The clock strikes midnight and she enters a new day alone.

Is the Incumbent awake, she wonders, just across the way?

It is around then that she notices the tendrils. In among the low-growing begonias, pink, peach and yellow, something very green is emerging. And then from the hanging baskets a trail of lacy foliage. She leaves it for a while, just in case they are meant. There are free seeds that come with her *Gardener's Quarterly* and she might well have scattered them. But next time she looks there are pods emerging and tiny green balls from the basket. The alien tendrils are coarser, stronger; some of the fuchsia are being throttled. Old Phil is standing there one morning, looking admiring.

'Veg,' he says. 'Just what I like. You had too much of that fancy stuff, if you ask me, Mrs F.'

She looks down. Nobody asked him, but she needs to know what he can see.

'Peas. And tomatoes up there in your basket things, and some herb, I think. Odd variety.'

How did they get there?

He looks at her with a sort of amused pity. 'Birds and

bees, Mrs F. Mind you, them begonias is a bit sad. Though me, I'm not one for begonias, though I like a nice chrysanth.'

It's true, the salmon pink of the begonias is rusty-edged. They are unhappy. Something is stealing their vigour.

'Why aren't you mowing the churchyard?' Margaret says, more sharply than she means, not because she's not cross, which she is, but because she doesn't want him to realise it.

'It's hardly any length,' he says. 'Too dry to grow now. Anyways, they sent a letter to the PCC. Bishop says live and let live. Birds. Butterflies. Harvest mice. Grass. Wild flowers. Local flora and something else. Weeds, even.'

She almost hisses. 'Live and let live!? In a churchyard? For the dead?' She knows, because Ginny has told her, that the new bishop is a socialist. He has come from Liverpool.

'What about respect? Do we want rodents and insects crawling all over our loved ones? Toads? Beetles? Slow-worms?' Slowworms had particularly stuck in her head when she read the bishop's document. Then she feels mean because Old Phil's wife was only buried two years back and, from all accounts, and there are lots, they didn't love each other at all. Loathed one another would about cover it.

Which is probably why Old Phil is grinning, revealing hideously neglected, stained, uneven teeth.

The next night is book club. Martin is banished to the Green Man. It's never been defined, but the book club is a woman-only affair. In the book club, Margaret is queen. It is her one success since she arrived.

They are a mixed group. Helen is the wife of the local GP and deputy headteacher of the primary school and Margaret counts her as a bit of a coup. There's Janine, who has a small architectural practice with her live-in partner, Ted. Sonia comes to most meetings. Even the vicar, also a woman, occasionally drops by, though she carries with her the sense that she might consider this duty. Beryl and Judy,

Donna and Penny walk up together. Sue comes because she never realised you had to be invited.

The idea is that once a month they meet, they discuss the book they've read, bring food and drink, then someone nominates a book for next time. That's how it was in Margaret's former home. There are arguments sometimes but Margaret has the veto. Donna had come up with the book they've just read. It was set on a Greek island, with a few tragic blips in its wartime past, golden sunshine, newcomers accepted by locals, reconciliation of an ancient feud, a love story and some delicious recipes. They all enjoyed it, so there's nothing much to discuss. They are thirsty from the heat and Twiglets. Margaret's sherry is finished, so they start on Ginny's prosecco. Penny bangs on about the Greek economy, Sonia hadn't much liked a church trip to Rhodes, and Donna met Rory in a bar on Santorini. She was wearing a bikini and some chap undid the clip as he passed behind her stool. 'I was mortified,' she says, happily. 'But Rory must have liked what he saw.' She laughs again, indicating the location of a bikini top with a vague hand. 'Then we watched the sunset. In silence. Amazing. If you see something like that, somewhere like that, it's a sort of bond.'

There is a small, tidy silence.

Janine wants, seriously, *Fifty Shades of Grey* as their next book. 'I'm not saying it's great literature,' she says, defiantly, 'in fact, it's a nasty bit of misogynistic, eroticised, capitalist branding, but it's a phenomenon. We need to read it to have a view.'

'I don't think we need that view,' Margaret says. She sees Judy and Beryl nodding 'no' and Donna nodding 'yes'.

'Donna's obviously read it.' Janine, a big woman, gives one of her laughs.

'We've seen the film,' says Donna. 'Jamie Dornan is soooo sexy.'

'Oh, come on, Marge,' says Penny, who has a degree in computers, which is how she came to work in an IT company in Oxford and believes herself an intellectual by osmosis. 'If you don't read it you're like one of those terrorists who blow themselves up because they think a book they've never read says they should.'

'No,' says Margaret and shudders almost imperceptibly. 'No. It's Helen's go, anyway.'

The GP's wife chooses a book by a modern French author. Houellebecq. She has to write the surname down. 'But it's all right; it's in translation. I haven't read it but my daughter's doing it at Warwick, and she says it's really interesting.'

Janine shakes her head. She can hardly speak for laughing. 'I don't think so,' she says. 'Your daughter is having you on. Margaret would throw a fit.' She beams at Margaret. 'No, you would, Mags. It's all casual sex. And sodomy and stuff. And he's a total misogynist. Much more than E. L. James, who is at least a woman.'

In the end, they decide on H. E. Bates' *The Darling Buds of May*.

Ginny asks the GP's wife what the name of the Incumbent actually is; it is too embarrassing to ask her outright so late in the day. But Helen shakes her head. 'Not one of ours. But anyway, I'd probably be supposed not to say.' Janine rolls her eyes.

'Felicity,' says Sonia, rather timidly. 'I'm sure it is. I thought, how appropriate, because she's always smiling.'

'Actually, Sonia, it's Verity,' says Sue. 'My aunty says so and she had a gran called Verity, so she'd remember.'

'Talking of smiling,' says Margaret. '*She* – next door', she lowers her voice, 'looks very calm and happy. I thought they were supposed to be recovering from a broken heart, that sort of thing?'

'And I thought you said at Christmas you were going to complain about the heartbreak?' says Penny. 'In case we were all murdered in our beds by that crazed-in-love jeweller? With her tools – for the murdering.'

'I just think … they need supervision.' Margaret feels defensive but, anyway, the book about Greece has instilled a profound sense of discontent. 'They don't fit in. They don't even try. What do they give to the village? This one doesn't even do art as far as I can see. Even repairs on the cottage get done by that unfriendly lot of contractors from Kenilworth. They're not using locals. Not Old Phil, or Dave at Pyramus and Thisbe Construction. Yet they're good enough for the rest of us.'

Margaret doesn't tell them that to Martin, and occasionally Ginny, she calls them the Encumbrances. It seems a bit small.

Margaret goes to bed, re-reads the bit in the novel they'd just done where Tassos and Jennifer make love on the sand as the sun rises, and she feels sad. Martin puts down his Kindle. Gives her a clumsy hug and the whole thing starts up again. She wonders what Martin is thinking about.

From spring onwards, Thursday is the day for mowing the churchyard. The bishop has indeed sent round a document asking for the older part of churchyards to be left as wildlife sanctuaries. He has invoked some powerful arguments, referring to the community as 'stewards of God's creation', and he has provided measurements: 'no grass to be cut below three inches, but most to be left uncut'.

Only Margaret, Mrs Probert and the Incumbent look directly out at the churchyard and the Incumbent is temporary. Huge horse-chestnut trees block the summer view from most other houses. The village and especially the visitors love the trees and, although they cast a shadow on her two mullioned upstairs windows, Margaret loves them too. Margaret has no real garden, not beyond the grass at the back, her front border and a world of matching baskets. She has put out a couple of tubs and two big logs, cross-sections of ash tree trunks, at the side of the house. This is, actually, public space but she does not want the aubrietia crushed by thoughtless parkers. The dustbins are in the ginnel. All other houses have gardens and ostentatiously put their surplus fruit and vegetables out to be taken, free. In autumn when it's dark, Margaret sometimes takes some fruit. She makes it into jam and then, in spring, puts the jam – greengage or plum usually – on the trestle by the lych-gate where village produce can be bought by visitors on an honesty system. This year it lingers rather but then, in a day, somebody buys the whole lot: eight jars of it.

At the back, however, the view is one-third hers and she does not want to look out on a wilderness and she won't. It's bad enough to think of the rows of skeletons that lie, albeit neatly, just beneath the surface. But the calm of the wide stretch of empty grass – there are very few gravestones in the bit near her house – fills her with satisfaction. She is composing a letter to the bishop to explain this, encouraged by his paragraph that explains the need for little mice to prosper in his imagined world of long soft grass, so that they can provide food for owls that swoop from nowhere. The bishop clearly knows it's a hard world of winners and losers out there. Residents and greedy incomers.

On Thursday, the motor-mower won't work. Old Phil swears it is always covered with a tarpaulin, but water has somehow got into the fuel line.

Over the following Sunday night, something really strange happens. Margaret is probably the first to notice, she thinks, on Monday morning. For a minute, looking out of the casement window in the bedroom, she can't work out what it is. But then she sees: in the churchyard there are flowers. Unofficial ones. Hundreds of flowers. Thousands, if you counted them, bloom by bloom, in the dawn. She leans out, turns her head sideways to look further. They are, seen from above, like a web of paths, small clumps of primroses, cowslips and fritillaries looping out from the entrance, linking graves and mounds and table top tombs.

As soon as it's a decent hour, Margaret walks out to find Old Phil. It is his job to weed. On the way she meets Sue, who cleans for Virginia. 'Ooh, have you seen the flowers come out?' she says. 'So pretty. Virginia's making little posies for the lounge. She saw them when she was walking the dog early.'

It's a fine day and by late afternoon people, not just tourists but locals, can already be seen walking up and down, looking or sitting on the consecrated grass. Sue's cousin Rick and the daughter of the publican – Sylvie, is it? – are lying entwined, glued to each other behind a handsome tomb. Margaret goes out to tidy them off but she sees some indulgent smiles being cast their way and decides that instead she'll tell Sylvie's mother, who, although she left the pub and who could blame her, still lives in the village in Avon View. These are Housing Association flats; just six of them on two stories and no one could ever have seen the Avon, even from the top floor. Sylvie will probably get pregnant if she's anything like her mother and so it would be the right thing to tip her off. She flicks her eyes away from where Rick is attempting to insinuate an eager hand inside the girl's shirt. Sylvie is shrieking, enough to raise Amabel Courthope d. 1782, her infant son, her husband John and his two subsequent wives, Elizabeth and Lettice, and their six children, from the dead. And what a kerfuffle that would cause, Margaret thinks.

Mrs Probert is darting about on the far side, like a long-legged insect, pinching off petals to crush in her flower press.

As Margaret leaves the churchyard she bumps into Janine. 'Isn't it funny?' Janine says, wistfully. 'What a lovely thing to do.'

She's glad Janine thinks somebody, not something, has made this happen. 'They're probably only from the garden centre,' she says. 'They're probably on special offer.' She hasn't checked, but they are not a miracle; for a second that was her fear. Plainly they have been planted, their small shroud of dark earth visible against the turf. She is not going to tell anyone that from above the flower whorls seem to spell 'delight'.

She pulls her bedroom curtains shut when she gets home. She has another headache. The curtains stay like that for the next three days, so she is not the first to realise that the churchyard has also acquired a nocturnal beauty. By night the ground is a place of stars; they are as tiny, and as bright, as the ones in the cloudless night sky. Dulcie, who is artistic, kind, but tends to reclusiveness and is not a member of the reading group, and lives on the far side of the churchyard, rings to tell her this. Her large timbered house, probably visited by the Bard, is sheltered by a hedge – wild rose grows through it – but she saw enough lights through the leaves to go out.

Margaret feels slightly sick. She has a sherry and makes herself go and look. Of course, she has to wait until it's almost dark, but it's not hard to identify the lights as minute solar cells, and others, hanging in jars in the trees, are also lit by solar power. She reaches up and hooks one down. Why, she doesn't know, though she has some thought of ringing the police, who might take fingerprints. She carries it home. There is a label, worn but readable, on the side. It says 'PLUM'. It is her writing. Her jam jar. One of the batch that disappeared a few weeks ago.

She opens the curtains a tiny chink. The lights, hidden

under the primroses, do make it clear that the word spelled out is 'delight'. Nobody eats plum jam that fast.

She tells Martin she has a migraine and goes to sleep in the spare room. It overlooks the war memorial.

Margaret can't decide whether the goings-on in the churchyard are a crime, a public nuisance or Satanism. Should she notify the bishop, or the police? At the back of her mind, she can't help thinking that it is no coincidence that they have a stranger in their very midst: the Incumbent. But she can hardly go and ask her if she's been planting flowers or has bought a hundred small solar bulbs. If she hasn't, Anna or Cecily or Felicity, or Verity, or whoever she is, will think she, Margaret, is a madwoman.

The *Gazette* sends a reporter and photographer to cover the story. Then Midlands TV sets up for a night. Margaret can hear them giggling, talking in their van by the war memorial in the square and she has been too inhibited to ask them to move it. 'It's strange, isn't it?' says Janine, looking at the van the next day, less ebullient than usual. 'There's BBC Points East and Points West, but we're nowhere. We're just pointless. You can't have BBC somewhere in the middle, just on the way to somewhere else. Even if you look at old prints, once we had woods all around. And we were lost in them.'

'But the Bard,' says Ginny. 'Look at all the coaches in Stratford. We're not on the way; we *are* the somewhere. He walked up our street.'

'He buzzed off as fast as he could to London,' says Penny. 'To the inns and the money.'

Old Phil refuses to remove the flowers or the lights and even the vicar seems happy to leave them. 'Thank heavens the plants are indigenous,' she says. 'The bishop was very clear on that. And the lights? Well "Let there be light", you know. I mean we can hardly extinguish them.'

Margaret doesn't know what 'indigenous' means. It was one of the things that annoyed her in the bishop's letter. The words that make it clear that power rests in long words. But she opens the curtains in her old room some nights to see if anything is going on. She feels she is the custodian of the territory of the dead. They deserve respect. They don't have much to say for themselves, after all.

In the other direction, where the living should be, it is strangely silent. The Incumbent doesn't seem to do anything. There's no sound of music, no banging about. Margaret could usually hear the Incumbents if she listened carefully. No smells of food.

At some point during the night she hears, or thinks she hears, a door close gently. She is ready. She pulls on a jumper, jeans and trainers. She doesn't need a torch, which would simply signal her presence. She leaves her own home with an equally quiet closing of the door. The moon is full. The churchyard still has dark corners, but nothing stirs among the starry grass. Margaret walks on. The river is only a short distance away. She is quite frightened of water. She doesn't know if she can swim. Last winter it flooded and the river came fifty yards closer to her house and seeped in among the oldest graves. But still, it is a light night.

She stands a little way from the bank in a sort of cave formed by the long fronds of a weeping willow. Her heart is being squeezed by night's strangeness, but she feels safer in there because, although it is muddy, she can hold on to the fine branches. Then she notices that there is, conveniently, a big log, a section of an ash tree. She recognises it, of course, as she sits down, smoothing her fingers over the raw wood. Anything seems possible and, indeed, something is about to happen. Because just as she sits, she hears a watery noise and then, in the shining black water, a monster, a pale, writhing snake, can be seen just upstream. It is huge, sleek, undulating. Tiny ripples of moonlight move outwards. She jumps up, slips, regains her balance and runs for her sanity.

The Incumbent walks across the square the next day. She looks thinner than ever. And happy, though she is not wearing a bra. Her small breasts and, especially, nipples show through her cotton top. Martin is on the corner of the square talking to Rolf. They keep looking back towards the cottages. It is obvious that they both notice the absence of a bra and they grin at the woman and she nods back, smiling prettily. Then Ginny comes round the corner. She stops and smiles. Everybody smiling these days. Exchanges a few words then comes on to Margaret's cottage. Looks at the front border, where the begonias have long expired; there is a smell of greenness and tendrils have spread across the path. The hanging baskets are weighty with green tomatoes. The stalks of emerging strawberries clamber across the doorstep. The white blossoms dying back to reveal small, green fruit.

Ginny says she can't stay, she is frightfully busy with a full house and one is an actor. A woman. They are all called actors these days, she explains, no more actresses. A proper actor with a speaking part at the Theatre itself. She's given Virginia and Simon tickets. It is not Shakespeare, sadly, but a new verse play about arranged marriages. Anyway, she came to see the churchyard when it was in the news and thought it was her sort of village for the expected long run of *Who Gives This Woman*. But, bigger news, she has just asked the Incumbent what field she works in and, when the Incumbent looked a little puzzled, suggested an option of writing, poetry, music, art or craft.

'Poetry *is* writing,' Margaret mutters, but she is also keen to know the answer. 'Life,' said Virginia. 'She just said "life".'

'What on earth does that mean? We're all working on life. And bloody difficult it is too.' Margaret is surprised to find herself swearing. 'Why doesn't somebody give *us* a cottage to live in free?'

Ginny shrugs. 'Creatives,' she says. 'A law unto themselves. And I didn't feel I could really ask what relationship had broken up. I mean, I know that's a condition of the trust, but you still can't really ask. Not outright. I told her about Simon's little escapades, but *nada* in return.'

Out of the corner of her eye, Margaret sees Old Phil, swinging an empty watering can as he crosses from the church. The grass is well over the stipulated three inches now. The primary school children, semi-supervised by Helen, who is sitting on the long grass, are shrieking around, doing nature projects. But at night there are the whisperings and gaspings of adolescents, and older people who should know better, behind the fine memorial tomb of Captain Richard Patrick Lorne Campbell. Captain of HMS *Androcles*, sunk off Java in 1862. Presumably he is not actually in it to be disturbed, but at the bottom of some far-off ocean. But Margaret is no innocent. The next thing will be condoms and cigarette packets and chewing gum. She wishes she could ask somebody to mark her words, but she is not sure anyone ever has.

Virginia calls back over her shoulder. 'Did Martin tell you your logs are gone?'

'I'm sorry ...?'

'Logs. Tree trunk slices. At the side. Your illegal logs.' Virginia's face is almost inscrutable but a smile lurks on the word 'illegal'.

It's stupid to go and look. Why should Virginia make such a thing up? Anyway, she sees Martin coming back. 'Hello, Ginny. The logs are gone,' he says. 'Someone is in your spot.'

'How can this have happened?' Margaret says, mostly to herself.

ELIZABETH SPELLER

'They'll just be in the river, old thing. It'll be kids. Or the telly people. The tubs are there. But sort of round the front.' Martin pats her as if she were a dog. But Martin's idea of reassurance doesn't hit its mark. Margaret is more upset that someone has done it than that the big chunks of wood are gone. There are other tree trunks. But is it someone who knows her? Hates her?

Someone unknown has parked in that space now, and with French number plates, and for the first time Margaret notices that on the side wall, something is climbing upwards: some sort of vine. How has she missed this? She knows it's probably because she often parks tight in to that wall as it's marginally nearer her front door. 'Where's my aubrietia?' she says. Suddenly she wants to cry. It's too much. Everything.

She is still spooked by the white water snake. Half of her knows she will never go near the river again. Half of her wants to check. All of her knows she was right about rivers being places of danger. She doesn't believe in the devil; her religious beliefs are very modern, but this, all of it, is more sinister than charming. It is what someone in a different sort of church would call a demonic force. That night she writes to the police, anonymously, the bishop, politely, and the clerk to the parish council, demandingly. They can't just let their village be taken over. What she would really like is gates. Gates across the road at its junction, that only locals can unlock. Visitors could park outside but at least comings and goings could be monitored. They could have CCTV, she thinks.

The next week, the stones appear. It seems that, in the night, two of the paving slabs on the main path have been defaced with writing.

The one nearer the church one says:

I know a bank where the wild thyme blows,
Where oxlips and the nodding violet grows,
Quite over-canopied with luscious woodbine,
With sweet musk-roses and with eglantine

Nearer the gate, on an identical paving stone, the incised words are:

There sleeps Titania sometime of the night,
Lull'd in these flowers with dances and delight;
And there the snake throws her enamell'd skin,
Weed wide enough to wrap a fairy in.

This time even the vicar seems unnerved. 'A biblical extract might have been more ...? Perhaps ...?'

'It is the Bard,' says Virginia firmly.

It is, however, also a matter for the council, Rolf and Sonia agree. You can't just let people pull up the fabric of the village and even if it is the Bard, it is, in its way, graffiti.

But Virginia brings the woman actor staying at Arden House, who materialises in a sea-green kaftan, declaring, 'How unutterably wonderful. What a gift! What beauty!'

Finally, at dusk, Dulcie comes out, drawn into the light by the commotion. She walks up the path, but sidesteps the carvings. She bends down, runs her fingers over the words.

'Professional,' she says, 'but hand-carved.' Then she looks distressed. 'Perhaps we should have CCTV?'

At last Margaret has an ally. 'Yes,' she says, 'oh yes, yes,' in a way that makes Martin look at her oddly.

'After all,' Dulcie says, 'we don't want these stolen or damaged, if word gets around, which it will.'

A bit of Margaret wants to cry again. Perhaps she *should* see the GP, she thinks.

Even Mrs Hicks and Sue have come for a look. There is a smell of something aromatic yet sweet.

Janine says, 'Look! Thyme between the stones. It'll take in the cracks. And there's Dulcie's wild rose! And, look, the honeysuckle on Margaret's cottage! Woodbine!'

And Margaret looks. She doesn't come round the back of her cottage often as it simply forms part of the churchyard boundary. But there the honeysuckle is.

'And cowslips,' says Virginia, looking around urgently, excited. 'And I bet those clumps are violets, not quite out.'

That night Margaret, who can only remember the word 'snake' in the mysterious carving, says to Martin, as he turns her this way and that in bed, shouting and saying things she wishes he wouldn't, 'it's not natural'. She means the things that are going on outside, but Martin ploughs on, grinning. His sexual approach has got much louder as well as much more varied over the last weeks.

When he's finished, and after a decent interval, she says, 'Martin, I can hear something going on down at the river. Maybe a scream?'

When he doesn't stir, she says, 'I hope somebody isn't throwing things in again. Dustbins. Or themselves. Who knows what with all these goings-on.'

She doesn't say that some nights there is singing in the churchyard, very soft and gentle. No song she knows.

With a sigh, Martin sits up.

'You can bally well come too,' he says, 'as I didn't hear a thing.'

Which is, Margaret thinks, hardly surprising.

But when they go out, Rolf is standing outside his house, swaying a little, and he agrees to accompany Martin, so Margaret can return to bed and safety. She looks up at Drayton Cottage but the windows are all dark. In the moonlight the vine looks like snakes writhing up the wall, their heads close to her window ledge. She decides to move permanently into the spare room. She pours a whisky, neat, and, as she goes past, looks out of the window of her old room and thinks she sees people walking, some in pale nightdresses and bonnets, two in wide skirts, sauntering in quite a lively way on the arm of a man in fancy dress: britches and a tricorn hat. A bent old man in a smock straightens up and looks at the church clock and shakes his head. It is midnight but the clock is not chiming. There are two young men in ruffs talking to each other with wild gesticulations, while leaning under the north window of the church a young woman with ringlets carries a baby in her arms. Four or five children play under the yew tree. But all this is in silence and the figures, though substantial, are monochrome. The glass, within its lead, is hazy in this room yet there are dark shadows thrown from the half-moon through the huge chestnuts. As the trees move in the wind, the shadows shift and change and, what with the whisky, Margaret's not sure and when she finds her glasses she can only see the unkempt churchyard and the nasty little lights and Simon walking up and down talking into his mobile. She can hear him laughing quite loudly. It'll be his usual. But something is changing and Margaret is frightened and excited.

The door crashes open. Rolf and Martin fall in.

'For God's sake!' Margaret calls out. 'It's after midnight. You need to pipe down.'

'Starkers!' says Rolf and both men snigger like school-boys.

'Naked!' says Martin. 'A naked woman!'

'So?' says Margaret. She thinks: how dare she? This has to be the end. It's an offence against public decency. Isn't it? It's the Incumbent. Surely?

'Beautiful,' says Rolf.

'Oh it wasn't her,' Martin says, not too stupid to see Margaret is upset, and tipping his head towards the front door. 'It was a sort of half-woman, half- ...' he can't quite put into words what the other half was. 'Shimmering. All white. Curling through the water. Turning onto her back …'

'And that's how we saw her wabs,' says Rolf, but Martin, of all people, says, 'Shut up, Rolf.'

Martin sounds more full of wonder than lust. 'It, she, whatever it was, might have been a mermaid? White from head to tip. Lovely thing, slipping through the willows where they touch the water, just ripples.'

That next morning he brings Margaret tea and he doesn't comment on her being in the other room. He just gives her a kiss. Strokes her hair. 'You know I love you,' he says, sounding a bit perplexed. 'Don't you? You're just the same as when I first saw you. The most beautiful girl I'd ever met. Blonde hair, those beautiful eyes. Way out of my league.'

The next day Margaret steps out to do some dead-heading and meets the doctor's wife. Or at least Helen is standing looking at her front border. 'What wonderful tomatoes,' she says. 'Could I take a few?'

Margaret realises she can give her own produce away now, which feels like a small balance in the way of things and allows her to say, casually, 'I've heard silly rumours there's a creature in the river. A sort of woman-like creature. But more creature than woman.'

Helen looks at her a bit oddly and Margaret's heart sinks. She is going to tell her husband and he's going to want Margaret on tablets.

'I haven't seen it myself, mind.' If anyone's going to look daft, it's going to be the men. 'But Rolf and Martin have. Last night.'

Helen looks knowing. 'Right,' she says. 'Rolf was in the Green Man all evening. Sonia was complaining.'

'Do you think you can get mermaids in rivers?' Margaret can't stop herself asking. But Helen is already shaking her head. 'No. My year threes did a project on mermaids and they're always of the sea. They're a rationalisation of sailors' historic fears and the sight of unfamiliar marine life. Dugongs, you know.'

Margaret doesn't know, but she nods.

'You do get naiads, I think,' Helen continues. 'Water nymphs. In freshwater.' She is matter-of-fact now. As if Margaret was one of her pupils being handed the great gift of education.

'There's one funny thing I've noticed,' says Helen, as Margaret pulls down some tomatoes for her. She points to a tiny tree against the west-facing terrace end of Margaret's house. 'These things in your garden, and climbing over your bins, they are all of a muddle – in a good way – some of them are right out of season, yet you've got them growing. It's like everything coming out at once. Even the pear tree.'

Margaret looks and wonders when the pear tree arrived and she thinks about the figures in the churchyard, who may just have been shadows, or whisky, all a muddle, all coming out at once.

'I expect you'll train it as an espalier?' says Helen. 'Pears are good for that. Aren't you clever! This looks astonishing now. You've got really green fingers. I never knew. Penny was saying you ought to win the village garden prize this year.'

As she turns away, she stops, looks back, then says, 'Why don't you both come to supper next week? We'd love that.'

Dulcie comes round, with Donna in tow. Donna looks pale and for a second Margaret thinks about the serpent, but she realises, close up, it's just the residue of paint from being a living statue. In her street life Donna tries to portray the female lead in every play that's on in Stratford. She's just finished being Hermione, which was easy, she'd said 'for obvious reasons', though it took Ginny to tell Margaret

ELIZABETH SPELLER

what the reasons were. But now Donna's struggling with
being a Punjabi housewife living in Birmingham.

Dulcie says, 'Margaret, my dear, it seems like an awful
intrusion, but would you let me paint your cottage? From
the front. It's at least sixteenth-century, probably older; the
black timbers, and your crooked windows and the glass
so marvellously distorted and now, with all this ...' She
spreads her arms wide, as if embracing the border. 'Your
garden seems somehow bigger than it used to. It's such a
celebration of past and present. I'm having an exhibition,
In-Perfections. In Shoreditch, you see. Oh, and Donna
wants to ask you a favour.'

She nods at Donna, who doesn't usually need encouraging.

Donna says, rather quickly, 'I just wanted to ask, if
it's not a cheek, whether our next book could be poetry?
I know there's Shakespeare and Michael Drayton, and
Rupert Brooke came from the county too. But a couple
more people want to come and I wondered if we could do
something special, like choose our favourite poem to read?
Ginny says her actor will read one. If we could have men,
well, it turns out Simon's a bit of a poet on the quiet. He
won a big competition about love.'

She looks to see how Margaret is taking to the idea of
men.

'Maybe out the front here if it's fine? Ask people not to
park for the evening? A sort of words party?'

Margaret just nods. She is giddy. Things are going so
fast; she is being tumbled into a different life.

She hasn't seen the Incumbent for a few days, but that
evening, from behind the curtain, she watches her come up
the path, so slender now, that she hardly seems to touch
the ground. She bends over, touches the lupins and smells
Margaret's white stocks. She breathes deeply and looks
upwards, not at Margaret but at the sky. Margaret wonders

if she might come to the next reading group, which might be a poetry recital, a party – a celebration. Of something.

She goes out later and cuts some stocks, wraps the stalks in wet newspaper and leaves them on the Incumbent's doorstep.

Martin is going to be back very late that night after his firm's dinner. Margaret thinks that she'll go down to the river. It's going to be a mild night and she can take a rug and a thermos – and go the long way round so nobody sees her. Then she'll wait. There doesn't seem to be anything malign about the serpent but she wants to *know*, wants to know if everything is of a piece, and she is much braver now. She waters the plants, puts tomato food in the baskets and when it gets really dark, which is late on these long days, she walks to the river. Nothing happens. It's peaceful. The air is soft, the sky shimmers with stars and a half-moon reveals a monochrome landscape stretching towards Stratford on the other side of the river. She's rarely out in the darkness alone and it all feels and smells new. There are a few ducks, tiny splashes and leaves drift by on smooth eddies. After a while she begins to ache from just sitting, so she walks up towards the bridge and after fifty yards she stops, suddenly. There, on the bank, a creature. It could be a swan. She saw one once, flopped like that. She'd been walking with her dad, not long before his accident. He told her it had hit an overhead power line and was dead.

Her heart is beating so hard there is drumming in her ears. Very carefully, she walks towards it, for now she's sure there are no feathers, nor scales, just smooth, almost opalescent skin. It is the serpent.

It's big and isn't moving and she considers running back for Simon or Rolf. But what could they do that she couldn't? She walks towards it, slowly, but certain now, even when it moves and she sees it has an arm, a very human arm. Afterwards she is not sure when she realised it was a woman. A slim, colourless woman, her face turned into the crook of her arm, but with a scalp like veined-marble.

Margaret squats down, touches the woman's shoulder, which is damp and cool, but she can feel tiny electric tremors under the unknown skin. Then she strokes her shoulder very gently. She looks down the length of one leg and sees the compass inked by the delicate toes. The woman turns her face. Margaret says, 'Shall I help?'

The Incumbent nods and, with Margaret's help, she turns over. Margaret doesn't like to leave her, but she wants to call the ambulance. The Incumbent shakes her head and a hand grasps at Margaret's clothes, as if to stop her. And then she whispers, 'No doctor. Stay. Please.'

So Margaret puts her blanket over her and she strips off her jumper and lifts the strange, naked head just enough for it to rest on the wool. Then she curls up next to her, holding one long-boned alabaster hand in her own rough, gardener's hands. They both look up at the stars. Margaret remembers more about when she was a child walking with her dad at night. He knew all the stars, pointing to them and giving them names. She hasn't thought of them for years.

'There's *Draco*,' she says, 'The Dragon. And there's *Serpens*, the Serpent.' The cool hand in hers squeezes her gently. 'And the Little Bear,' she says and her heart aches. And now, as she looks at the misty path of the Milky Way, she thinks she hasn't looked upwards for decades, but there it has been, always, and more memories are tumbling down.

'*Willows whiten, aspens quiver, Little breezes dusk and shiver, thro' the wave that runs for ever, By the island in the river.*' She speaks as much to herself as to the woman beside her.

At some point, after Margaret has pulled the blanket higher up the Incumbent's shoulders and kissed her softly on the forehead as she would have kissed the small child she never had, they both drift off.

They can't find anything in Drayton's Cottage to indicate where the Incumbent comes from. Nor can they find the address of the trust. Margaret notices, when she goes in, that the painting of the door to the churchyard dead has been altered. Now, beyond its opening, where there used to be dark gravestones, is a field of flowers. The typography has been covered completely, as has everything else. It's all white except for Margaret's stocks, which are in a green jug. Upstairs the bed is made and on a chair what the vicar at first takes to be a cat, but Margaret knows is a red wig.

Helen's husband has come from the village surgery. He picks up the bottles on the small table by the bed. He nods as if he knew what he'd find. He turns to Margaret, who everybody is being immensely kind to as if it's not a lot of fun finding a dead body outside, at night.

'I don't think we need to wait for the results of the PM to know. It was cancer, I should think. Palliative stuff this. Powerful, for pain and sickness.' Then he says, tapping the label, 'Her name was Selene, but the label's partly rubbed off.'

A month later they get permission to bury her in this place where she lived and died. Nobody else has come forward to claim her. The whole village turns up, plus lots of interested visitors, including the press, although the vicar is very firm about cameras, because of course the story got into the papers – and lots of actors, because Virginia's actor has told all her cast and the playwright, who is already thinking he has the bones of his new play right here. The narrow street over which Rolf and John, Simon and Simon's son, Pete, post office Doug and Martin carry her coffin has been strewn with flowers, and greenery is woven into her wicker coffin. There's a lot of crying for the idea of this woman no one knew.

Later, it's Margaret, with Martin's very tender arm around her, who reads the poem she's chosen, that she once learned by heart at school, forgot, and has now remembered. She looks up from the graveside twice and over the fresh russet earth sees her friends, who know her, and, to the side, in the deep shade under the trees, a cluster of faintly familiar faces, somehow insubstantial in smocks, ruffs and bonnets, holding the tiny hands of children. She only wobbles a couple of times and ignores the actors, all in elaborate Jacobean black. Because Margaret is the chief mourner; not because she claimed it but because that's how it has turned out. Like everything else.

She walks in beauty like the night
Of cloudless climes and starry skies
And all that's best of dark and bright
Meet in her aspect and her eyes ...

Kiss and Part

'Colossal Wreck'

by Maria McCann

The trouble began on a day like any other. Jane Doe sat down at her laptop. Before starting work she looked round, as she always did, at her darling little office – such a reliable source of pleasure, with the honeysuckle twining at the casement and the faded rose wallpaper, that she seldom noticed, nowadays, how cramped it was. On an inlaid table to one side stood a pot of Earl Grey, a china cup and saucer and a selection of expensive biscuits. The writing was going well: Jane had already sketched in the atmosphere of the ancient fishing port and was about to introduce her villain, Pierre Durand.

> Approaching the *Libellule*, Beth could see its owner sprawled in a sun-lounger, a drink by his elbow. As she stepped onto the pontoon he turned. His eyes were hidden by dark glasses, the mouth beneath them stretched in a wolfish smile. 'Bonjour, mademoiselle.'

It was at this point, she would later realise, that failure set in. At the time it seemed nothing serious, just a momentary lapse of energy. Beth had to be invited aboard and ruthlessly impressed but, try as she might, Jane could not summon up interest in Pierre's luxury yacht. Normally this sort of thing involved some online research, perhaps a phone call or two to a friend who, like Pierre, was a connoisseur of boats. Hardly a demanding task. She had only to avoid obvious howlers, though even those might go unnoticed: the sort of woman who knew her way round such yachts was unlikely to read Jane's novels. Still, she prided herself on getting things right.

Minutes ticked away as she fidgeted, drank tea and checked her email. Research was by now second nature to her, yet she could not make a start. Her procrastination grew more leaden and mulish, taking on a personality of its own; it sat in the room with her, sucking up oxygen, until she at last understood that she was bored.

She sat motionless. She had never before felt bored while writing, so why now? Could it be that this was a boring book? The question was followed by a rush of others, each more unsettling than the last: were *all* her books boring? Were her readers? Was there something innately ridiculous in romantic fantasies? Was she, in fact, a boring writer, writing for ridiculous people?

Jane blushed. Regarding one's readers with contempt was itself contemptible – and navel-gazing, she reminded herself sternly, was an excellent way of sabotaging creativity. Better leave the yacht for a while and work on Pierre himself, since the boat must surely reflect the man.

But Pierre, when she read back through her notes, provided even less comfort. What *had* she been thinking? No woman capable of tying her own shoelaces would venture on board with such a leering oaf. Frowning, she began to type.

'May I help you, mademoiselle?' The man pushed back his sunglasses. His dark eyes regarded her impassively. Was it her imagination, or was there also something sad about them – a hint of regret?

Yes! Regret! He should present, initially, as a rough diamond, a man who only needed a little TLC: women were suckers for that sort of thing. Before she knew her true desires, the heroine would be snared by his charm and her own generous, unsuspecting nature. Pierre must exude a certain charisma, if only because you couldn't have a romantic heroine nakedly excited by a man's money. Such rapaciousness was for the Other Woman.

Pierre was now working satisfactorily – Jane even liked him a little – but changing him meant she also had to reshape the heroine. Sensible little Beth with her 'who, me?' modesty had previously seemed endearing, but having reworked Pierre, Jane knew that Beth was a pain and she wanted to slap her. She pulled up the first chapter and sipped from her third cup of tea as she scrolled up and down, trying to pinpoint the problem. A suspicion grew in her that she'd unwittingly borrowed the character from *Little Women*, name and all. Beth must be sent packing, back to Marmee ...

A tombstone green with mould, carved with Beth's name, flashed before Jane's eyes. No! Not *that*, not now.

She forced herself to concentrate. Nothing here she couldn't fix: she was an old hand at such adjustments. Her heroines were traditionalists at heart, facing traditional ordeals (what feminine ordeal, apart from childbirth itself, could be more traditional than choosing the right husband?) because her readers liked things that way. They were mostly older women who mourned the loss of 'proper romance, without all this jumping into bed' – romance, in other words, that led first and foremost to the altar. There was a perilously fine line, however, between old-style and plain *dull*, especially in a novel where passions could not be allowed free rein or, to put it more bluntly, things couldn't be spiced up with lots of sex. To compensate for that, both hero and heroine needed a certain sparkle, but with Beth,

Jane's instincts had failed her. How could she have missed it before? For any woman who had not slept through the last thirty years, Beth was about as sparkling as a mug of Horlicks. Jane began making notes on a new heroine: the half-French, innocent yet sensuous Eloise.

> The woman who looked back at her from the mirror had a tiny waist and flower-blue eyes beneath inky lashes: if photographs could be trusted, Eloise had Maman's eyes, and her delicate olive skin, but Eloise's mouth was too full for conventional beauty.

The voice that breathed from this conventionally unconventional mouth was soft, almost childlike. Eloise could not, of course, be a sophisticate, a full-blown Frenchwoman: she was if anything naïve. Raised by an aunt, she thought of herself as English but her true nature, unawakened until now, was about to burst forth (though for all practical purposes she would, of course, continue to be very English indeed). There would be a job, as yet unspecified. Eloise would discover an appetite for Sun, Wine and Happiness (Jane's fingers rattled over the keyboard as the familiar formula fell into place) and would Plunge Into Life.

What sort of Life?

Apart from the inevitable love interest, nothing came to mind; Jane's mind went blank when she tried to imagine adventures for her charming new heroine. Eloise would of course marry the prickly and passionate hero, Laurent de Mazel. The reader expected *that*, it came with the turf, but there must be something fresh in the lead-up to it. All Jane could see clearly was Eloise blossoming. And blossoming. She went right on blossoming, all eyes and lips, until something treacherous in Jane began to root for Eloise's rival in love, the 'fiery temptress' who was to seduce and entangle the hero before being conveniently mopped up by bad-boy

Pierre. Even as she realised this, she knew that things were wrong elsewhere, and that the thrilling virility of Laurent had, well, flopped. He was as useless as the rest.

That evening found Jane prostrate on the sofa, staring up at the ceiling. Apart from the brief surge that had spawned Eloise, the book lacked energy and so did she.

What *was* going on? She ran occasional workshops for aspiring novelists and had seen other writers in her pitiable condition, wrestling with chaotic manuscripts. The first question she would put to them was: *Whose story is this?* Sometimes they stared at her in bafflement, causing her heart to sink. A woman had once replied, 'Well, it's everybody's, isn't it? I mean, they're all in it together.' Not a promising answer, but now, for the first time ever, Jane found herself in sympathy with it. They were, indeed, all in it together, and she hated the bloody lot of them.

* * *

Night had fallen by the time she pulled up and turned off the engine. The place was so silent she could hear rain pocking against the car roof; in the darkness the little square of houses appeared flat and unreal, like an abandoned film set. Jane sat watching water trickle down the windscreen and fighting a strong, if doomed, urge to stay in the car. But she was a practical woman with a lost mojo and a contract for four more books; she had come this far and she was going to see it through. She took out her phone. Within minutes a Miss Hosking arrived to let her into Number 35.

'There's everything you could want,' Miss Hosking said, 'and if there isn't, just ask. We aim to please.'

'It's so quiet.'

'Quiet' was an understatement: it seemed to her that she could almost hear the air settling.

'Oh, yes. Everyone tells me it's wonderful for writing.'

'I'm sure they do,' Jane said, absorbing the comfort and practicality of the arrangements. The cottage had a single downstairs room, L-shaped and fitted out to serve as office, living room and kitchen in one: only three steps from desk to kettle. Staffordshire pottery spaniels smirked from the windowsills and behind the little dogs the blinds were drawn, creating an impression of snugness. To her right, a wood-burning stove and a basket of logs. To her left, the work space, complete with printer, inviting her to sit down and get stuck in.

When Miss Hosking had handed over the key and left, Jane went upstairs to the attic bedroom. It filled the entire upper storey, a long sloping space patterned with William Morris willow fronds. Again she was aware of the silence. Her beloved office sometimes suffered from traffic noise, but this place was soundless as if sealed, a cosy Victorian womb. The bedroom had three windows, each facing a different way, their blinds drawn against the night.

She had made the right decision. She looked forward to raising those blinds tomorrow, to flinging open the casements and gazing out onto new surroundings, a new day, and – please God – new ideas.

Drifting about waiting for the muse never works. Having hung up her clothes, she hurried downstairs to unpack her writing paraphernalia: laptop, paper, ink cartridges, shoes. Behind her, near the cottage door, the boiler purred. She set up her laptop, made tea and cradled her writing shoes in her hands. They were years behind the fashion but that didn't matter. They weren't accessories but magical objects whose power lay in their crippling narrowness, their vertiginous heels. What mattered was the feeling they induced in Jane, that sensation of head-to-toe femininity for which her private shorthand was *All Woman*. She slipped them on, read through the last section she had written and raised her hands over the keys.

Nothing. And now that she looked at him again, Pierre still wasn't working: he'd gone a bit too soft, not enough of a threat. Like an idiot, she hadn't kept a copy of the previous version, which meant Pierre would have to be rebuilt from scratch.

Never had anyone fallen so out of love as Jane Doe had with *Undying Passions*.

* * *

On waking next morning, Jane felt a visceral relief. A bell had chimed during the night, not once but repeatedly, its sound slicing into a confused and suffocating dream about something subhuman concealed in the bedroom. Now, though, her night terrors receded like spent surf, depositing her safely in the high bed. On her right the blinds glowed gold, backlit by morning sun. She sat up and gazed around: calm, clear reality and – by the look of it – auspicious weather. She crossed the room and lifted one blind, only to drop it and recoil. What she had taken last night for the darkness of a country garden was a graveyard full of tombstones.

Jane retreated to the bed.

Number 35 was also known as Church Cottage. She hadn't realised the implications of that address – she was forever not realising things these days. Even if she left the blinds down throughout her stay, how could she sleep another night, knowing that only a pane of glass separated her from *that?*

Downstairs, when she got there, was worse: the kitchen windows shared the cemetery view, only from close range. Careful not to dislodge the Staffordshire dog on the sill, she peeped under a blind and at once noticed a floral sprig, tied with red ribbon, lying on the grass about five feet away, presumably from one of the old graves, since there didn't seem to be any new ones. The ground rose ominously against the back wall of the cottage. No wonder it was so quiet. Quiet as …

She mustn't panic. Over the years she had developed strategies: distractions, displacements. She could check how far the graveyard extended – whether she could take walks in the village without having to pass it, pass *them*. Yes! Make a cup of tea, then blow away the cobwebs, freshen her brain, buy something nice for dinner – there was a Waitrose just down the road. *And get away from here.* She drank the tea, ate an apple and went in search of her winter boots.

Her walk was unsatisfactory. The graveyard dominated her end of the village; the only way to avoid seeing it would be to walk up the road with a bag over her head. She did, however, get as far as the supermarket where grim-faced people were shoving trolleys piled high like skips. This wasn't her corner store in Bristol, it was stocking-up-for-the-month, pistols-at-dawn-over-the-last-pack-of-kale shopping. Feeling pathetically underequipped with her handbasket and backpack, Jane selected a few healthy staples – low fat, no added sugar, lean protein – then dithered for five minutes at the confectionery shelves before snatching up a pack of Mars bars. Then, narrowly escaping being mown down by a 4x4, she crept back to The Square, averting her eyes from the war monument which, though inoffensive in itself, marked one corner of the graveyard. The sun had shifted; the cottage parlour, when she entered, was dark. Her laptop sat sullenly where she had left it, open to dust but not to inspiration.

Jane steeled herself: she had come to *work*, her stay had to produce *results*. She gripped a biro and drew diagrams of three-act structures. She free-associated. She made lists of possible characters: two new romantic leads, three rivals, all of the purest cardboard. By five o'clock she could do nothing but yawn and rub her itching eyes. The obvious thing to do was sleep, but she was a determined woman and decided she would try sinking into a 'creative trance' for twenty minutes or so.

She moved to the sofa. For a while she was conscious of the occasional church bell – that was St Helen's, she now knew, presiding over the churchyard – but soon the chimes, too, faded from her mind. She surfaced from sleep just before nine without a single useful idea, her creativity having apparently dozed along with her during the entire time.

She struggled up from the sofa, massaging her aching hips. There *had* been a dream, but nothing that helped – something about Simon Forshaw. Poor Simon, he'd wanted so badly to marry her. Should she have – no, ridiculous, how ironic! What was this, the loneliness of the long-distance romance writer? Marriage to Simon would also have been cardboard. You had to feel more for a man than she did for him: she hadn't even bothered to correct some-one who'd sneeringly referred to him as Simon Foreskin. Was that, she now wondered, emotionally cold? *Could* a cold person have written four novels of passion? True, she was sometimes conscious of a numb, detached feeling – she'd had it for years – but wasn't that just tiredness, the same as everybody felt? It had never stopped her writing. Was it possible that the numbness, or whatever it was, had spread and had finally reached the point where –

Inspiring thoughts were what she needed and that wasn't one of them. She couldn't be bothered now to make a proper meal, so she brewed tea and unpeeled her first Mars bar, then noticed with surprise that she was still wearing her walking boots. No wonder she'd had no ideas. She performed the ritual – shoes, china teacup, chocolate – and the sugar rush filled her like love. Now All Woman, she restyled Laurent de Mazel's hair and career: he became a gifted painter, freed to follow his genius by the death of his father. Unimaginative, unforgiving Papa had wanted Laurent to work in a bank, no, *way* too obvious, what was the matter with her? He wanted Laurent to work on the *estate,* that was it, the estate Laurent had now inherited and would one day share with Eloise. He – Laurent, not Papa – had unflinching integrity and a short fuse.

Something wild flashed in his eyes. As he turned away, Eloise remembered what he had said about freedom and living for Art.

Virile now, definitely virile, and as difficult as such heroes generally were. In real life, Jane thought, they would be impossible: imagine asking Heathcliff to pick up the cat litter on his way home. But this was fantasy, in which men could be at once wild, virile and domesticated. As much as the shoes allowed, Jane wriggled her toes with excitement. Once more the magic was drawing things together. Eloise was also a painter, of sorts, no, too much like competition. Watercolours? Too wet, in every sense. A designer, then?

'I design textiles,' Eloise murmured. 'The colours here are so intense, I'm sure I'll find inspiration.'

Alone in the passionate South, wearing beautiful, original clothes of her own design. What could be more adventurous, yet more feminine?

This was a *good* Mars bar.

Now those two were sorted, she could turn her attention to Pierre Durand and Temptress Giselle, who would create the mix-ups and dangers and then mop up each other's greed and libido by the end, leaving things nicely balanced. By now, Jane was in benevolent mood; if only she could get the book written, she decided, she would allow them to be happy together.

She began to re-plot the stars that must cross the path of true love. Once she realised that Pierre was an art collector, with a network of shady friends in the trade, his role became clearer. Giselle was more elusive. For some reason, Jane pictured her in black lace. A widow? Whose? How had he died? Why did she need to be a widow, anyway? For money, of course; riches got without the daily grind of earning them. Yes. A spoilt, ruthless woman ... That was as far as Jane could get, for now. Giselle's dead husband, important for the light he might cast on Giselle herself, remained a blank. She needed to know how he'd –

– and as suddenly as she had got onto her roll, she was off it. The colour drained from her imagination, leaving the clichés threadbare in the grey English light.

Shit!

* * *

She'd spent too long thinking about the dead husband. *The thing*, as she called it, was unpredictable – sometimes she escaped entirely – but when it struck, it struck.

The graveyard outside the window couldn't have helped.

Her problem was that anything connected with death, if dwelt on for long enough, could trigger panic. Sometimes, as now, it wasn't so bad, merely a freezing in her mind; at other times it approached terror. Either way, it put paid to any creative work. Occasionally it attacked her in the company of strangers, and excuses had to be made. In such situations Jane put the whole thing down to her unfortunate name – she had been seventeen, she would explain, and in a Film Studies class before she realised that a *Jane Doe* was not a Bambi-like creature wandering the forest but the nameless woman buried under the ferns. That much was true: while other students laughed, Jane had sat speechless and shocked. Her name, that she had always thought pretty, signified death and decay. It had been one of the most hateful experiences of her life.

In reality, the realisation about her name hadn't sparked her phobia; *that* had existed for years before. The name added to her troubles, however, and seemed to lay her under an intimate, unspeakable curse.

Any reference to death or dying, any thought along those lines, might bring on *the thing*. Particularly bad were death's accoutrements and trappings. Tolling bells, tombstones, maggots, rot, the Reaper – all filled her with dread. The word *macabre* could have been coined to describe the taboos that constricted her life: she was unable to watch horror films or attend funerals. When, in a TV drama, a dog in woodland suddenly whined and began to dig, Jane reached for the remote.

The novels she wrote under the name of Jane Darke were her escape from all that. Her nom de plume was a knowing joke: there was nothing dark about her books. They were pure froth, celebrations of pleasure and passion in which British women yielded to the charm of suntanned Frenchmen and Italians, in the process consuming much good food and wine without gaining so much as a kilo. The women were canny, however, and (since Jane's selling point was *retro* romance) they only yielded up to a point. Men might strut around bare-chested, storm, rant or even command: they still had to wait until the wedding night. In Jane Darke novels, the battlefield of the sexes was so crowded with power plays and manoeuvres there was no room for corpses.

And yet, death had secretly wormed its way into her fiction. Jane had found this out by accident one night when she was entertaining her friends, Julia and Paul Sankey. The Sankeys had arrived early; it was understood between Jane and Julia that this was never a problem and Julia was not above rolling up her sleeves and helping, if need be. On this occasion, however, everything was under control. The three of them were drinking and chatting in Jane's kitchen as the scent of roast lamb rose on thermals and wafted temptingly about the room.

The two women were close friends. It was Julia who, without telling Jane, had sent her first, self-published novel to the romance blogger Fanny Hill, who had tweeted ambiguously that you could give a Jane Darke novel to your grandma. If this was intended as a sneer, it backfired; there were lots of grandmas out there whose grandchildren didn't know what to buy them. Slowly but surely, the wave began to build. Older women recommended the book to reading groups as 'proper romance, the way it used to be' and younger ones read it in a spirit of satire – but they read it. At last, in a dream-come-true ending worthy of her own fiction, 'Jane Darke' had been offered a publishing contract: old-fashioned romance was back from the dead and living on the Med. As a result, Jane considered Julia Sankey not only her dearest friend but also the Fairy Godmother of her writing career.

Smiling at the Sankeys, she took out the lamb and set it to rest. Paul waved the wine bottle at her and she nodded her acceptance of another drink. Julia was talking about a crime novel she was writing, in which a young boy was kidnapped and accidentally killed. 'I've been reading up on bereaved parents,' she said, 'but I still feel a bit – I mean, of course it would be unspeakable, that goes without saying, but unless you've had kids yourself, you know? I usually avoid dead kids. Like you don't do parents.'

Jane said, 'What?'

'In your novels.'

'I didn't know you still read them.'

Paul said, 'She needs some light relief after all her cadavers.'

Jane repressed a shudder at the word *cadavers*. 'Well, it's very sweet of her. But no parents, Julia? Really?'

Julia laughed. 'Join the club. Someone pointed out to me that all my policewomen have names beginning with R, would you credit it? Rebecca, Rosie and Rachel.'

'Not intentional?'

'Not in the slightest.'

They agreed that the creative mind worked in peculiar ways. Jane said, 'With romance, though, would you *expect* to read about their parents? I mean, it's all about the mating game.' Mentally she was listing the heroes and heroines of her last three books, who were all, as it happened, orphaned long before the start of Chapter One. 'Actually,' she said, 'I see what you mean. Perhaps it's because I'm adopted.' Julia looked uncomfortable. Jane laid a hand on her shoulder. 'It doesn't bother me. Mum's Mum, as far as I'm concerned. I don't remember my natural parents.'

Afterwards she had sat mulling over those orphaned heroes and heroines. So much death, and she had failed to notice! Could it be true that her characters were orphans because she herself was orphaned? Surely not. Some choices came down to instinctive crafting, so deeply embedded in the writer's practice as to be second nature. Fictional orphans are useful creatures: unrestrained by parental authority, they are free to choose their adventures and their loves.

It was over a year since that conversation, but Jane still fretted about it. Because of it she had given Laurent de Mazel a father for as long as he needed one, though by the end of the novel Papa was only seen in flashbacks, being, well, dead. But now, sitting in a darkened cottage with bones stacked against the walls, she realised something else. Of all the fictional women she had read about, and of all the March sisters, she had borrowed the one who died young.

* * *

Though very quiet, Number 35 was not silent as she had first thought. Occasionally someone trudged down Duck Lane, which ran alongside the house and curved round the graveyard. The chimes of St Helen's, which continued throughout the night, had just sounded eleven.

Jane was tucked up in bed. A reading lamp cast a soft halo onto the leaf-patterned quilt, which exactly matched the papered ceiling: there was a great deal of soothing greenness in this room and the delicate pattern of willow foliage gave her much the same comforting sensation as her Victorian roses at home. The bed was so high that she had to climb into it, but once wedged into that intimate, sloping space, with the blinds firmly down, she could almost forget what lay behind them.

Whenever she thought about her natural parents, as she was doing now, she had the sensation of staring into mist. She had done her research; she knew what had happened to a little girl called Jane Jeans when a car turned over on a road across the Somerset Levels. She had made a point, years ago, of going to see the place, and stopping there, and looking up and down. The road, a long straight strip of tarmac, ran between banked-up drainage ditches, with fields either side. Cows grazed nearby, as they had presumably done on the day of the accident. There had been no signs of collision with another vehicle, just one car, upside down.

Jane Jeans had been brought out unharmed, if that was the right word. Presumably the memory of the collision lived on in Jane Doe, though she could not retrieve it: the drag of rubber, the screams as the car flipped over, the buckling of the roof as it hit the tarmac and the sudden silence of her parents.

Their bodies had been cremated. Jane could not help thinking this was a mercy. She could never have visited their graves.

Little Jane's new mother, Mrs Doe, was biologically her aunt, sister to Eileen-who-died-in-the-crash. Jane knew Eileen's name from childhood, though she wasn't sure how; it was seldom mentioned in the house. As she grew up, she realised that Mum and Dad – Mr and Mrs Doe – were not sophisticated people. They assumed that others saw things exactly as they did. They believed, as their parents had believed, that the best way to heal emotions was to ignore them: least said, soonest mended.

Though they tried, they could not shield her completely. The accident was reported in the papers. People driving by had seen the car, and had phoned the police. Neighbours gossiped. In time the story percolated and mutated and the bizarre accident on the Levels passed into local folklore. At school a boy asked Jane if she'd heard of the bloke doing handbrake turns whose car was found upside down. 'Killed him and his missus,' he said, 'and when the moon's full you can still see 'em driving along, holding the little babby.' There was a terrible silence, cut by a girl's giggle.

By the time Jane reached her teens, her fear of anything 'morbid' (Mrs Doe's word) was long-established. Kindly people said she was a sensible girl and would grow out of it. There was plenty of time, after all. She did well in her GCSEs. Then came Film Studies A-level, with *film noir* and the definition of *Jane Doe* which made the students laugh. Jane left the lesson feeling sick but still in control, and managed to eat some lunch. The crisis came later that day, during English Literature. She went white, began to shake and had to be taken home.

What was it? Mrs Doe demanded as Jane sat ashen on the sofa. Was someone bullying her? No, Jane, said, no. She couldn't explain. The class were studying Shelley's 'Ozymandias'. She'd just felt weird, really weird, she said, when she read the ending:

Round the decay
Of that colossal wreck, boundless and bare
The lone and level sands stretch far away.

* * *

Now here she was, with her horror of the macabre, in a cottage sinking into a graveyard. That was probably enough, she thought, without musing on a car crash, so from her bedside table she picked up a history of the village. She leafed through until she came to a section headed 'Tombstones and Memorials' and was about to close the book when she remembered something: Julia Sankey claimed to have cured herself of arachnophobia by studying spiders. Perhaps if she went at a gentle pace, knowing she could stop whenever she chose …?

The first paragraph wasn't too bad. Someone called Daphne Bramwell had recorded the various stones: what a task, Jane thought. The second paragraph started more ominously with the words 'unmarked mounds', suggesting lurking skeletons beneath the feet of the unwary. Most burials, said the book, were unmarked. People had been buried for centuries, *centuries*, just on the other side of that wall, and it was their remains that had banked up the earth against the back of the cottage. Shuddering, Jane put down the book, then steadied herself and read on. She'd seen something about Number 35, where was that? Ah, yes. 'Indeed, when the garden wall of no. 35 collapsed a few years ago, the owner found bones tumbling into his garden: "I tapped them back with a mallet and told them to lie quiet".'

The garden wall. That yard where her washing line was, so harmless and ordinary-looking, full of tumbling bones, of cemetery filth. She skimmed down the page, looking for something, anything that could take her mind off it, but succeeded only in finding 'by 1955 the graveyard had become so full that there was no room for any more burials'.

There they were, then, a great roiling, seething heap of them, hidden, packed in rot, pressed up against the wall, fingering it, knocking, seeking a way through, their long yellow teeth grinning at her from the other side. If they could get through the garden wall, why not through the wall of the kitchen?

Jane drew up her knees beneath the quilt. Her phone lay beside the pillow but she could hardly call on friends to protect her. Why should they? Because she had stupidly come to stay in a house next to a graveyard and, even more stupidly, chosen a history of tombstones as her bedtime reading? 'I've given myself hysterics, come here immediately' – was that the sort of thing a self-respecting adult could ask?

Not that she was an adult, just then. Other people were adults and she needed one of them to chase the dead away; at that moment she sincerely regretted not marrying Simon Foreskin. She managed, however, a half-decent imitation of adulthood. She gave herself a good talking-to, stressing the necessity of staying where she was and the danger of driving at night, tired, along unfamiliar roads. The last thing she needed was a car accident. She turned out the lamp, pulled the duvet over her head and lay staring into the darkness, waiting for sleep. From below she could hear faint tapping sounds.

* * *

Of course there were dreams. In the night she heard her own voice saying, 'Tough on death, tough on the causes of death.' Or was it her adoptive mother's? Familiar, anyway. That was followed by something about Duck Lane – a woman, not Mrs Doe, talking low and insistent about Duck Lane.

On waking, Jane slid down from the high bed and went to the window facing away from the church. The houses opposite were bathed in a chill, sweetish light. In slippers and dressing gown she descended to the ground floor and drew back the curtains on the same side, but the room remained gloomy. The table and the rest of the furniture regarded her with an air of reproach – what kind of slut had come to live among them? – as, her heart pounding, Jane raised the blind separating her from the yard.

Where had it happened? The yard was small and irregular; the wall she wanted to see was obscured by the edge of an outhouse. She went to the back door, which had a glass pane in it, and looked again. Now she could see the white-painted wall holding back the banked earth. A mouldy green stain had infected its whiteness. Was that it – the rupture between worlds that had allowed them to come 'tumbling' (the terrible cheeriness of that word) into everyday life? Breaking out, breaking in, the unspeaking and unspeakable come to light. *If you're not careful,* Jane warned herself, *you'll be scared to go out there.*

That mustn't be allowed to happen. The door leading into the yard was the only exit from the cottage; if she couldn't use it, couldn't pass through, she would be effectively a prisoner, unless she wanted to make a spectacle of herself by climbing out of the living-room windows.

No. She was not climbing anywhere. She was going to stay and work. She'd made a start already; making a start was everything and this morning she intended to go on in the same spirit. She must get her rituals established here, make it her place, and then things would get better; she might even forget the churchyard. Well, temporarily. But even if the churchyard spooked her every minute of the day, *she had made a start*. She forced down some cereal, poured a second cup of Earl Grey and went over to the laptop.

The writing shoes stood ready by her chair. She slipped her feet into them and logged on. She'd been working on Giselle – wait a minute! For the love of God, what an ugly name! Presumably not to French people, but look at it there on the page: to an English eye, it suggested gizzards and gristle. What about Manon? *Manon, mon amour.*

Now *that* she liked; it sounded like kissing. A dewy, pouting creature of eye-boggling curves and undulations rose before Jane's eyes as she clicked on 'find and replace'. She paused. Was that right, though – curves and undulations? Half the point of having a French rival was her terrifying thinness: Manon sounded too bosomy. The rival should have hipbones sharp enough to shave with. How about … Léa? A whiplash of a woman, Léa worked out every day, cooked brilliantly and was at ease in every situation. She had a dismissive shrug, a lethal sneer and (Jane conceded) perhaps a formidable bosom too: thanks to cosmetic surgery, an anorexic physique topped by immense breasts no longer raised an eyebrow.

Léa it would be.

To avoid further trouble, Léa was no longer a widow. She was the spoiled daughter of a rich, indulgent father, now living (not dead, *not dead*) in Paris. Designer clothes, designer everything. Was that it, Jane wondered? Was that all Léa occupied her time with – improving her figure, cooking and dressing up? She needed some sort of prestigious or at least interesting occupation. Not a lawyer, surely? Jane couldn't think of anything that might express the essence of Léa as she imagined her. She ran through lists of professions: doctor, artist, journalist, photographer, therapist, racehorse breeder, diamond merchant, jewellery designer. Jewellery designer felt almost right but it tied Léa to a workshop, which might prove tricky when it came to plotting. Nothing quite fitted. And then, just as Jane was about to give up and condemn Léa to idleness, things clicked into place: she was a restorer of precious fabrics, a job she enjoyed for the introductions it provided into some of France's most exclusive homes. She had worked for Laurent's father in his country house, repairing the *tapisseries*. Everything about her, from her disciplined body to the studied chic of her wardrobe, suggested a sophisticated visual sense, though as a designer, Eloise had a creative spark Léa could not match.

Jane sat back smiling, her foursome in place: a textile designer, a restorer, a painter and an art dealer, people who might very well meet or at least have acquaintances in common. That would be a great help with getting them together, though she did wonder whether she had overdone the arty aspect. She was well rid of boring Beth, but it was also possible to make the heroine too interesting; retro romantics wanted reassurance that a man like Laurent de Mazel could be ensnared by the most ordinary of females. Jane would have to be careful with Eloise – give her sound British common sense and a diploma from a college, a work ethic rather than effortless brilliance.

Well, what was wrong with that? It was how Jane thought of herself.

Now for the plot, an aspect of her work that had always a predictable element. Though far from identical, romances had certain things in common, such as the triumph of true love. That was the point, after all – nobody wanted to read a romance in which the heroine drowned and the hero married her rival. Because of this very predictability, Jane preferred to start with character. Julia Sankey, who had to juggle subplots and red herrings, first worked out the story, then fitted the characters into it; Jane did the opposite. If her lovers and rivals came right, then the plot, which she pictured as a vine, would practically write itself, strands springing from the characters, twining round them and climbing, with the occasional knot and twiddle, towards the bright sunshine of Happy Ever After, where everything joined up at the end. She just had to imagine the knots and twiddles likely to sprout from this particular foursome.

When she stopped for lunch, her mind continued happily preoccupied with *Undying Passions*. She already had the major disasters lined up, as well as some early skirmishes and embarrassments. If the heroine is placed at a disadvantage on first meeting the hero, perhaps made to look foolish, the hero can either come to her rescue (the St George model) or appear cold and unimpressed (the *Pride and Prejudice* model). As a rule, Jane preferred unimpressed heroes, who could then be humbled as part of the woman's inevitable triumph. Laurent de Mazel's genius made him arrogant at times. His past affair with Léa, still unresolved, had taught him to be wary of women. Wounded warrior, to be healed by love ... He hadn't time to waste on bumbling English-women. Precisely how Eloise would bumble wasn't yet clear. So far Jane had only thought of her trying to buy fruit in the market, with inadequate French. It wasn't exactly gripping. Perhaps her car could dent his. Did she even *have* a car? She could hire one. She wasn't careless, of course, just unused to a left-hand drive. Better than that, some drama, a collision –

Lone and level
Lone and level sands

Jane blinked. The sexy shouting match between Laurent and Eloise died away into silence. It wasn't sexy but stagey, contrived and predictable.

Everything about the book was contrived and predictable.

* * *

She was lying under a heavy quilt that pinned her arms to her sides. She knew she must not open her eyes. In the darkness a woman was muttering, the sound indistinct and uneven. Jane caught the word *he*, which was repeated obsessively: he this, he that. At times the woman seemed to be sitting in the bedroom chair, rather like a sickroom visitor. At others her voice would fade into the far corner and murmur there awhile before drawing closer and closer, at last coming right up to the bedside.

He has a stone just against the tower, a nice sunny spot, my father said. They put daffodils.

Jane lay very still.

I never told. On account of my sister. If you do, you'll know about it, he said.

The voice was drifting off again. *Bad dream,* Jane told herself. But though she screwed up her face into a rictus, her tried and tested method for surfacing from nightmares, she remained trapped beneath the quilt and the muttering continued, coming back once more to the bed.

We went down Duck Lane to the river. My sister cooking the dinner. He said there was a heron.

Jane tried to shout, 'Go away!' but no sound came from her mouth.

He said not to tell.

Beneath the bedcover, Jane lay with her eyes screwed shut. *My sister cooking the dinner.* The voice crazed and crackled, breaking up on the air like a badly tuned radio, and was gone.

* * *

Breakfast was a melancholy business. She felt like a hang-over sufferer, dry and queasy and faintly ashamed.

She had been stupid to stay another night in a place that was haunted, or perhaps not haunted, in which case she was stupid to cause herself so much terror. She eyed the pottery dogs perched between her and the graveyard. Wasn't that something dogs did – guard the entrance to the underworld? 'Do your duty, Cerberus,' she said to the near one. 'Keep them away.'

But Cerberus was only a soft-faced spaniel, a lap dog. In the cemetery a bird was singing; peace hung in the morning air. The crooked beams above her, the leaded panes giving onto The Square – all spoke of continuity, of generations come and gone. The cottage was the sort of 'character' residence people paid a great deal to acquire these days. Putting aside the mouldy wall, which she would never have noticed had she not read about it, there was not a single sinister detail. Nor was she alone. Outside were other cottages inhabited by other people, solid, respectable, comfortable people who would be kindly and reassuring to a frightened woman – at least, until they heard what had frightened her.

'Once they knew, they'd think I was mad,' Jane Doe informed her slice of toast.

Was she mad? If so, she'd been headed that way most of her life. But this was silly. You didn't go mad from dreams. True, the sealed claustrophobia of nightmare could last into morning but it soon dissolved, banished by real life. It was unfortunate about the churchyard – could hardly be *more* unfortunate, for someone afflicted by *the thing* – but she was awake now and could work, just as she always did. She was a writer, a professional, a woman who received fan mail for sitting at a laptop in pyjamas and high heels. There were worse lives.

All she had to do was keep writing. She cleared away the breakfast things and settled down to her draft.

She had still to revisit the meeting between Eloise and Laurent de Mazel (not at a market, *not* in a car). Perhaps a château? Léa was doing some restoration there; Laurent, still her lover though tiring of her imperious ways, had come at her invitation to see a painting not on display to the public. Jane typed *research paintings* in red. Eloise would, of course, come to the château to soak up patterns, colours, inspiration for her new designs. The place was open to the public and Eloise, being the unprivileged hardworking Brit that she was, would buy a ticket like anyone else.

Here Jane paused. She had once worked at a country house and her impressions of day visitors were unfavourable: they left grubby marks on the walls and fatally lacked glamour. Eloise must somehow stand out from the sticky, gawping crowd, but how? Impossible for Léa to invite her, introduce her to Laurent or even know her – easy to write but psychologically wrong. Eloise would be poaching the lover of a woman who had done her a kindness, and romantic heroines had to be nicer than that.

She typed: *painting being moved from room to room, so temporarily on view? E the only one to notice it, goes to look more closely, meets L?*

Many a couple had met in a more haphazard way. Besides, it was typical of her stories: Jane Darke heroines were always deserving and – because they lived in a just universe – always helped on their way by something magical. The joy of writing traditional romances was that this magic never wore off. Except for subplots, such as the affair between Laurent and Léa, she never had to write scenes of disillusionment and bitterness, because the lovers went on being mutually infatuated, basking in their shared aura all the way to the altar, before soaring off into the blue skies of limitless emotional fulfilment. For these and other reasons, Jane had been attacked for encouraging young women in unrealistic hopes. Fair comment, she thought, if women confused her books with reality, but she didn't think they did; there was enough other stuff out there to ensure that. They wanted entertainment, that was all, and the young ones weren't even her core readers. Older married women, the sort who knew how tough life could be but flinched from Julia's stalkers and serial killers – those were her constituency. For them, the latest Jane Darke was a brief holiday from everyday life – like a girls' night out, only cheaper.

She wrote on until lunchtime, when she put on her boots and coat to walk, head twisted away from the churchyard, down into the village. She went through the park and along by the allotments, then to the pub, where she had a glass of white wine and a chicken pie. Coming back (head twisted in the opposite direction) she felt in control, happy and purposeful, ready to sit at the laptop until midnight if need be. If she met her word count, and made herself tired, she'd sleep soundly.

Through the afternoon she continued to work. Having restructured the characters, she saw clearly the plot vine that would weave around them, right up to the happy ending. For now, however, Pierre sulked on his yacht, dissatisfied with his latest artistic acquisition, while Léa, suspecting Laurent of another love interest, plotted to retain his affections. Under the fierce Mediterranean sun, conversations swelled with suppressed desire and bristled with carefully orchestrated misunderstandings; food, glistening with oil and perfumed with herbs, enticed the appetite; tanned skin was kissed by salt spray. Back in grey, chilly England, Jane lit the stove. Suppose, she thought, she were to look in at the window now and see herself busily typing: *romantic novelist in rural hideaway.* That stove would put the finishing touch to a picture of picturesque productivity and domestic bliss.

At last the moment came to turn off the laptop and get ready for bed. She printed out everything she'd written, did the washing-up and fussed round the kitchen, then opened the stair-foot door with the sense of an approaching ordeal. In times past, she thought, a woman probably felt like this on her wedding night. Here we go. Hope it isn't too bad. All over before the morning.

***

Staring once more at the papered ceiling, she found herself thinking of her adopted mother, who even now resisted talking about Eileen-in-the-car except in such terms as, 'Well, we were sisters. You know how it is.'

Once, the teenage Jane had retorted, 'But I *don't* know, Mum! How would I?'

Mum had said merely, 'Your friends have got sisters, haven't they?'

In the end, Jane thought, nobody was to blame but Mr and Mrs Jeans. But to have everything about them bricked up, as it were – it wasn't right. It felt like having part of herself stolen, the part of her that had also been theirs.

No use chewing it over now. In the hope that a relaxing

read would keep away nightmares, she had brought a novel to bed, a comedy about a compulsive thief and his unsuspecting girlfriend. She allowed herself to float on the surface of the story until her eyelids began to droop, then pushed the book aside and turned off the light.

Almost at once she was in a restaurant with Simon Forshaw, standing facing him across a table. The place was tricked out with roses and pink ribbons and each table-setting included a candle in a sparkly white candlestick.

'It's Valentine's Day,' said Simon, pulling out his chair to sit.

Jane looked more closely at their candlestick: it was plastic. All around her couples were ogling one another, the women with 'sixties beehive hairstyles and seamed stockings. She saw one woman kick off a high-heeled shoe and run her foot up her partner's leg.

Simon smiled. 'Aren't you going to sit down?'

She walked past him to the next table, which was also free, and took the seat directly behind his so that they were sitting back to back.

'Just you stay there,' she said.

After that came a confused sequence of walking down steps, though not with Simon, while clutching a mallet.

She woke irritable and sweating: the room was too hot. She flung off the duvet and spread out her arms and legs, searching for cool spots in the bedclothes. As she did so, she heard a faint scuttling in the far corner of the room.

That was all she needed, a rat. She lay still and the noise came again, closer now, and not so much a scuttling as a shuffling. In an instant Jane had reached for the lamp and switched it on. At first she was blinded. When she could open her eyes properly she forced herself to sit up and scan the room. Everything lay innocent and open: no sinister shadows, nothing lurking at the foot of the bed.

She turned off the lamp, lay down again and pulled the duvet over her head, her heart pounding. Was it possible to die from a nightmare? You might, she supposed. Nobody would know. That shuffling noise had been horrible. She thought about her cheerful novel. She had just turned the lamp back on when the crackling began.

The words *her blood ran cold* flashed into her mind: a cliché, but an accurate one. Icy waves seemed to wash over her skin as the crackling persisted and grew louder. Now she could hear a distant man's voice whining, *I have no …* Jane curled up, her hands pressed over her ears as the voice continued more clearly, *No mouth. I have no mouth –*

'Go away,' she hissed.

All of us. Speak for us.

'You're speaking now. Shut up.'

Speak for us. We have no mouths. We have no mouths. We have no mouths –

The voice was inside her head. It multiplied – she could hear a woman now, and children, wailing, moaning, growing more urgent until suddenly all their voices were in her throat, rising on her breath, pressing on her tongue, pushing through teeth and lips.

'Speak for us,' she screamed.

Her eyes fell open. She lay panting and moaning, seeing swirls of dots spin across her eyeballs in the darkness. The lamp was off. She had never turned it on, then: everything, from throwing off the duvet to the voice that had burst from her, had been part of the nightmare. She waited but there were no more shufflings or cracklings. They had what they wanted.

* * *

In the morning she made coffee, phoned Mum and said she would be paying a visit. 'I'm looking forward to a good old talk,' she said.

'Are you, love? Is it lonely there?'

'There's company in the evenings.'

'That's nice. Is Simon with you?'

'Mum, we're finished. I told you that ages ago.'

'But you were so well suited.'

'Yes, well. I have to go, Mum. Talk soon.' Jane put down the phone and went round raising the kitchen blinds. She was shocked to see flares of yellow just under the windows: daffodils had flowered since she last looked out. She straightened the pottery dogs on the sills. Behind them, the tombstones stood out sharply in the cold morning light.

Going to the printed script of *Undying Passions*, she read through the opening chapter. It could be made to work, was working already: her little puppets would perform their mating dance in the time-honoured way. Justice would be done and True Love triumph. The readers would be delighted. The only problem was that, after the voice that had screamed from her in the night, she could not continue with it.

She put *Undying Passions* onto the shelf above the desk, then turned on her laptop and opened a new document.

Colossal Wreck
By Jane Doe

Research would be needed, but it could wait. She wrote barefoot, without breakfast, unconscious of her surroundings.

* * *

The poet arrived on a raw afternoon a week later. Miss Hosking came to let her in. The heater in the poet's car had broken and her fingers were purple, so before unpacking her clothes and laptop she lit the stove and switched on the kettle. Waiting for it to boil, she gazed from the kitchen window. So many stones. As always when she saw a graveyard, a wave of tenderness went out from her to all the people once as distinct and sentient as herself, now stripped back to bones and clods of earth.

It was the next day when she found the script. She lifted it down, thinking it was unused paper, and saw the name on the front page: Jane Darke. The poet telephoned Miss Hosking to ask what she should do: would Jane Darke be coming back for it? Miss Hosking said to hold on to it, just for now. An hour later she rang back. No, Jane Darke no longer needed the script, though she appreciated being asked.

The poet sat at the kitchen table, reading. A designer was leaving her home in search of inspiration. Her parents were dead. She seemed almost a child, this heroine, as if some part of her had never grown up. As for the hero, Laurent, he had *the proud eyes of a young lion.* The poet smiled, closed up the script and straightened its edges. It should go into the stove, but she felt curiously reluctant to burn it – not yet, not today. For the time being she put it back on the shelf and, as she did so, she heard a faint tapping in the kitchen wall.

Kiss and Part

The Visitation

by Maggie Gee

I

A grey lid of cloud lies low on the land.
Ruth circles back towards the village
where she will wait till night, if need be.
If there's no hope, come let us kiss and part.
Fields of ash hold up the crow-black skies.
Time for one last attempt, before hope dies –
yes, she just needs to make him understand.
Like other men, perhaps he doesn't get it,
Ruth is prepared to spell it out. Love.
L-O-V-E. I love you. Bob, I love you.
A rabbit cries, pierced through by claw of hawk.
She'd dreamed a cottage garden gauzed with sunlight,
path a blue blaze of lavender and catmint ...
Bob would glimpse her from a leaded casement.

In the same instant, a latched door swings open;
laughter; he's chasing up the path to hold her.
The cold fiancée is away (in London?)
Bob would invite Ruth in to meet ... his mother.
Yes, his mother, white-haired, sturdy, patient,
ready to treat her like a favourite daughter.
While Bob's in the kitchen boiling water,

the woman stretches out a pale crepe hand
to take Ruth's own, smiles and sweetly whispers
'Truly, dear, I've never really liked her.
My Bob needs more. You are the one for him.'
Later Ruth tells them both about the baby.
Settled at tea in a green dreaming garden.
scones and strawberries, a roo-cooing pigeon.

Shared tears of joy, brief glitterballs of light.
Bob's cowlick fringe as thick as thrushes' wings.
His eyes are smiling from the child inside her.
'How did you know I longed to be a father?'
'Now your family will be my family.'
Feathered cirrus like faint angels' breath
blesses his future union with Ruth
on the unfinished, edgeless lawn of dreams.
Through the gold-leaning summer afternoon
maybe they'd sit *à deux* discussing names;
the mildest, sweetest lovers' bickerings
as the sky tincts with rosy pink above her.
'She is the one,' says Naomi, his mother.
'God, she's beautiful,' he sighs. 'I love her.'

In the event, though, there was nothing,
nothing. Nothing can come of nothing.
No one was there to welcome her; thin rain,
the houses clustered by the grey churchyard.
Their eyes looked small, the eaves frowning.
She had imagined detached islands
of thatch, white plaster and full-blown roses;
but these cottages stood fast against her,
shoulder to shoulder, close-set, crouching.
Blocking the church, a yew-tree black as ravens
flanking wet conker-trees, a dripping rowan.

THE VISITATION

A brindled cat slunk past, feral, silent,
eyes flicking malice at the anxious stranger
whose sapling arms cradle her passenger.

Thickets of scarlet buds blew and flickered,
cross-hatched, thorny, defending the windows,
a dew of blood from ancient battles.
Now she's no longer sure of the number
seen on an envelope in early summer;
she's a scholar, she must remember.
If there's no hope … they'd been too long apart
after the hasty tryst (first time on Tinder)
led to a dovecote flight of sweet, brief meetings,
growing more tender, she had thought, each time.
'So, we're both in the academic game …'
Ruth's bird-like calls of passion; his hoarse, deeper,
clawing the duvet to him as he came,
and for the first few times, he'd called her name.

Odd she should come here first after a man.
This village was the home of Michael Drayton,
one of the bands of brave Elizabethan
bowmen of poetry, her older passion,
Marlowe, bold Kit, sweet Will: *who pulls me down?*
She loved their metaphors, their rakish spirits,
cantering through the fields on steeds of words.
Drayton had ranged too far in *Polyolbion*,
thousands of lines beset with bards and druids,
which she had often started, never finished.
Did our beginnings ever know our ends?
Drayton was single, married to his art.
Now she is haunted by his hungry sonnet.
If there's no hope, come let us kiss and part.

It's August now. Ruth saw Bob last in June.
She'd talked of Henry James and Stevenson.
Yes, he had 'got engaged', brushing it off
as a mere trifle: 'There's no where and when.
Honestly, Ruth, it might just/well? never happen.
You are fantastic.' 'Yes, but what's Anne like?'
'Oh, not a bit like you. More cool and cautious.
Chilly, my mother says. I've known her ages.'
Somehow he'd been too busy in July,
but when she sent Bob texts, he would reply
with flirty messages and heart emojis.
After a month had passed, she vomited
one morning on the printout of her thesis,
purchased a test, and sobbed with happiness.

2

Through the blanched field of corn, ready for harvest,
Ruth follows some man's path, a v-shaped parting
dark as the roots of Anne's sharp beach-blonde hair –
her photograph had fallen from his jacket.
'Why do you carry this?' 'Oh, just a habit.'
Ruth's walking fast, her scholar's eyes are blind,
she cannot bear to see where she is going.
What was it, Henry James's 'distinguished thing'?
She'd sent a message first a week ago:
'I'd love to see you, darling. Tell me when.'
There was no answer so she sent again.
She knows they have a cerebral connection,
and she is strong, and not like other women,
he a professor, not like other men.

And yet, and yet. Is she too innocent?
Nay, I have done, you get no more of me.

THE VISITATION

She starts to worry as the week crawls by.
Her breasts are growing bigger by the day,
which, if he'd only meet her, he'd enjoy.
Maybe he's ill, or buried deep in study.
She understands. (One day they'll work together,
Writing their books; the children will be clever,
reading at two and off to bed at seven
leaving their parents free for adult heaven.)
No, she won't wait. She'll beard him in his den,
his country hideout where he lives alone
in pleasant Clifford Chambers on the river.
(But Sweet Will whispers, *Men, deceivers ever.*)

If Bob's not willing, there will be no child.
Her body's hot, but oh, her mind is cold,
Hey nonny no. No, she'll sigh no more,
one foot on shore and one in chilly stream,
she will be rational and kill her dream.
Beside the wheat the muddy Stour runs,
Too brown, too tangled, calling her too soon.
Of course he will be happy once he learns.
She turns away. Inside the sonnet burns,
Nay, I have done. You get no more of me!
And I am glad, yes, glad, with all my heart,
That thus so cleanly I myself can free.
Harder, too hard, to have the child alone.
Her purpose settles stupid as a stone.

That morning she had forced some breakfast down,
driven the roaring B-road, turning off
to sudden quiet. The village, secret, tight,
not one of its inhabitants about.
At last she'd found the number – no one home –
to ring, and ring, and louder, ring again.

Behind green curtains, had she glimpsed a hand
clawing the stuff that hid it back across?
But no, she thought, he'd said he kept a pet,
which left pale hairs; a kitten must have leapt.
Ruth longed for some kind minion in a pinny,
mother or cleaner, to emerge and greet her.
Outside the house, a neighbour's crimson Mini
(Bob, so he said, had never learned to drive)
proved that at least one person was alive.

And then the rain. It stopped (her sorrow lifted),
then started harder, grimmer still, and steadied.
How could she linger in the unpeopled square
where each blank window saw her sad and naked?
No, they were yokels, rustics. She has pride.
She is a serious young academic – yes,
and in her womb grow seeds of genius,
their two brains squared. She'd marched off down the
    road:
St Helen's Church, a Lutyens Manor House,
veers right – great acres of ripe wheat, too bright –
try left. A snicket leads her by green water,
dinnerplates of dark leaves and tight white flowers,
two swans, a mill, a family house, *not ours*,
then funnels on through ivy, hawthorn, briars.

So black, so deep. She has not been invited.
All afternoon she walks, too proud to weep.
At last the kindness of wide fields of grass
and the strange sideways eyes of yellow sheep
who safely graze beside their strapping lambs;
tall thistles poke from horse-apples; the sun
suddenly lobs long rays beneath the clouds,
somewhere there hides a rainbow, a good omen

making Bob's safe return to her seem certain.
Bees re-emerge, blurring the B-road's buzz
and all grows wild and Ruth can keep her child.
She had a breakdown once. The cars are loud,
her urban shoes are thin, the path is steep.
And there is far to go before they sleep.

No worries, none. The cars are deafening now.
That road might be the one that brought her here.
She'll take that well-worn path out of the fields
and find a quick way back beside the traffic.
It's six o'clock already. Time to go.
She knows him well enough, she prays, to know
he's no deceiver. *Oh, then sigh not so,*
but let him go, and be you blithe and bonny,
converting all your sounds of woe – but no.
Until she's seen him, no hey nonny.
Over the stile Ruth hoists herself and baby.
Past her dash giant jeeps, a petrol tanker.
(Ten years more worldly, blanker, her professor,
groaning in orgasm, professed to love her.)

3

Ping. And ping. Over the traffic noise the text-birds sing.
Across the road the path looks easier,
there is at least a low crash barrier, a bank
to hold away the savage metal river
scouring away the mossy world of Drayton.
Since there's no help, come let us kiss and part.
Split-second thinking. Shall she stay, or cross?
Instead she takes her phone – a brief caress –
then feasts in terror on her lover's message.
'Busy today. Am sorry. Also, news. Out of the blue

decided to get married. In Barbados! Want to thank
you Ruth. Sleep tight, sweet pea! Great memories.'
Someone is staggering. The wind is stunning
noise and the maw of fate and endless nothing.

Nay, I have done, you get no more of me.
Leaf in the eye of time, she sails the void,
her babe aboard, trialling the pathless crossing
over the kindly Lethe that brings death
to careless walkers and the suffering.
Ruth casts them both far out, an offering.
She's tried it twice before, once as a girl,
rejected by best friend for being too keen,
once as an anxious, under-frivolous student.
Yes, she's in luck. A pause; there's nothing coming,
And I am glad, am glad with all my heart –
for life's been beautiful, although it's short,
she's loved her poets, lived their poetry –
that thus so cleanly I myself can free.

Gasping, half-laughing, she is halfway over
half on her feet, half-kneeling for the blow.
She thinks of him, her tall half-time professor:
surely he has been half in love with her? –
oh hurry, Ruth, for what is this new noise –
she's crawling now, her thoughts are generous,
shake hands for ever, cancel all our vows,
and when we meet at any time again –
no, they'll not meet. Only another metre
left to traverse, and they are still all right,
but something red is flying on towards her,
going too fast around a nearby corner,
coming to brush our dyad with death's wing
and bringing Ruth that last 'distinguished thing'.

THE VISITATION

On, on, the crimson dragon bears on down,
a customised Mini driven fast by Anne,
who's cooking dinner for her man tonight.
He'll want a sauce. She's tired, hardly looking,
screams rounds the bend and in the evening light
dark dog or fox is dragging towards the verge –
Christ, now she'll be some animal's undoing –
Anne is upon it as the angles meet
of time and space and fortune at Ruth's feet.
A flash of bleached white buzzcut, crimson light,
a blaring wall of warning from the horn –
Be it not seen in either of our brows
That we one jot of former love retain –
and speed and noise dissolve in wails of pain.

Ruth sees it rushing at her, bloody death,
Now at the last gasp of love's latest breath,
when, his pulse failing, passion speechless lies –
one second's choice. She makes it, or it's made,
some pitying angel flings them both aside,
sprawled on her knees, saved by the palisade
some careful council jobsworth had decreed;
the skidding car jets pebbles at her head.
She lies quite still. She is alive. Alive.
And in that instant finds she wants to live.
when Faith is kneeling by his bed of death
the child within her turns his bud-blind face
and innocence is closing up his eyes
Ruth opens hers, and sees the sheltering skies.

Since there's no help, come let us kiss and part –
Nay I have done, you get no more of me;
And I am glad, yea glad with all my heart,
That thus so cleanly I myself can free;

Shake hands for ever, cancel all our vows,
And when we meet at any time again,
Be it not seen in either of our brows
That we one jot of former love retain.
Now at the last gasp of love's latest breath,
When, his pulse failing, Passion speechless lies,
When Faith is kneeling by his bed of death,
And Innocence is closing up his eyes –
The bells ring seven. Light and night collide.
White clover, white. Ruth and the world abide.

And what is faith, she thinks, if it's not this?
Within her, circled, precious, helpless, held,
floats in her belly still the marvellous child
and he can have no place upon this earth
(her hair is full of dust, her eyes are wild)
unless her body brings him safe to birth.
The light increases, pigeon streaked with pearl,
a halo round his head, most sacred-small,
gold the cut stalks, gold the wind-shivered barley,
gold the late sunlight's radiant offering,
for it is life, the one distinguished thing –
and here is heaven, and he is part of it.
Now if thou would'st, when all have giv'n him over
From death to life thou might'st him still recover.

Kiss and Part

And the River Flows On

by Joan Bakewell

Liza was wearing a veil: she had insisted. It covered her
eyes, opaque, concealing her expression. Just as well. She
didn't want anyone seeing: curious as to her expression,
whether she might even drop a tear, or at least pretend to.
She wanted them to admire the veil, of course, its stylish-
ness, its originality. Typical of her, they might say; she
hoped they would say. She expected to be noticed. That's
why she had chosen the veil ... As the hour approached,
she had taken the pert little hat carefully from its box and
set it gently on her fine blonde hair, newly washed, newly
blonde. Then spread its trimming of fine black net with its
scattering of small black dots across her face. Facing the
hotel room mirror she had squinted through its texture to
see its effect. Good. She was almost ready.

***

Ginny, in contrast, had set out scarcely ready at all. She
hadn't had time to get the car serviced, but at least she had
had a posse of immigrants swill it clean. She hadn't thought
about what to wear. Did people care these days? And who
would notice? Well, her mother certainly would and she
felt it important to please her. Especially given her mother's
frailty. Perhaps her critical eye might not be as keen as once

it was. Yet ever the dutiful daughter, she searched out a simple dark coat and, a nice touch, pinned a brooch on the lapel: amber stone in pinchbeck that Father had given her. She ran a brush through her deliberately tangled hair to give it just enough seemliness for the occasion.

She and Gerald had decided their children should not come with them: taking a day off school could generate all sorts of administrative crises, possibly prompting an official reprimand and marking them down as 'tricky' parents by the surly headmistress. So Jocelyn and Piers would stay at school and Karen, their amiable neighbour, would take them in for tea and, unavoidably, sticky cake and television when they returned. 'I'll give Granny your love, eh?' Ginny had called, but their heads were bowed over their iPhones and they didn't respond.

Gerald, self-employed and glad of a break from his desk, offered to drive. But Ginny insisted: after all, she believed this event belonged to her family, and she was both reluctant and assertive in seeking to own it. She set the satnav for the village in the Warwickshire countryside, adjusting the car's mirrors. As she drove away, they reflected back the pink stucco and brimming window boxes of their Victorian terrace home. When she returned, things would have changed. But then, things change all the time, don't they? How could a single day, even one so freighted with significance as this one, make much of a difference? Only a tiny anxiety niggled at the back of her mind. But traffic concerns took over. Gerald adjusted the radio and they settled back to the soothing predictability of Classic FM. As they drove on in silence, he placed a hand gently on her knee.

* * *

Emmeline Thoroughgood had organised the funeral. Thoroughgood Associates were a theatrical agents and Emmeline its ebullient presiding diva. Justin Shirley had been one of her most celebrated clients. More than that, he had been, since his giddy days fresh out of RADA, the recipient of her unqualified adoration and, ever more needed, her tolerance. He had been one among the clutch of northern working-class talent that first hit the English stage in the early 1960s and went on to sustained careers as stars in modest British films: early success had enflamed a nascent ego.

He responded to the adulation with a fine attention to his professional skills – and a reckless sharing of his success with a series of vulnerable women. His skills would hold him at the top of his profession through decades when others were fading into neglect and alcoholism; his vulpine charm would garner him a series of wives and a bevy of children that even his starry income could not support. His northern values – probity, honesty, plain speaking – would struggle to survive such demands. So he was touchingly thankful whenever one of the wives took her own independent course. But he remained fitfully loyal and generous to his children. Ginny loved him. Her younger brother, Desmond, struggled with resentment and pique. Their mother, even in her years alone, kept her own counsel.

* * *

Emmy – the telling abbreviation of her name had lost none of its power to amuse her theatrical clientele – had been responsible for the obituaries. She had persuaded disenchanted friends and jaundiced critics to pen paragraphs of unqualified praise. At the moment of death it is right and proper that we remember good things ... and exaggerate them almost beyond credibility. Thus it was that each of his four wives was described as bringing happiness and fecundity to the marriage. His second, Liza, the set and costume designer on the debut of a Pinter play in which he starred, had in reality been the one credited with bringing him back from near-suicidal depression. Fifteen years on he had led a national company in a revival of the same Pinter play and garnered a crop of bad notices for his hesitant performance. 'It's the pauses, don't they know that yet ... the Pinter pauses,' he had complained.

His wretchedness had seemed inconsolable, so she had snatched him from the dispiriting company of more successful colleagues and taken him to a small cottage in a small village, where he could act out the role of an anonymous urban refugee without fear of being confronted and asked for an autograph. She had cancelled a commitment to design an avant-garde rendering of *Le Misanthrope*, and donned wellies and anorak to stomp by his side through muddy fields in search of true values ... or whatever it was they felt they had lost.

In the end they had failed to find it and were divorced a year later. But something precious about that encounter lingered, sustaining a distant but fond friendship between them. That's why, perhaps, some thirty years later Justin had left instructions that his funeral be in St Helen's Church, at the consoling heart of the village where he had once come back from the brink.

Now his ex-wife was touched by her own broken memories. Through the brittle frailty of age, she could snatch at something gone, and regretted: a feathering of light through green leaf, a fleeting shimmer of sunshine on a moving stream. Snatches of mood still reached her. In flight from traffic and chatter they had been content and quiet together, he nursing a wounded pride, she tending his disappointment. The days had lolled along, seemingly of limitless hours, only marked by the sweet chiming of St Helen's clock, each stroke holding its place in the mellow air until it was time to make space for the next. There was no hurry in its progress: there was no hurry in their lives.

They rose early from white sheets on soft mattresses, surveyed, even admired, each other's long-familiar limbs. He made fresh coffee. The crust of the freshly baked bread crunched beneath a weight of unsalted butter and home-made raspberry jam. The coffee settled within the Italian percolator before being dispensed into sturdy white cups. Why had they neglected to enjoy such things, the precious details of daily life? Later they would walk along the river-bank, marking where long purple flowers stooped over turgid pools, crossing a bridge from tangled hedges into meadowlands where their arrival stirred lazy sheep to move from their path. The days ambled slowly: a dog barked, a family of swans glided by, their teenage cygnets ungainly and grey. They sat on a splintered bench. They smiled, without speech. There was no need.

Through the spreading days, Liza watched him furtively, monitoring his moods, encouraged by his silence, taking it for the return of some inner consolation. Slowly she came to realise this was more than a crisis of a bad review: it crystallised a lifetime of lurking self-doubt. He at his most needful encountered her at her wisest. The moment was not to last. Their return to hectic others and the tumultu-ous round of their chosen lives broke the spell. But now something stirred from long ago that deserved her con-sideration.

Emmy had phoned her with news of his death and the funeral arrangements. Liza was taken off guard: 'But why St Helen's Church? Did he say?'

'I know, it's truly odd, but then he was getting a little odd. We all are, aren't we, darling, as the years go by?' Liza ignored the hint. She knew she was forgetting things. So, yes, perhaps things were getting a little odd. But oddness wouldn't explain this. This was a message, a message that Justin had left behind for her. A reminder of what had mattered long ago. She had promptly phoned the only inn in the village and booked a room for the night before the funeral.

'No, thanks, Emmy, I won't want one of the formal cars' (she knew they were intended for theatrical moguls), 'I'll get there under my own steam.' She promptly hired a Jaguar XL and bought the neat little hat trimmed with veiling and its scattering of black spots.

Ginny was not entirely surprised by the hat. And not impressed. It made too much of a bid to be noticed, threatening, even intended, to steal the thunder from Justin's fourth wife, the mousy Amy, and their two pale children. Ginny had spoken to her mother on the telephone on the night they heard of Justin's death. They had been practical, matter-of-fact together, the distress of one meeting the anguish of the other and resolving itself into platitudes. But something about the edge in her mother's voice suggested more than grief. Liza had always spoken with a low throaty rumble, what people might have called a smoker's voice, although she didn't smoke. Now there was a drifting vagueness about her speech that conveyed a mind distracted. Ginny struggled to focus the conversation: they spoke of how the funeral might take shape, whose responsibility would it be, might either of them even be asked to contribute. (Liza spoke keenly of 'Fear no more the heat of the Sun'.) Why was it not in St Paul's, Covent Garden? Ginny had wondered. Her mother stayed quiet about her personal theory. Better keep that to herself, lest people think she was completely dotty.

Desmond, younger than his sister Ginny by four years, was a GP in Shrewsbury and not keen to turn up at all. His days were already exhausting enough and now he would have to find a locum for his daytime surgery and leave his wife to handle the parents' evening that night. No one had asked if it would inconvenience him, indeed no one expressed any awareness of him at all. His beige personality had a way of passing people by. He expected to be a drab figure among the glittering Shirley clan, and although he accepted that with tepid resignation, he felt the burden of immediate responsibility. He knew his mother would expect his support, literally his arm to lean on. She was getting old and, he suspected, arthritic. She was also more forgetful than ever and he wondered whether it was simply cognitive decline or something more threatening. He closed his mind to that idea the moment it occurred.

* * *

The village, a long cul-de-sac, meanders from the New Inn at the junction with the main road, towards the manor house at the other end. There is no through traffic but always a goodly clutch of cars in the inn's car park. Its reputation as a gastropub attracts a regular fan base. On the morning of the funeral the space would boast a higher than usual medley of Volvos and Lexus, even a vintage Bentley. Liza's Jaguar would sit unashamedly among them. The theatrical fraternity was turning out in style.

At the other end, flanked by an ancient Tudor rectory, stands the simple church of St Helen's, rich with all that makes the British parish church so precious: just inside the heavy oak door, a list of rectors starting in 1274 with Robert the Wise; a fine Jacobean pulpit, and towards the altar two brasses on the wall; further along, a painted Elizabethan tomb: kneeling parents face to face, the folds of her black mourning gown tipping over a velvet cushion; their three children, two grown to adulthood, and one who died a baby, wrapped in pink and white swaddling clothes. And hidden away on a lower wall, a plaque commemorating the visits of the poet Michael Drayton, about whom speculation was rife. Had he loved the lady of the manor? Had he cavorted here with his neighbouring playwright colleague, one Will Shakespeare? Had he, like him, come and gone to London when the summer plague hit the city? Perhaps Emmy would have found an appropriate poem to read at Justin's obsequies.

Between the inn at one end and the church at the other, houses of diverse styles line the street: a row of Victorian redbrick terrace houses; a number of half-timbered houses with picket fences and tangled front gardens; one or two grander houses, stuccoed walls and a curving porch; a number of Lutyens-style houses with tall chimneys and angled windows; even a crop of more recent build. And beside the church a three-sided square; the only way beyond it, a narrow lane of tiny cottages winding through close-packed hedges and gardens towards the river, where swans pass and on the opposing bank horses and sheep graze. Somehow they all converge into the lyricism of the English country village. And it was here that Liza had brought Justin back from the depths.

The sunlight woke her. She had tossed under the floral duvet and been up in the night as she regularly was these days. There was no going back to sleep. The enormity of the day dawned with the sunlight: Justin had not been central to her life for many years, but they had consulted about the children's teenage years. She had watched the trajectory of his success; they exchanged warm greetings when the occasion warranted it – she on his knighthood, he on her BAFTA award; they had grown distant while in some ways remaining close. Now he was not even in the world, leaving a yawning place in her emotional life where he had lingered long after the divorce.

She found she was confused by his going; he had after all gone from her home, her bed, long ago. She had learnt to live a life in which he was not present. So what in all honesty was she thinking now he was not there at all, and regretting it so powerfully? How was it that people who had left our lives could be continuing somehow in their place while living strong and effective lives somewhere else entirely? Is that what memory was about? Was time somehow tricking our minds into thinking nothing was entirely over? She had never made sense of the scientists' claim that time was curved. Yet somehow it seemed to be curving back on her now and coming back in more than passing sentiment. She felt like a bereaved widow.

This certainly would not play well on the stage of public events. Justin's death had earned a place of regret on the news bulletins of the day and his funeral a week later would command a camera feed for the networks. *The Stage* magazine had sent a journalist. The older denizens of the West End theatre, of TV soaps and British films were brushing down their darker clothes ... increasingly used as they got older – and preparing a succinct but generous phrase for the moment a microphone was waved towards them. Ginny and Desmond were resolved to shepherd their mother through such mayhem with the minimum of fuss and attention. They were unsure whether she felt the same. The little hat had them worried: a deliberate attention-seeker from one who after all had once had an international reputation for stage and costume design. Not everyone would remember that, but Liza certainly did.

'You look very nice, dear.' Ginny and Gerald had been ushered into her hotel room and Liza had appraised her daughter: Ginny had cleared the first hurdle. Her mother's tone indicated a mellow if melancholy mood. The edgy irritation had not materialised. Ginny raised an eyebrow at Gerald, knowing she must return the compliment: 'And you look lovely, Ma.' Then more tentatively but confronting the crux of the day: 'Father would be so proud.'

Desmond, added his required comments, more clumsily over-egged the pudding: 'Oh yes, Ma, he always admired the way you dressed.' Liza saw no manoeuvre, but it came.

'We need to protect your hat against the breeze, Ma, so why don't I drive you in my car right up to the church rather than walk? Then you can slip in unnoticed without any risk.'

Liza was not interested in 'slipping in unnoticed' and not averse to taking the risk. But her arthritis was playing up, so the car did indeed seem a good idea.

It was a fine May morning with a cheerful light breeze, teasing at her veil as Liza made for Desmond's Volvo. He tucked a rug round her thin legs, their purple blotches muted by her fine black stockings. 'Comfy, Ma?'

'Yes, yes, don't fuss.'

She looked wistful. 'I'm trying to bring to mind those happy days … They were happy, you know, when we were here together. Had I told you how we used to sit beside the stream, how it would sooth his worries?' She had, many times. But he listened again with resignation.

Desmond had long closed his mind to his father's departure from the noisy family home. It seemed, in memory, as though one moment he was there and laughing, bossing his son around over toy trains, the next he was ponderously explaining how he would be coming over each weekend for outings that turned out to be visits to windy playgrounds and lavish treats at McDonald's. Desmond always returned with subdued relief to his warm home and his mother's chill indifference to his outings. Now he brooded moodily on what exactly he had liked about his father. He remembered with a grim smile the Christmas his father had been Dame in an up-market Christmas pantomime with jokes about Mrs Thatcher. Yes, yes, he would hold on to the fun that had been. Though even then it had not felt close.

* * *

The first cars crept unobtrusively into the village, like purring black panthers. One or two stopped at the inn, calling imperiously for coffees, sometimes a stiff brandy. Meetings and greetings, of which there would be many, took on an appropriate ritual, a ritual half-improvised, half-formal. Smiles were kept to a minimum. Even those who knew each other well offered only a subdued acknowledgement. In the process of greeting, some clung together briefly, their bodies offering subtle reassurance rather than anything that might suggest pleasure. Sometimes a hand reached out and held the other by the neck, their locked heads nodding, expressions grim. The women sighed; occasionally there were shrugged shoulders. 'Did you expect? ...', 'Had you heard? ...', 'When had you last? ...'

Implied honours went to those who had most recently been in touch, an awed respect for those who had shared celebrated performances. There was a surreptitious enquiring as to who else might be coming. The cast list was expected to be long and it was natural to wonder who would star.

* * *

At the other end of the village, the church of St Helen's was a house divided. Were the proceedings of the morning to be primarily a religious ceremony or would theatricality prevail? There were strong advocates on either side: members of the parish council cherished the orthodoxy of the *Book of Common Prayer*; the undertakers extolled the virtues of inclusiveness and, more pressingly, compromise. So the incumbent vicar of the church had been prevailed on to be elsewhere. He had conceded with a reluctant spirit. While relieved of conducting a service he suspected might not accord with his evangelical tendency, he was sad to miss the church-door moment of shaking hands with departing stars of stage and television for whom he cherished something of a schoolboy crush. To allay his disappointment he had agreed to turn up for the lavish spread that was to be provided afterwards in the Jubilee Hall, his evangelical tendencies giving way before the prospect of champagne and *foie gras*.

His place at the altar and beside the coffin was being taken by the Revd Simon Simmons, newly ordained to the ranks of the clergy after an earlier incarnation as a pop musician. For five years he had been the lead singer in the group Simon and the Stylites, his explicitly sexy lyrics sitting incongruously with tunes not too distantly derived from the hymns of his Methodist childhood. His partner Timothy worked on the same listings magazine as Justin's young widow, Amy, and at his suggestion Simon had been called to the bedside to give secular comfort to the dying atheist. Now he would match a thoughtful and ambiguous theology with the voluble tributes of family and friends. Amy and her children had drawn up the printed order of service which reflected the skills of her print background and the range of poetic and dramatic tributes various actors were keen to make. It was agreed there would be three hymns, three personal tributes, two prayers and one pop song.

* * *

Desmond's car drew up in the small square beside the church and he moved quickly to help his mother from the passenger seat. They had arrived early in order to choose a good place. He led her slowly past the war memorial and through the creaking wooden gate into the churchyard. In the interests of grass-cutting, some of the tombstones had been set aside, yet a disordered array still stood recognisable as the traditional place where the English laid their dead.

As they moved to approach the church porch, Liza paused beneath the two towering horse-chestnut trees that flanked the path. She looked up, through the thin veiling of her hat. The trees were in their full May-time glory, their green leaves brilliant, their candles coming into the promise of flower. Her memories, all green now, came flooding back: the green of the river, of the weeping willow; the green of the glossy magnolia leaves, sheltering the pregnant pink buds; the green of the meadow gardens, their crops of dandelions splashing yellow into this green world.

'Why did I dress like this? ... Why all this black and city stuff? It's not how we were ...' She looked around in horror as though it was all a mistake, a slip in time, a sudden brain storm.

'But Ma, it's a special occasion. You want it to be a special occasion,' Desmond struggled to reassure the now dazed woman. 'And you look very smart, the hat especially.'

He gave a tug at her elbow and felt the thin bones beneath her sleeve. She returned to the moment and let him guide her on.

Others were arriving now, in pressing numbers. It's not done to hurry or overtake at a funeral, so this has to be done surreptitiously. A minor television presenter with her garish partner stepped on the grass to gain a stride ahead. Desmond and Liza moved into the small neat space of the little church. There they found access to the pews blocked by three discreetly suited young men who, in return for the printed order of service, claimed the right to direct arrivals to specific pews.

Desmond, his hand on his mother's elbow, felt his spirits sag in fear that her role, her status, might go unacknowledged. At its worst she might be denied access at all and invited to join the groups of villagers and media already assembling beyond the gates to hear the service relayed by speakers. The television presenter and her companion were already being turned away. Liza drew herself to her full height, which was modest.

'Ah yes,' said one of the young man in black, a flick of flaxen hair falling forward as he stooped to speak to her. 'Liza Shirley, isn't it? Please come this way.'

Desmond turned anxiously to search out Ginny and Gerald, who were still to arrive. But if he hesitated, the reserved space might be lost. He took his place beside his mother in the forward rows of Victorian pews. Not at the very front, of course, but forward enough for honour to be served. Liza resolved to gaze straight ahead, unwilling to encounter the embarrassment of half-remembered faces and forgotten names. She clung to memories of Justin and his presence in her heart and in her past.

Desmond fidgeted with the order of service. Its cover displayed a photograph of Justin in the role of Prospero, and below:

We are such stuff
As dreams are made on, and our little life
Is rounded with a sleep.

A seemly lack of grandeur, Desmond thought. And a gentle dig at the official funeral service, with its promise of resurrection. He glanced down the list of speakers, checking for those his mother had known, had worked with, been close to. There was a smattering large enough to give the comfort of feeling among her own: not her family, perhaps, but her tribe.

And here they were: worthies from the RSC and the National Theatre led the roll call, a company of like-minded spirits called by some compelling instinct to celebrate language, human discourse and the tempestuous vagaries of life. Such things had happened in their private lives too. Liza was no exception there. She suddenly felt good being among them. Her sense of self blossomed. Now her eyes wandered eagerly around the gathering congregation, recognising, nodding, a shy smile and small frown for someone known but only half-remembered.

The congregation stood as Justin's immediate family arrived. Liza, not wishing to seem nosy, waited to glance sideways as they passed Amy, hatless, her blonde hair tamed into a bun at her neck, held there with a spray of white spring flowers. She wore a grey linen coat and dress. The grief was in her face, not her clothes. Her two children, one on each side, were holding her hands, drawing comfort from the warmth of her skin and its familiarity. Their father's hands had at the last been cold and still. Liza knew grief was terrible wherever it fell: theirs stabbed at her own. She felt her body quiver and sway forward. She held fast to the pew in front.

The organ had been playing softly throughout the morning. Now Bach's Toccata broke forth: powerful, commanding, reminiscent of great tragedy, impressing its audience, keen as they were to be impressed by the profundity of its emotion. If there had been fleeting glances at others, if there had been flimsy reminiscences buzzing in bowed heads, these were gone. Suddenly and as one – as in great theatre – the audience was united in its sense of moment, the moment a great man, great loss, was being acknowledged and revered.

* * *

It was when the singing started that Liza changed.

There was the usual church choir turned out in scarlet robes, the boys with pie-frill collars. But there was also an informal choir up from London of those who had shared the stage with Justin in works by Sondheim and Bernstein. They had arrived early in the hope of bringing some order to an unwieldy collaboration. They were not entirely disappointed. The sound was both well-meaning and robust. It was certainly loud, prompting other performers among the congregation to open their throats and let forth. The sentiments came easily.

And did those feet in ancient time, Walk upon England's mountains green. Didn't they all share this easy patriotism born of the post-war pride in which many had grown up? Liza was at one with them. And something more. Listening intently, she turned her ear to the mellifluous sounds and let words she had once sung by rote reach into her inner heart: 'pleasant pastures', 'our clouded hill', 'I will not cease from mental fight', 'England's green and pleasant land'. Wasn't it all suddenly a call to love the places she knew with new strength? This place, particularly, the place where Justin and she had shared an illuminating moment, an incandescent experience ... That's how it was, surely. Her grief grew precious to her, it as if reaching her through the words she was hearing.

There was a reading from T. S. Eliot. Liza found the language unfamiliar and hard to decipher. But her mind snatched at what she needed:

the communication
Of the dead is tongued with fire beyond the language of
   the living
Here, the intersection of the timeless moment
In England and nowhere.

Yes, yes, the timeless moment, this was it. And in England. She thought of the world beyond the church, turning physically towards it, seeking the brilliant green of leaf and lane, the shivering trees she knew were there, running down to the stream. She squirmed at the formality of the service. But in the moment, there was Justin, lying not far away, the coffin set on two trestles, topped by a vast spread of white and yellow flowers, dressed out with gypsophila and fern, all fixed firmly in place with a twining of unseen wires and florist's thread and ribbons. Was man subduing nature or did the wreath's evident beauty show nature transcending man? Funny that! Liza fidgeted uneasily with her veil. How odd she had thought that mattered. That she had made so much fuss, when what mattered was Justin, in the flesh, once alive, now dead; his proper body, so full of meaning for her, lying now no longer beside her but not far away either. Justin, and flowers, and green meadows, and England.

Suddenly there was a change of mood and it made her smile: Justin's two young children – they must be about twelve and ten – and a gaggle of others on guitars and a violin, their slight voices recalling times their elders had known: 'Thank you for the days ...'

There were smiles of recognition along the pews: The Kinks, of course. Must have been released around 1968! That was a year! Justin had begun to make his name in the sixties. So had many of those around her. It had been a hey-day for some, a golden start for others. What an inspired choice. How quirky people were these days, rejecting much of the formal liturgy, making choices of their own. She thoroughly approved. And as the sweetness of the music swayed over them, Liza's mind wandered. Images came swimming into her mind: Justin leaning over their newborn, holding tiny fingers; Justin raging at the ruin of a favourite sweater; Justin popping a cork after his first leading role; Justin brushing leaves from her hair as they lay in the grass. Now he was gone and only she knew these things had happened. When she went, the images went with her. They had no presence in any other memory. Gone.

She shivered with a sharp thrill of fear. Everything, everyone, vanishes. One day soon someone would write Justin's biography. Some bright young journalist would go rooting around in theatre programmes, seeking out reviews, asking for letters, interviewing relations, friends, the acting fraternity. But what would he know of tiny fingers, ruined sweaters? Why should he care about leaves in her hair? The real Justin was slipping away, caught as briefly as a wisp of smoke in the clear air.

Beyond the church the lane quivered with greenness; the stream meandered through meadows of dandelions and buttercups. He had recovered here: recovered what was fine and talented in his life. And of that she would be his last, his only witness.

Seriousness returned. The congregation rose and their rising voices confirmed her thoughts.

Time like an ever-rolling stream,
Bears all its sons away ...

Her reedy voice joined theirs. She felt elated.

* * *

There was confusion outside the church. There usually is, Liza knew. She had been to many funerals recently. People milled around, greeting each other with sudden smiles hastily mellowed into sighs and hugs. She hid her face, eager to avoid the sighs and hugs. Where were Ginny and Gerald? She dispatched Desmond to find them. Soon there was a general move towards the Jubilee Hall, where a reception was provided: media people and villagers craned their necks to identify those they knew from TV soaps and historic fantasy dramas. A discrete acknowledgement was made by lesser stars. The grandees kept themselves aloof, fearful of requests for autographs or fawning praise. The scene was one of spontaneous confusion such as any film director would struggle to create.

Liza, rather than hover alone in their midst, moved swiftly and neatly towards the lane she knew. It ran alongside the church, down to the river, down to the spot where Justin and she had walked so often.

Her eyes were shining.

Ginny was furious: 'You know she's frail, Desi. She's also amazingly forgetful.'

'Yes, I said I'd bring you back, but she is alarmingly vague these days ...'

'Yes, that's my point. She won't remember where we agreed to meet up. Did we even agree? Oh, God, this is hopeless.'

Desmond refused to be panicked.

'I think she remembers lots, you know. Odd to say it, but I think she was quite excited by the service.'

Gerald grew impatient.

'We need to find her, Desmond. All the more if she's lost her marbles.'

'Oh, don't say such things.' Ginny shared his fears but didn't want them spoken. 'Perhaps she's gone along to the reception. She knows the place, after all.'

They ambled off, still squabbling, in the wrong direction.

* * *

The path down to the river had become overgrown since Liza had first known it. Brambles caught at her clothes.

She raised a hand to move an intrusive branch out of her way. But the path itself was sturdy and sure. She felt its old familiarity. The small gardens dotted along the way, individually different, but creating an aura of eternal fruitfulness as she remembered. The old apple tree was heavier than ever, stooping low to totally obscure the collapsed outhouses that she knew were there. It reminded her of Samuel Palmer and Linden Lea, scraps of a childhood memory that re-emerged in her late years and ageing mind. She started to hum the tune ... *the apple trees do lean down low in Linden Lea* ... and here too, she thought, smiling at the persistence of nature, the eternity of green.

The river was like a vision, flowing slowly, catching the stray leaf that dawdled down, pulling at the reeds along the bank. The freshness of its green darkened almost to brown in the shadows. On the far side the weeping willow drooped its branches into the water. Beyond it the meadows reached towards the open countryside: fields and pathways, even in the distance a small clutch of trees. It was how she had remembered, how she had loved it, how they both had loved it.

Some hours later as the sun went down and the sky turned to gold, they found her hat on the riverbank.

Kiss and Part

The Creature

by Jill Dawson

She was beset by annoying little ailments. She was thinking this as she pushed the old-fashioned latch to keep the skinny wooden door from flapping open and noticed the sore spot in her fingers. My fingers hurt. My gums hurt (that new toothbrush perhaps?), there's a bruise on my buttock where I fell two days ago in the car park. I'm not myself. I'm falling apart. And why? Stupid reasons. Jeff. Too busy. Too something. Why on earth had she promised to cat-sit for Raymond? But that had been agreed last year, and things so different then. How could she have known what lay in wait for her?

Raymond. How kind he was; the meals he brought her, the long phone conversations, just listening really, just breathing. Now off on a cruise and she hadn't really taken it in. A whole week. She'd said she could feed the cat, but she'd somehow pictured herself dropping by, calling in with cat food every few days. Not twice a day. Not staying in Raymond's funny little house. Not having to bring wine, loo roll, make up fires, fill Raymond's fridge with her olives and new butter; struggle with the pedal bin that didn't pop up; take baths in Raymond's rickety old bath. When you pulled out the plug, the water running down the pipes was like an animal growling. Primitive, that's what it was.

And talking of animals: my God, Georgio. A cat so melo-dramatic that when she arrived and saw it arching its spine and displaying its full glory on the wall opposite the house, well, just looking at it reminded her of a Ted Hughes poem. *Green tigering the gold.* What kind of cat has a striped tail, striped legs, and looks like it's made of slatted blinds? A tiger cat. A super-cat. She was freaked out by it. Raymond had explained there was a tin opener and a big bag of stuff for the litter tray and Georgio needed some dry food and some wet food and – it sounded easy. It would be fine – she should get over herself! – if she opened a bottle of Raymond's pinot noir and made up a fire with his logs. That cat was more a tiger and its jelly food stank so power-fully of something savoury it disgusted her, but weirdly made her hungry, too. Cat food! I'm *definitely* not myself.

Falling over in a car park, for God's sake. Stone cold sober. Am I turning into an old person? Raymond said: have you been to the doctor? You're only fifty-four. Perhaps it's something neurological. A brain thing. You know, a balance thing. She didn't tell him about the auditory hallu-cination. The time she'd heard Jeff, so clearly, talking to her in the kitchen. Bollocks, she said. Yes, I'll look after the cat. Bring me something nice from your Caribbean trip and don't get a venereal disease.

STD, he'd corrected. Raymond. He was ten years younger than her, and they used different terms these days. No one would use an old-fashioned phrase any more like 'going bonkers'.

Now she jumped as someone trundled past the cottage window with a wheelie bin. Unfamiliar noises. The sky dark-ened, or rather the sky over the graveyard flowed to green, like being underwater. The blossom from a huge cherry tree dangled and twitched. When Raymond had asked her the cat-sitting favour she hadn't known his house backed onto a graveyard. She hadn't reckoned on the significance of graveyards, how differently she'd feel about them one day.

After she'd fed Georgio, he went out for his nightly prowl. There was a cat flap. Raymond said beyond the meals – morning and evening – she wasn't to worry. She *did* worry. She didn't like the creature; she felt better when the cat wasn't there. The sound of the cat flap startled her, as did a log snapping in the fire. It made her heart race. Once, babysitting as a teenager, the owners hadn't told her they'd a cat and she'd heard one sneezing behind a curtain. A sneezing ghost! She could still remember how shaken she'd felt as she peeled back the curtain to confront it; she'd never liked cats after that.

Raymond hadn't been there to let her in: he was already at Southampton checking out his Standard Berth. He'd left the key in the back garden, on a hook in the log shed. Just for one week, and the idea was she'd catch her breath, after the funeral and all, and it would be good for her, a change of scene, and she could go walking in the beautiful country-side nearby, have a meal at the pub. But she'd brought the wrong boots and another little ailment now arose: a painful verruca on her left foot, choosing this moment to start smarting, playing up. My body is turning against me, she thought. It's revolting. *I'm* revolting.

Everything startled her. The timer went off on the cooker and she hadn't meant to set it. Georgio – Devil Cat – came back once, pranged the flap again like a prankster, and then went out. The church bell chimed the hour, reminding her of school, of some horrid boy dinging on a triangle. Her heart hammered afresh. If Raymond had been there he would have said, Darling, who knew you were so skittish? *Who knew?*

The floor was cold: red tiles. The walls were a utilitarian blue, the colour reminded her of school or hospitals, though there were nice touches: a deep-red velvet sofa and flowered curtains with little red birds on them. Raymond was a sad loner, she decided, and pictured her own house, now on the market, recently despised, but immediately revaluated, resuscitated: the light, the snarly wild garden. The daffodils with their healthy yellow heads: so friendly in comparison to those dark, sickly bluebells under the nodding cherry in the graveyard.

She was ready. They'd discussed it and Raymond had advised, and it had seemed for the best. A fresh start, moving on, not staying in the past, putting Jeff behind her (when Raymond said this she had a strong picture: Jeff standing behind her, his hands on her breasts, warm hands, now lifting up her nightdress, pressing himself against her. She banished this, though, because it felt wrong to think such thoughts, such trivialising, debasing thoughts about the dead. And then this banishment was followed by a silent howl of anguish. Only Jeff would be able to share this memory, only Jeff would let her be smutty and eroticise everything; Jeff who knew that this was a left-over trait from girlhood and vaguely dysfunctional, and knew why).

Never mind that: a week at Raymond's cat-sitting was just the break she needed. She still had a month of compassionate leave from work, there were notes she could catch up on. This was the break before the bigger break, before the new life began.

So she should pour another glass of red, put a log on and maybe read a book or something, or open up some of her notes, write them up. She dismissed as ridiculous the idea that she was too spooked to go outside and open the log shed. The sky over the graveyard was soupy now, not green any longer but actually a heightened, intense blue, with spiky black trees. As she looked at it she saw her own face in the window-pane wearing the glasses that she forgot she wore these days. And then another face. Huge eyes. A girl. Oh my God. And moments later – a loud rap at the door. And another one: someone rapping wildly. *Let me in, let me in.* And Linda's heart again began hammering, hammering, hammering.

* * *

She went to the door and listened. Actually, it wasn't a loud rap. More like a bird, tap-tapping. It was possible it was just a branch, knocking lightly. She listened again and it continued, distinctly. Her feet were cold on the tiles; she put her slippers on and stood there again, shaking and listening. What was it? Should she let it in?

The cat sneezing behind the sofa: her girlhood self-aroused in terror. *What will happen if I open the door?*

There were two doors. Firstly, a wooden interior door that opened to a little space with the boiler in it. Linda said: Hello, who's there? into the wood, and lifted the rattly little latch on the first door, pulling it towards her. It opened with a theatrical creak. Then she was in the space, the strange dark space between doors and it smelled of warm apples and some other smell from her childhood. And she was looking at the other door, the outside door, with a black square of window in it.

And in the window, shadowy: a girl's face. The girl was pressing her face up to the glass. She was calling: Anybody home? Please – help me! Please, can I come in?

Don't be ridiculous. It's probably a neighbour. Let the girl in. So she did.

Linda let her in, and the girl stepped into the apple space and then over the WELCOME mat and into the front room. She was shaking, she'd been running. She was breathless, she could hardly speak. She brought a great rush of outdoor air with her, chilled air. She was vague at first but also a big presence: loud, blustery. She doubled up for a moment.

'Oh thank you, thank you!' she said, when she unfolded herself. Her shape seemed to settle, like a genie materialising from a bottle.

'Would you like to sit down?' Linda asked. 'Can I get you something?'

The girl nodded. Yes, she would like tea, she said. Could she have a cup of tea?

Linda went to the corner of the front room – the kitchen part – to put the kettle on. The cottage was small and the downstairs was just one big room with a window and sink on one side; a cooker in a corner. She did not like to turn her back on the girl, who had sunk immediately onto Raymond's red velvet sofa. The girl had moved two cushions – blue tapestry cushions, embroidered, she suspected by Raymond himself – to one side. It was a gesture that Linda saw out of the corner of her eye and struck her as ... calm. Not the gesture of someone in distress. Not the gesture of someone exhausted, who had been running. She was suspicious, but she made the tea anyway because the girl was here, inside now, and what could she do?

As she brought the tea she tried to study her, surreptitiously, without the girl noticing. She guessed her age as about fifteen. Her hair was straggling, reddish-brown, slightly wet. (And yet she hadn't noticed rain when she glanced out at the churchyard.) There was a speckling of freckles across her nose; she was skinny, long-legged, dressed in a denim skirt and halterneck top. Her clavicle was very prominent, almost as though she had some kind of oddly constructed skeleton. (Which was a weird thought, Linda conceded.) Was she pretty? Hard to know. Her teeth were a little crooked, though her nose was straight. She was the sort of girl Linda had been, too: nondescript, a girl who needed effort to create herself. She looked practically naked; she should have had on a jacket of some sort, it was only May, the night air was crisp. She was definitely under-dressed. Bare legs. Espadrille sandals with cork soles and laces that tied up her calves. One was undone, and one of her legs had scratches, smudges of mud and was bleeding.

'They were chasing me,' the girl said. 'I didn't know where to go.'

'Do you take sugar? I brought milk ...' Linda said, at the same time.

She had brought Jaffa cakes, too. A tray that trembled a little as Linda set it down on the coffee table – she pushed aside Raymond's *Radio Times* and *New Statesman*, and placed the tea in front of her.

'What's your name?' Linda asked.

The girl shook her head. She had a slightly crooked face; something about it was asymmetrical, wonky. From one side she looked sweet. Standing face on, directly in front of her, less so. Her eyes were searching, a flat grey colour that might have been green in another light.

'Do you know Raymond? I'm cat-sitting for him,' Linda volunteered. Perhaps this girl was in the habit of calling on Raymond; hadn't expected to find anyone else at home. He could be her uncle for goodness sake, her maths tutor. Raymond did indeed tutor some local children, for pin money: a perfectly reasonable explanation.

On cue, Georgio appeared. They both jumped as he popped through the cat flat, a rabbit from a magician's hat. Linda laughed, but stopped herself quickly. The girl didn't laugh. She reached for the tea and sipped in little slurps. She didn't acknowledge the cat or stroke him. Georgio wove in and out of Linda's legs until she went to the kitchen to pour some of the dry food, shaped like little fish, into his bowl.

Perhaps a kind remark was called for. Linda came back to the girl on the sofa and tried again.

'You sure you're all right? Who was chasing you? Where do you live?'

'I live in the village. But can I stay here? Can I stay with you?'

Linda found herself trembling afresh, it was so boldly put. She did not feel she had a choice. Her heart was knocking around in her ribcage. The girl seemed to lack … moderation, or humility or something. She was just so direct. It was a bit much. It was not something Linda was used to. She'd been a teacher, and now she was an Ofsted marker. She was respected at work. She was accustomed to teenagers, and this girl was nothing like any girl she'd ever come across.

I'm not myself, she thought again.

'Why do you need to stay here?' Linda asked, and tried to make her voice sound kind, rather than accusing. 'Who is chasing you? If you could tell me, I'd know what to do. Perhaps I ought to ring the police?'

The girl shook her head again. 'My name's Ginger,' she said. 'It's a nickname. Please don't call the police. Just let me stay here, right? On your sofa. I won't make a peep. I'll be gone in the morning.'

Once, people had called Linda 'Ginger' too. It was funny to remember that her hair, these days a soft, cropped grey, had been red enough to warrant teasing years ago.

'Won't your parents worry?' Linda asked. 'Shouldn't I ring them, if not the police?'

The girl shook her head more vigorously. She wore gold hoop earrings, which rattled like keys.

'You're bleeding,' Linda said, gesturing to the scratches on the girl's leg. 'Let me go and get some plasters, clean that up for you.'

The girl began unwinding the ribbons of her canvas sandals, nodded. She smiled at Linda and flashed the wonky teeth as if she was a great beauty. Perhaps she thinks she is, Linda thought. She remembered being fifteen: she'd believed the same thing.

* * *

Linda came back with a little first aid box she'd spied in Raymond's bedroom and blankets she'd found in a chest.

'I was just walking on my own,' Ginger said. 'I was walking by the river – you know, at the bottom of the cottages. I like to be by myself. I didn't know it was going to be dangerous.'

Linda opened the box and found antiseptic wipes. She took and opened one out, offered it and Ginger began cleaning the scratches.

'Yes, there was a murder there once. I remember reading about it. A long time ago, though. Forty years. And only one, after all. English villages. Pretty safe, I suppose.'

Linda said nothing more, thinking that when the girl's head was bowed, she might be more willing to talk.

'Who knew you can't even walk about in your own village on your own? Is it a crime? I want to be a travel writer when I leave school and I'm gonna go to really, you know, faraway places …'

The girl finished cleaning and accepted a plaster, unpeeled by Linda, to stick over the long pattern of scratches.

A dim memory was tickling at Linda. Her first trip to the States. Florida. Eighteen. She'd woken early and gone for a walk on the beach on her own without the other girls, leaving them at the campsite. And some bloke, a weird bloke, had come out of nowhere and started chatting her up. Told her she was beautiful but her skin was burning.

She'd been lying on her front, afraid to budge because her bikini top was undone and he'd offered to put sun cream on her back for her. And then when she said no, he'd jumped on her, straddled her, punched her …

Long ago. She'd never told anybody, until she met Jeff. Jeff had held her and stroked her hair and understood when she'd wailed: I just wanted to walk on the beach on my own in the early morning. And he took that from me, because I never quite dared set off like that again.

It hadn't been a rape. Mercifully, the strange beefy American had been interrupted by her screaming and she'd managed by some miraculous manoeuvre to throw him off, jump up, grab the bikini top, start running … Seems incredible now, the narrowness of her escape. She remembered the guy had been watching her; she knew he was just standing there, openly masturbating. She felt that he *chose* somehow not to give chase; he easily could have done. But perhaps he'd just been surprised that she didn't cave in, that he couldn't grind her to nothing in the sand as he'd expected.

'Who was chasing you?' Linda asked again.

'Just boys. Two boys. Or men – I don't really know if they were men. To me they looked big and tall and I didn't know them.'

'Why don't we take you home and you can tell your parents? Or really you should tell the police.'

Ginger's face clamped down again. No. No police and no parents.

'They didn't do anything,' she said. Then added: '*much*.'

A pause then she said: 'My parents would ask me what they did. The police would make me tell them … I couldn't tell them.'

This Linda recognised too. The man on the Florida beach? She'd staggered back to the campsite, the soles of her feet now burning because she'd had to abandon her flipflops.

And why hadn't she mentioned it to anyone? She hadn't wanted to make a fuss. She was embarrassed. She was ashamed. Or perhaps in the end, she'd agreed with the American man that she'd been foolish – foolhardy – that she'd asked too much to want to walk on a beach alone.

'I tell you what,' Linda said. 'Why don't I pour us a tiny glass of Raymond's whiskey? I think you might still be in shock.'

Raymond's cottage was beginning to seem more welcoming. Every time she thought of something, she realised it was there. She fetched the bottle; she'd noted it on her arrival, next to a little glass of bluebells that Raymond had thoughtfully left for her. It seemed a sign. She poured an egg-cupful for Ginger, and a bigger one for herself and added ice.

Ginger slugged it and pulled a face. Linda sipped at hers and asked carefully: 'What did the boys do?'

It seemed she caught the girl off guard, or the whiskey had loosened Ginger's tongue. She answered at once: 'They grabbed me. I was so surprised! I just couldn't understand what they wanted. And they sort of tried to get my skirt up, and I was pushing it down and they were trying to put their fingers inside my knickers. It was horrible. It was ridiculous.'

Ginger was blushing, the pure tomato red that only a teenager can achieve. Linda looked away.

'And then I wriggled away from them,' she said, 'but they chased me, so then I ran, and I ran across the graveyard and I saw the light on in your cottage and I saw you in the window and I thought if I pretend I know you, they'll drop back. If I go in the cottage, they won't follow me. I was praying you'd let me in.'

'Fucking bastards,' Linda said quietly. So you're still out there, somewhere, are you, she thought, draining the rest of her whiskey.

* * *

She'd put the blankets on the sofa and the girl draped them around herself. But still, Linda didn't like to go up to bed and leave the girl downstairs. She felt uneasy, but couldn't put her finger on why. The girl's clothes: what was it about them that seemed strange? The church clock chimed midnight, and still Linda sat quietly talking to the girl, about the village, the boys; Ginger's hopes of being a travel writer.

'What's worrying me,' Linda said, on her third whiskey, 'is that your parents will surely fret if you stay out all night. And they'll ring the police and then I'll be in trouble for not letting anyone know you were here.'

'They won't bother,' Ginger said. 'They don't care about me.'

'Ah, I'm sure that's not true,' Linda said, but it was a reflex, it was the sort of thing she had been used to saying as a teacher. She was not sure at all.

'I've stayed out loads of times. I have a boyfriend. They know, and they don't care. They'll think that's where I am.' Ginger's eyes were green in the light of the fire, as Linda had known they would be.

'How old are you?' Linda asked, feeling sure she knew the answer. 'Fifteen,' Ginger shot back, and Linda nodded. I saved you, she thought.

The whiskey was making her swimmy and she'd added too many logs to the fire. They were jammed into the woodstove and it was blazing like a furnace. The room was hot; Linda's cheeks were blazing too and her eyes watering. Sleep kept stealing up to her and she wondered if she hadn't nodded off a few times.

'I had a boyfriend at your age,' she told the girl. 'But it wasn't a good idea. He was older than me. I was just lonely. He put a lot of pressure on me. I think now he was quite a troubled person but I didn't understand that then. He said things like: if you loved me you'd let me do this and that, and so I did. But I regretted it. In today's terminology I think he'd be described as abusive.'

Why on earth was she talking about this, after so long? Only Jeff, only Jeff knew these stories.

'My parents scream and shout all the time,' Ginger said, sleepily. 'They only care about each other. I'm just in the middle. One minute it's: Leave then, I'll be fine without you. Then the next, my dad says: women. You can't live with 'em and you can't live without 'em and they're all kissing and cuddling and making up. It's disgusting. I hate them.'

This was familiar too. It might have been Linda's story. Her long-ago parents, her father an alcoholic, her mother bitter, enraged, always enraged, especially during those teenage years. This had been the unhappiest time for Linda. Her life began at the age of twenty-nine, when she met Jeff. A blind date: a pub. And when he walked in, she could barely believe her luck. To be as handsome as that: tall, leonine and yet – a nice guy! Not a weirdo or pervert or freak! A man to show her what men could be. For the first years she had fought him, she could not believe that she could deserve him. But in the end, he soothed her. He was enough.

Handsome Jeff with his flirty playfulness, his steadiness, his steeliness, his sweetness. Jeff: in a shirt of hyacinth blue, hiding flowers behind his back. Her reward just for hanging on in there, for staying. For not taking a handful of pills and finishing herself off, as she'd once considered, on a night very like this one, when she had been exactly Ginger's age.

She'd forgotten that.

Ginger was asleep: a humped shape under her blanket. She made soft snoring sounds and the blanket rose and fell. It was too late to telephone the parents now, so Linda had better hope Ginger's story was true and they wouldn't contact the police. Linda felt she should get up, sober up, make some cocoa, but the thought formed and she did nothing about it.

She longed to weep and wail, that was the trouble. Howl in an ungainly way, intemperate, not like the polite crying she'd done at the funeral, not like the crying of a grown woman. With Jeff gone, what to do with this young self that no one wanted? Here she was, in the room again, as raw as she had been when she'd first met him, all soothing ended.

* * *

Yesterday, on arriving, before she unlocked the cottage, she had had a quick nosy around the churchyard. She'd thought: I need some inspiration for what to put on Jeff's stone.

A robin had puffed its chest out as it watched her. The sun poured over the studded daisies on the grass and they were the same kind of lawns that had been there in her English childhood: buttercups, dandelions, clover. A lilac tree spilled over a low wall. Blossom scattered like pale pink fingerprints. *Dearly loved husband and soulmate.* Surely a modern inscription, that one. Soulmate? Bloody ridiculous word. She found herself sniffing, derisory.

She was not a religious person, that was the problem. The quiet twitterings of birds accompanied her as she pondered the question of what she could, in all honesty, bring herself to have carved in stone in memory of Jeff. Raymond would help her, Raymond – gently mocking too, an atheist to her agnostic self – would surely have an idea of what might do? In Loving Memory of … In Jesus' Keeping … Resting in the sleep of peace … Until we meet again. No, there could be none of those for her. No meeting again, she didn't believe in any of that bollocks.

There was one little pot with a simple message that she liked: *Mum and Dad, Dearly do we Love You* and one modern one that almost hit the right note: *Goodbye, my Love.*

On one mound, clearly a child's grave, was a toy windmill, flicking sunlight around the graveyard. Somewhere nearby she heard the sound of a drill and even, she thought, a cockerel. The ramshackle churchyard with the trees swaying, the birds twittering up a storm, was not spooky in daylight. It was full of movement, it was alive, a place for the living, not ghosts. What could she say to Jeff that she had not already said? She'd thanked him and loved him; that would have to do.

Since there's no help, come let us kiss and part.

* * *

In the morning the girl was gone, the blankets neatly piled on the sofa, next to the cushions. Linda came downstairs and stared at the place where she had been and the whiskey bottle on the floor by the fire. She made herself a cup of tea, the cat softly weaving around her ankles, moaning to be fed. On the counter top there was cold tea in the tea cup and, on the tray, an unopened packet of Jaffa cakes.

She had known the girl would disappear like that. It was as if she'd never been there at all.

The Turn

by Catherine Fox

St Helen's, Clifford Chambers, stands on a low tump of
Warwickshire land, just above the reach of the flood-prone
River Stour. It is not flashy, but it is still a functioning
church – unlike its nearest neighbour a mile away over the
meadows, sold off thirty years ago and turned into a house.

On this June afternoon in 2018, the 15th-century wooden
door of St Helen's is unlocked. Feel free to go in and look
round. There's not a great deal to see, but do admire the
Elizabethan monument to – whip out your Pevsner – 'Sir
Henry Rainsford (1622) and his wife … facing one another
across a bulgy prayer desk'. Remember to sign the visitors'
book as you leave ('Beautiful church. Lovely peaceful
atmosphere'). Please donate generously, and shut the door
behind you.

Outside, the churchyard is under constant surveillance.
Glance up. That stone dragon on the tower above the
door has been keeping a sharp eye on things since the mid-
fourteen hundreds. She – trust me, the dragons of the C of
E are female – sees another visitor arrive, shortly after you
have driven off. He is middle-aged and wearing red trousers.
He's coming up the path now, big brogues crunching the
gravel, then clumping into the porch. The latch clacks. He
enters. The door thuds shut behind him.

Christy mooched up the aisle and stopped with a theatrical sigh by the altar rails. Then he glanced down at the slab he was standing on.

Here lyeth ye Body of ye Reverend
CHRISTOPHER SMITH

He let out a squawk of laughter and turned for someone to share the moment with. Nobody. Birdsong outside, a strimmer in the distance. Apart from that, the silence of a June day. He stood frozen, like someone caught in the act. His heart pounded. But what was that? The pounding of another heart. The church clock. Tock. Tock. Tock. Tock. Beating in the stone body of the tower.

He patted his chest and looked down at his feet again.

CHRISTOPHER SMITH
above Fourty years Rector of
this Parish, who died 22nd of
April 1729
in ye 66th year of his Age

Christy spent a superstitious moment calculating that if this were a warning, he only had nine years left. Christopher Smith. The full name treatment, rapped out as if he were a naughty child. *Christopher Smith, come here this minute!* And those capital letters. CHRISTOPHER SMITH. Like a shouty email from the bishop. No, that wasn't fair. Lovely Bishop Steve had been lovely. Lovely, lovely, lovely. (Why couldn't Christy stand him?) Steve was *appalled* by the blunder and very understanding about Christy's emotional meltdown. He had arranged cover, picked up the phone to a fellow bishop and packed Christy off on this little rusticating break.

Above Fourty years Rector of this Parish. Those were the days, eh? Vicar of the same place, man and boy. Dying in post, buried in your church. And here was Christy, a flighty eight years into his current post in Harbury, on the brink of jacking it all in.

He massaged his chest and laughed again. Walking like a ghost over his own grave! He continued to potter about, snooping. He didn't need Pevsner to read a church. There on a pew by the organ was a cardboard box. To the untrained eye, it was full of sticks and rubble. But Christy knew it at once for the dismantled Easter garden. He took a sneaky picture and sent it to the 'Von Smith Family Singers' WhatsApp group set up by his children. 'Guess what this is?' Then, having checked again there was nobody about, he went and lay on his back on the memorial stone and took a selfie, playing dead beside his name. He whizzed that one off to the group too. 'Gave me a real turn!'

The church clock chimed three. Turn, turn, turn. He got up and dusted himself off. Turn again, Whittington. Turn again, Christy Smith.

'Thou turnest man to destruction!' The words rolled orotundly round the empty church.

Oh, shut up, brain, do. Sometimes Christy wished he could switch off his confetti cannon of quotations. It was like a nonstop ticker tape parade wherever he went, celebrating Christy Smith, tap-dancing priest and wag extraordinaire, ta da! He couldn't really tap dance. Except in his mind's eye, where he was endlessly dancing in his tails as if no one was watching.

No one?

You mean *apart from God*, surely?

No. God doesn't count. God and I are on a break.

No one watching apart from his mum, then. Mum, mum, watch me, mum! She had been his first audience. His ever-delighted mum (You're so clever, Christopher!), so skilled in downscaling her expectations of him (Oh well!). How was he going to tell her about *this*? He pictured her disappointment. She'd disguise with silver linings (I expect it's for the best. This way you'll get to do X). Like the flowery sheets she draped over any heap of knickknacks and bric-a-brac en route to the bazaar. Knickknack bric-a-brac, give a priest a job. God, he was sick of himself, poor jack self, all cobbled together from flashy fragments. A counterfeit, a plated person.

There you go again.

He went and sat in the choir stalls facing the organ. His phone buzzed. Tansy (at drama school) sending a link to a website called 'Look at my fucking red trousers'.

'IMPUDENCE!' Christy messaged back.

He stared up at the east window. His phone buzzed again. A pic from Tansy's twin, Hereward (choral scholar at St John's, Cambridge). 'Lol. Look at my fucking red cassock!' This was immediately followed by one from Lysander (still at school, current preferred pronouns: they/them/their; possibly gender-fluid, possibly trying to piss Dad off): 'Look at my fucking red lippie!!!'

Christie stared down at his poor trousers. What was wrong with a nice cheerful red? Honestly, his children were utter cads and rotters, every man Jaqueline of them.

He sighed, and went back to staring. Something nagged him about that window. There were four glass panels in the Victorian blond Christ manner: Nativity, Transfiguration, Ascension, and – odd choice – the Cleansing of the Temple. It felt like a puzzle. *What's wrong with this picture?* The clock ticked. He sat there a long time, barely moving.

* * *

Early on the following morning the villagers of Clifford Chambers saw him leave the house. Another priest, was he? They were used to the comings and goings of the Bishop of Barchester's bolthole (so handy for Stratford!). The woman who came in to change sheets and leave fresh eggs, she would check the visitors' book after he'd gone to find out who he was. *Do sign our guest book!* urged the bishop's hand-written note.

Christy riffled through to see who had preceded him. The guest book at Church Cottage went back to 1985. In it were recorded the visits of friends, family members, fellow bishops with a little + in front of their name, even when they were off duty relaxing in a bolthole. Oh look! +Steve Lindcaster, and his fragrant wife Sonya. Presumably it was she, not +Steve, who had drawn hearts and flowers around the words '*GORGEOUS AS EVER!!!*' but one never knew. There was an esteemed parade of academics and writers escaping the hurly-burly to finish long overdue books and a generous sprinkling of painters, dancers and assorted arty types of every persuasion. Some were rather famous. Ooh, get *you*, Rt Rev Well-Connected!

The village was used to the carry-on. 'Staying at The Cottage?' they asked any stranger found wandering the footpaths, lonely as a cloud with a Moleskine notebook. The guests only ever came in ones or twos, as the cottage was tiny. No rowdy kids or stag do's, mercifully. Mostly they were quiet; or, if not, they made an arty kind of noise, practising their cellos or singing marvellously under the moon beside the river ('By thy banks, gentle Stour'), then considerately calling it a night just as the neighbours were beginning to think of complaining. Scarcely any went skinny-dipping in the millpond; and, as far as anyone knew, only one had sprinted round the green at midnight clad only in his piercings and tattoos.

The latest guest looked to be in his late fifties. A bit of a dandy, the village thought, when he parked his Morris Minor on the tiny square and carried his leather satchel and carpetbag to the cottage. Tall. Red trousers. Floppy silver curls.

That was him now, in baggy shorts and T-shirt. Curtains twitched. A glint from a pair of binoculars. Off for a run. Warming up – unless that was as fast as he could go. Dodgy knees, perhaps. An actor, rather than a priest? He certainly looked familiar. The dog walkers gave him a nod as he turned right by the manor and headed down the muddy lane. Christy had one of those faces that people always thought they recognised; not handsome, but puzzlingly familiar. Where do I know him from? Have I seen him in something?

Christy had been aware of the 'Who *is* he?' glances last night in the Mucky Duck, when he'd stopped for a gin after *The Duchess of Malfi*. The bar had bristled with bona fide luvvies. Such a treat, the theatre. He really should get his act together and go more often.

He jogged along the lane, trainers squishing. Like the actors' feet sloshing in blood last night. Good grief, what a gore-fest! The audience on the front row were tucked up under blankets in case of spatters. No doubt Tansy would've been able to estimate how many gallons of fake blood they'd got through. It was not a play Christy had at his fingertips, though he must have studied it during his a-diller-a-dollar undergraduate career.

Apparently, this RSC offering was *a complete travesty*. The woman behind him kept hissing to her friend, 'But this isn't what the play's *about*!' He resisted the urge to turn round and enunciate like a famous luvvie, 'Nevertheless, it *is* what *this production*'s about, darling.'

How glorious to be sure what things were about! Oh, to grab from the tricksy flotsam of postmodernism two solid handfuls of What's What. Didn't part of him envy the woman's certainty? Meh, as the youngsters so eloquently put it. That would require him to care. About anything, really. And he seemed to have lost the knack. Pff! Gone. A bit of a catastrophe in his line of work, you'd have to agree. Like a flautist with embouchure collapse.

He slogged on, panting, even though it was flat. *Madam, I go with all convenient speed!* A lark ascended, somewhere out of sight. Christy stifled the burbling rush of lark quotes. How long had his dire condition gone undiagnosed? Had he been in denial for years? Yes. Deep down, he'd known something was amiss when he took the Harbury job. But he'd soldiered on these eight years, preaching witty, erudite sermons, visiting the sick, seeking Christ's sheep dispersed in this naughty world &c, &c. He'd kept on tootling down the middle of the Anglican road without disaster. The building was still standing. They coughed up their parish share to the diocese. What more could you ask?

But the symptoms were all there. His congregation were still belting out the repertoire of their 1980s heyday. The music group were all in their fifties; their fresh-faced fifties, compared with the robed choir of warbling septuagenarians. The youth fellowship, once sixty to eighty strong, now barely mustered half a dozen.

There was no denying it: All Saints was a holy escalator. The current members, for all their vigour (and, let's not pussyfoot about, their *money*), were ascending through middle age, late middle age, old age (what do you mean? seventy's young!), to the top, where they popped off into glory.

And nobody was coming up behind.

So here he was, *by no means* in disgrace, no, no. Christy spread compassionate hands – his +Steve impersonation – as he jogged. (Lovely Steve, my successful doppelganger, who *did* go down the passage and open the door into the episcopal rose garden, the jammy devil.) Christy was to think of it as a mini sabbatical. A chance to reflect. A gift.

Gift indeed! Christy knew a retirement carriage clock when he saw one. Tick, tick, tick. Your days are numbered.

Here lyeth ye Body of ye Reverend
CHRISTOPHER SMITH

What if he knew he only had nine years left? How would he spend them? He could stubbornly stay put. He had common tenure. Unless he fiddled with the accounts or someone's person, Bishop Steve couldn't get rid of him. But Christy didn't have the temperament to stick around where he wasn't loved and wanted. Backward, turn backward, O Time in thy flight! Wouldn't it be nice just to be the beloved priest of the same little flock for forty years, like his namesake!

And I bloody could have been! he realised suddenly. He *would* have been vicar of St Helen's, if he'd only got the Stratford job when he applied. It was part of the same group of parishes as Holy Trinity. Now that was pitiful, still smarting with disappointment after all these years. However, in his defence, it was Christy's first brush with being turned down.

That's to say, academically and professionally. He'd been turned down by girls aplenty as a callow youth. But he got on so well with girls! *Why* wasn't he 'boyfriend material'? (Why, *why* hadn't he 'been a fit' for Shakespeare's church? Didn't he *ooze* fitness?) Let's just be friends, Chris, the girls had all said. He'd been Chris back then. Everyone was Chris or Dave in the 70s. He'd always replied, Gosh, *of course* we can just be friends, Caroline, Mandy, Tessa, Yvette! There. He could still list them all, tragic buffoon that he was.

He eased through a gap in the hedge. Nettles twingled his bare knees, ow, ow, ow! It was a wooden kissing gate without the moving part. A non-kissing gate, if you will – how apposite for this train of thought. He jogged over the long green swathe of the gallops. Wind rushed in the poplars (my aspens, dear!) like a waterfall. A reflex made him check right and left for the ghosts of horses, thundering by from the long-gone stud farm. Tall grass bowed. Dog daisies, cuckoo buds of yellow hue. It was possible Shakespeare himself might have walked these fields, made dens down by the Stour. The cuckoo then, on every tree ... Christy kept a hopeful ear cocked, but they'd probably already transacted their beastly cuckoo business and skedaddled back to Europe. Wild roses in the hedge, a whiff of elderflower. A yellowhammer: little-bit-of-bread-and-no-cheeeeeese!

Oh, England, my England! He missed the countryside. Which was absurd, considering his own parish was pretty much surrounded by rural Lindfordshire. Well, if nothing else, the 'gift' had reminded him to get out into fields and lanes more. That said, even in this rural idyll he could hear the permanent white noise of distant traffic, unacknowledged on the edge of things.

He passed through the second non-kissing gate and onto the track again, beside a field of ripening rape. He caught its faint cabbage-y stench. A narrow strip of poppies clung to the field-edge. The lark still poured down its song.

What were you doing wrong, you poor, aching, randy boy? Trying too hard, probably. Standing too close with your big blue eyes, your floppy brown curls, your rosy farmer boy cheeks. Too tall, feet too big. Spouting poetry, clowning, doing your Pam Ayres impression, trying to snog them when they just wanted to be friends.

With the benefit of hindsight, they were nice girls. Kinder than he deserved. He'd tangled with unkind girls at university, oho yes. Married one, in fact, and sired three healthy brats. Christy pranced and let out a whinny. (There was nobody about.) Admittedly, even the kind girls had compared notes. Literally. They'd compared the passionate letters he wrote them – back when randy boys wrote passionate letters to girls they fancied – and they'd giggled hysterically. Could they really *all* be snake-hipped temptresses? Oh, I shouldn't laugh, they snorted. But he's like a big puppy, isn't he? And his tongue! I know! I know! The driller!

Exit eavesdropping swain, mortified.

And the moral of that tale: be careful how and where you rehash your material. That had stood him in good stead over the years with sermons. And secondly, never drill with your tongue, gentlemen.

* * *

His hours went by, structureless. He missed his parish. (Sudden paranoia: Was everyone dancing in the aisle and singing 'Huzzah, he's gone!'?) He missed his family. Not that he saw much of them during term time, now the twins had flown the vicarage nest, and Sander was off boarding at Hogwarts. What dreadful children they were. Jesu mercy! Vicarage kids from central casting, forever on final warnings, getting wasted, suspended, busted, barred. (So proud, my darlings!)

Most of all, at all times and in all places, he missed his bad woman. She, too, was escaping the vicarage. Off at last to run her dream, ploughing her inheritance into that bonkers performing arts school of hers in Netherstone; notionally commuting back to Harbury each weekend, to keep up appearances for Christy's sake. He'd texted to say he was here, so there was a chance she'd pop over. He left the cottage door unlocked, just in case.

SEND HELP! he WhatsApped the children. SEND KETTLE CHIPS! They replied with their customary sensitivity, BUY UR OWN. GET A LIFE FFS. WTF DAD

UR A TOTAL LOSER. He was going mad in this little backwater. Oh, it was not good for man to be alone! Thrillingly, he discovered there was a shelf of Angela Brazil school stories in the bedroom. He selected *A Terrible Tomboy* and got rather caught up in it. He re-read Shakespeare sonnets – it would be rude not to, this close to Stratford. There was no TV to distract him. He tuned the ancient Roberts radio from Four to Three, to shut out the Trump-and-Brexit hideousness of world events. (A gift was not a gift if you still had to endure John Bumptious at breakfast.) In the evenings he fidgeted about on the internet – at least there was Wi-Fi – sternly renouncing porn, the flesh and the devil. Frankly, he had his work cut out already curating the mental archives. He could do without a new deposit of oinkish ephemera to catalogue.

The reward for his chaste browsing was to learn that Michael Drayton had local links too. Interesting! So, Drayton had hung out in the manor in Clifford Chambers, had he? His muse – his 'Idea', he called her – Lady Anne Rainsford had lived there with her husband. Aha, that fancy Tudor monument in St Helen's, to the left of the altar – that must be theirs. He'd better go back and get a proper look. Not really stood the test of time, had he, poor old Drayton. Vast howling deserts of unread verse, with just one lonely pyramid of a sonnet jutting up:

> Since there's no help, come let us kiss and part.
>> Nay, I have done, you get no more of me;
>> And I am glad, yea glad with all my heart,
>> That thus so cleanly I myself can free.

Christy closed the tab. That'll do, thank you, Michael. A tad too near the knuckle, when one was splitting up from one's wife (probably); and quite possibly in the process of divorcing the good old C of E as well. Was there a service for that, of un-ordination? He pictured himself kneeling, and Bishop Steve, like a film in reverse, wrenching his hands back off the reprobate head in front of him. 'Shake hands forever, cancel all our vows'. He wasn't divorcing God, obviously. That would be a nonsense, like divorcing the air. It's over, air. From now on, I'll be making my own breathing arrangements.

A gift, a gift, a gift. Chance to reflect. Perhaps he should weep, down by the River Stour. Hang up his lyre on the willows and weep when he remembered Canterbury. It had slowly dawned on him that the job he'd trained for in the 80s no longer existed, and that if he went forward for ordination training now, he'd be turned down. The rose garden had been fenced off for the likes of him. Colourful characters (especially ones with dreadful wives and children) were never going to be offered a bishopric in this brave new world of Renewal and Reform. (Query: Was he kidding himself? Maybe there was *no* era in which he coulda been a contender.) Oh, it was all growth strategies, management-itis, and Evangelical Yay!

But that's a *travesty*! It's not what church is *about*!

Nevertheless, it *is* what *this iteration* of the church is about, darling.

Let's face it, we are almost finished. Still the established church, but consigned to the very edges of national life, like a narrow strip of poppies. Was this not cause enough for tears?

No tears came. He rambled up the gallops at dusk, swishing his hands through the grass heads, watching the strange spindling dance of the ghost moths. They flickered, almost luminous in the twilight. An owl called. Christy turned and walked home among the flitting bats. The village was dark and still. There were no streetlights, but his eyes were accustomed. Honeysuckle wafted from a garden wall as he passed. A few stars, and he could just make out the gold of the church clock face gleaming on the black tower between the lime trees. He filled his lungs. His breath shuddered, as if he'd been sobbing hours earlier. Night air all around him, in his nostrils, his lungs, bloodstream, heart. I have nothing to say to you, air. Stop stalking me.

* * *

Another day dreamed past. He was eating healthily, because on a godly whim he'd only brought healthy food to the cottage. There was no weakening at the 9pm witching hour when the kettle chips crooned their siren song – far too pished to drive anywhere for supplies – and by daybreak comestible godliness had reasserted itself. And thus the hideous quinoa cycle continued.

He lay wide awake at three in the morning, then slept in the afternoon. Long trancelike hours. Memories broke off submerged wrecks and floated to the surface. Leon.

He found himself awake in the wee small hours wondering about Leon Cardine, of all people! Where was he now? Christy was sufficiently bothered to reach for his iPad and google the name. Not a trace. Still holding yourself aloof, Leon? I hope you've not gone to a poetic early grave. Leon had seemed so gilded, so destined for brilliance, with his enigmatic smile and Cambridge classics exhibition. (Christy had squeaked into Oxford by the back door of Regent's Park College.) Why did we lose touch?

He put his iPad back down and switched off the light. That A-level results summer. How young we were. Jesus, the days that we have seen!

MRS CARDINE: Nothing wrong with a parson's son. *(She rumples CHRIS'S hair)* Come to France with us.

CHRIS: Golly! Really? *(He stands too close, too eager)*
Gosh, if you're sure. Thank you *so* much, Mrs Cardine.
TANYA: *(the daughter, tosses her silvery blonde hair,
leaves the kitchen muttering)* Oh, for God's sake.
MRS CARDINE: *(lights cigarette)* Call me Vivien.

He never did manage to address them as Pip and Vivien. It
felt too cheeky. How star-struck he was! He realised with
hindsight that the Cardines weren't that posh. They were
just posher than the Smiths. But before Oxford opened up
the Burke's peerage of poshness, Leon was an aristocrat.

Their house still cropped up in Christy's dreams. (Joan
Fontaine voice: *Last night I dreamed of The Old Rectory.*)
It was a *real* rectory, that one, not the godawful 60s
parsonage the Smiths lived in. There was another covetable
classic of the genre here in Clifford Chambers, just across
the graveyard from the bishop's cottage. Half-timbered,
beyond gorgeous. But a nightmare to heat, as Mrs Smith of
the Silver Linings wisely pointed out.

His bus passed the house on the journey to and from
grammar school. Christy sat on the top deck and looked out
for it every day. Tudor chimneys above high yew hedges,
a glimpse of higgledy-piggledy roofs and attic windows.
Long before he'd met Leon, Christy yearned to live there.
By the age of twelve, he'd built it up into a National Trust
property, like the kind his parents took him to.

He smiled in the dark. What a comedown, the first time
he crossed the threshold! We walked to it, didn't we, from
Rob Watkin's party, a mile across the fields among the
dancing ghost moths. Lost souls of fairies, I said, and you
laughed. Yes, I made you laugh. That's why you tolerated a
clodhopper like me.

There we were, hurrying, to beat the coming storm. My
jumble sale silk shirt clung to me horribly. I could smell

the previous owner's armpits. No matter. I was about to duck under the plush red rope and touch things at last. Tinkle a riff on the spinet, quaff from the Georgian crystal. Instead, I stumbled into the snarled-up Jungian shadow of the mudroom. Things falling on my head, tangling in my big feet. Piles of mess with no floral sheets over them. Then the rustle of old newspapers underfoot in the dark kitchen. The doggy stink. Cats slinking.

You gleamed milk white like a ghost moth yourself. Your skin, your pale hair. I followed you through the house, giggling (too much cider), plucking at my sweaty shirt. Stumbling up, up, up the crooked attic stairs. Stifling under the eaves. Tiny window open. The to and fro of lightning behind the clouds, silent, like searchlights.

Lying naked beside you. Light flickering. Oh, the heat!

'You know people think we're homos,' I said.

You said, 'Who cares?'

* * *

On the afternoon of Christy's third day in Clifford Chambers, he lay on the bed staring up at the papered ceiling. William Morris willow. The room brimmed with green. It was like being underwater. Leaves crowded at the tiny windows, as if the outside was trying to creep in. Suddenly, everything dimmed. A thrush carolled on in the graveyard. Then came thunder, like cosmic sceneshifters at work overhead. A rush of rain on the roof.

I loved him, didn't I? Boy crush, bromance – the right vocabulary didn't exist back then. If he'd made even the slightest move, I would've. Or would I? No, more likely recoiled. There was no knowing, so long after the event. I am so tired, he thought. All my bones have deliquesced. I am a jellyfish, and no man. Oh, but I was made for love. Always have been. That's all I know. I am a giant roving magnet, forever fighting the tug of the nearest attraction. I am a crush waiting to happen.

Hang on.

He checked his phone, then slumped back bonelessly. Yes, it was the anniversary of his last Finals paper. There'd been a spectacular storm that afternoon, too. Rain crashing down onto the champagne-spraying students. Mortarboards hurled like Frisbees, up, up, up and away.

They were probably still out there somewhere, those mortarboards, orbiting Jupiter, tassels floating …

He woke himself with a vast snort. Cora was standing by the high Edwardian bed in the green gloom.

'Absolutely not snoring,' he said. 'I deny it.'

She bent and dropped a kiss on his forehead as if he were a child. He was a child.

'What happened?' she asked. 'Are you in disgrace? You've not been spanking teenage girls in the vestry, have you?'

'What? No! What are you on about?'

'Ah. You've not seen the *Church Times*, then.'

'Oh God.' Spanking? Really? A copy had been delivered to the cottage, but it was still in its plastic on the kitchen table. 'Not guilty, m'lud.' He felt a grubby spurt of something all the same. No priest was an island. Any man's sin diminished him. Not forgetting the victims, he reminded himself.

'Thank God for small mercies,' said Cora. 'So what *are* you doing here?'

I have been very zealous for the Lord, but the people have forsaken the covenant and I alone am left! 'Mini sabbatical.' His chin trembled. Ah, there it was at last, the maudlin surge. He could always cry in front of Cora.

She tipped her head back, exasperated. 'Look. Sorry to be heartless, but I am pressed for time, Christy. Any chance we can fast-forward over the breast-beating, to the bit where you explain coherently, then agree to bravely –'

'Gasp! A split infinitive?'

' – TO BRAVELY SOLDIER ON. Like you always do?' She poked him. 'Try it. I'd say, "for me", but why would you do anything for me anymore? Yes, I know you would. But you shouldn't. Come on, bunk up and tell me what's going on.' She gave him a shove. 'Look at that. It even has little steps! Little steps to climb into bed.'

'Up the wooden hill to Bedfordshire,' he said.

She lay beside him. Their hands found each other and they laced fingers. Muscle memory. He glanced at her beaky profile. Her glorious Elizabeth Siddal hair had faded, as if spun back into old straw by a vengeful dwarf. Christy had always felt sorry for Rumpelstiltskin. All that spinning for the heartless queen, and nothing to show for it. Did you know, in the original version, poor Rumpelstiltskin *tore himself in two*, trying to pull his leg out of the ground? He almost said it, but that would require tedious explanation.

The rain began drumming again. Cora lifted her head and looked around her. 'Sweet little place. Fabulous bath. I hope you've lolled in it drinking champagne.'

'Does prosecco count?'

'No. I stuck some Bolly in the fridge. Make sure you drink it.'

'I will. Thanks.'

'What's this you're reading?' She squinted at the Angela Brazil on the bedside table. 'You do know you're mad, don't you?'

'It's a serious exploration of gender dysphoria, I'll have you know. Not to mention a fearfully ripping read. She gives Jones minor a pasting behind the cricket palings for bullying her brother.'

'Yes, dear.' Cora finished looking round. 'Well. The bishop has good taste. Or else he married into it.'

'Like me.'

'Like you.'

He listened to her breathing. To the drumming rain. To the thrush, still singing Go, Go, Go in the churchyard.

'Anyway. It was autofill,' he said. 'An autofill blunder. The senior staff were emailing one another, trying to identify underperforming parishes. Then the archdeacon accidentally copied me in.'

'Underperforming! Says who?'

He clenched her hand and bumped their fists up and down gently on the bed. 'It's OK.'

'Well, fuck 'em all, I say. They can't get rid of you, can they?'

'No, but ...'

'They don't deserve you.'

'To be fair, it was underperforming *parishes*, not priests.'

After a moment, he felt a quiver. Then a ripple. Then Cora let out her famous honking laugh. Horrid goose-girl with her honking laugh, her bony face, her mad too-close-together beady goose eyes. Why did he still love her so hopelessly, now it was all so well and truly hopeless?

'Ha, ha, ha! Sorry. Just the idea of you *under*performing! God, you're the biggest ham in Christendom. Your whole life is an English comedy of manners. With your Morris Minor –'

'What, pray, is wrong with my transport of delight?'

' – and your red trousers! You're a humbug.'

'A *HUMBUG*?' he Bracknelled.

'You see? I *knew* you'd do that.' She nipped his thigh.

'Ow! How's life in Neverland?'

'It's Netherstone, as well you know.' She yawned. 'Loving every bit of it. Insanely brilliant fun. But it's like running up a down escalator, keeping tabs on everything.'

'Oh no, and now I've dragged you away. Sorry. I –'

'Stop. Fast forward. Will you be OK, Christy?'

'Oh, probably.' He swallowed. His throat ached to weep and howl. 'Somehow or other.'

'Good. Listen, mad idea – why don't you join us, and play chaplain?'

He winced.

'*Be* chaplain, I meant, obviously,' she said. 'Not play.'

He bumped their hands up and down again on the bedspread.

'There's Netherstone parish church, too.' She yawned even more widely. 'They haven't had a proper vicar for yonks. They'd bite your hand off. You could probably get house-for-duties, or something.'

Excellent. I could *play vicar*. Buy a horse and ride round the parish in a stovepipe hat! He blotted the tears stealthily. Had she noticed?

She was asleep.

Oh, Cora. Posh girl, bad girl. My muse, my Idea. He watched her beloved face. You never could grasp the fact that I'm not acting. It's all real. I am Christy Smith, priest. A big old humbug, but a priest through and through.

Before long, she would wake, and they'd go through their little ritual: 'Yes? What are *you* gawking at?'

'At your ineffable beauty.'

Their first exchange of words. She had just gate-crashed a Summer Ball by jumping down into the quad from a high window, wearing a green taffeta ball gown. A pre-Raphaelite belle dame sans merci. Long hair. Wild, wild eyes. Nearly thirty-eight years ago. How was that possible?

Not boyfriend material. He hadn't needed telling. She was above his touch. Cora Dorrington-Mayne. A susurration followed her everywhere: *She's* the one whose brother ... Everyone seemed to know but Christy. They told him soon enough. *Her brother. Secure hospital for life. Terrible, terrible business. Both parents!* But Christy had been granted

CATHERINE FOX

a moment of grace and saw her first unframed by tragedy. Just a wild girl in a green dress dropping into his life.

Not boyfriend material. He was far too nice. Cora needed bad men. But she'd snogged him gamely enough between disastrous affairs. Years after Oxford – he was bishop's chaplain by then – she'd come to him with a proposition. He was single. She was sick of having her heart broken. Furthermore, her biological clock was ticking like a time bomb. So how about a marriage of affection, not passion? They were good friends. He was kind. He made her laugh. Why not make babies, stick together till the parenting job was finished, then take stock? What did he say?

'Yes. Provided you understand one thing: I adore you.'

'I know. I can stand it, if you can.'

Where had the time gone? Here they were, taking stock already. But he would never stop adoring her. As he watched, he saw her eyelids flicker. Some dream he couldn't share. Your crazy performing arts school. I do understand, you know. You're gluing together your smashed childhood. Shards of idyll. The dressing-up box, the paper puppet theatre; tea in the tree house, and the hammer sleeping safe in the toolbox. Why wouldn't you package up the eternal golden summer of *Before*, and give it away to countless children?

And yet. Please let there be an *And yet* ... A *But still* ... A volta in the sonnet of our love.

Now at the last gasp of Love's latest breath,
When, his pulse failing, Passion speechless lies ...

Now, if thou wouldst, when all have given him over ...

If thou wouldst. If thou only wouldst, Cora. Ah well. This too shall pass. We are but dust. One day, his Idea would die. And so would he. God willing, there would be some kind person to sit beside him and watch them go. Just as he had sat by deathbeds and seen the soul depart. Felt that pause, where eternity seemed to lean in.

The storm had rumbled off into the distance now. A bee droned in at the window, and out again. He could smell the roses on the fence below.

* * *

Sunday came. He was emphatically not going to church. But the church was there, literally just *there* through the cottage window, Union Jack fluttering on the tower flagpole. He stuck two fingers up, then converted the gesture into a simpering wave when he saw a dog walker staring. So sorry, madam. I thought you were God. The clock struck nine.

He'd heard it chiming the hours, day and night, since his arrival. As ever, it felt like a homecoming. Plinking his heartstrings, promising an eternal ten to three and reliable honey supplies. Nothing he could do about it: English bells were hardwired into his brain. There was the dreaded Thursday night practice right outside his bedroom window when he was a child, like skip-loads of scrap metal tumbled down a mineshaft. Lord, the letters of complaint his dad received! One man – demented by the racket – broke into the bell tower and hacked the sallies off the ropes with his wife's dressmaking shears. Mrs Smith, round-eyed, had impressed on Christy just how shocking that crime was: 'With her best dressmaking shears!'

Later came the more decorous cacophony of cathedral bells, right outside his bedroom window *again*, when he lived on Lindchester cathedral close. Back when he was a promising young bishop's chaplain on flightpath A, going places. Before he threw in his lot with Cora and had to watch the likes of Steve overtake him on the inside. That was three bishops of Lindchester ago. Bishop Neville. Not a married gentleman. Mouth-puckeringly dry as London gin, but kindly enough in his way.

He became aware of some undefined bad feeling creeping up on him. What could have triggered that? Ah yes. The *Church Times* still lay on the kitchen table, under a pile of fast food fliers and BT bills. So many ghastly cases. But tilly-vally. He was *not* reading the *Church Times* on sabbatical. It was full of classified ads for Passionate Evangelists.

He made a cafetière of coffee and tried to visualise his current flightpath. A derelict WW2 aerodrome runway in the middle of nowhere, nettles sprouting through the concrete. With +Steve buzzing over like Biggles in his spiffy biplane, trailing a banner saying DIOCESAN STRATEGY, while Sonya strewed hearts and flowers down onto the over-performing pioneer ministers.

Bitter? Moi?

He ducked to look out of the kitchen window again. The gravestones were at eye level in the mown grass. I'm not going. He drank his coffee. There didn't appear to be any bells to summon the faithful of St Helen's these days. The sally-ravaging shears could be retired to the needlework box to rust in peace. He ate a godly banana. (Why hadn't he bought croissants, damn it all?) He watched an elderly couple cross the churchyard.

Why was he still here, alone and palely loitering? Did he not have his trusty Morris Minor? He could drive any-where. To Penzance. To John O'Groats. Wait, better still to Portsmouth. Get the ferry to France. Tootle down through Normandy. Spain, Italy. Obviously, he'd need to return home for his passport first. But in theory.

Oh, he might as well go to church. It would fill an hour. He gulped the last of his coffee and picked up the cottage keys. He'd have to fob people off, the way clergy always did on holiday. I'm a teacher. End-of-life care provider. I manage a local branch of a multinational charitable organisation.

The churchyard gate stood open. He looked up at the lime trees against the blue. They were – *pace* Housman – the loveliest of trees. Just on the cusp of turning from hectic spring juiciness into the calmer hues of summer. Before long, they'd be in blossom. That ravishing smell was forever associated with Petertide ordinations. Thirty years since his own priesting.

I'm an underperforming has-been about to take voluntary redundancy.

He went down the path and clumped into the porch. If hounded, he'd say, 'Currently between jobs. Resting, darling,' and leave the red trousers and floppy hair to do the rest.

He went in, was welcomed and chose a pew halfway up the aisle on the right. Someone was playing the organ. Christy did a swift professional scan. A basket of brightly coloured musical instruments on the chancel step seemed to promise an All Age service. But not a child in sight.

Common Worship Holy Communion nurdled by. He sat and stood, mentally revised the sermon into the way *he* would have preached it, said the responses and sang a little too showily in his fine bass-baritone. The power of the Lord? Is moving in this place? In what way, pray?

You sing this at your church too, said Mr Snide, his inner Peg-or-Two Monitor. Who do you think you are? All Saints is dying on its feet, for all your good old-fashioned parsoning.

No work too hard for him! chided the hymn.

Christy sighed and walked up the aisle. He knelt at the altar rail. If the work of reversing decline wasn't too hard for the Lord, one was forced to conclude he had washed his hands of the whole Anglican caper. There were nine of them there in all, counting the organist and the curate. This really was Christy's dear old C of E in declining microcosm. Who could blame the likes of +Steve for urgently deploying the jump-leads while there was still time?

He looked up at the east window, and now the answer struck him. From transfiguration to ascension, bypassing death. There was no crucifixion. No resurrection. And no coming again in glory.

He held out his cupped hands.

The body of Christ.

The blood of Christ.

Amen, amen.

He walked back down the aisle and sat. A woman turned and leant over the pew in front. She squeezed his arm.

'I'm so glad you came. One more. Just *one more* makes a difference.'

* * *

'I went to church this morning,' said Christy. 'And now I'm drinking champagne, as per your orders.'

'Chin, chin. Are you in the bath?'

'Possibly.'

'I can hear swooshing.'

Christy swooshed some more. Cara's honking laugh came from the phone on the shelf. 'Are you pleasuring yourself?'

'No, but I did just fart. Which is always pleasurable underwater. Waddle-boddle-waddle-boddle-waddle!'

The phone honked again. 'What are you, eight years old?'

'Currently seem to be around eighteen,' said Christy.

'Why? What happened when you were eighteen?' she asked.

'One had a bromance.'

'What? You never told me!'

'Nothing to tell,' said Christy. 'He was called Leon

Cardine. He went to the local public school. We met at the Anglican-Methodist youth fellowship.'

'It's Brideshead all over again!'

'I know! I went on holiday to France with his family. I was in love with them all. Especially his older sister, who despised me.'

'Poor Christy.'

'*Entre nous*, I got horribly homesick, because his parents spent the whole time fighting. Leon and I escaped when we could. We used to swim in the altogether, under a row of poplars, tackle a-waft in the warm water. It was gorgeous.'

'And?'

'I told you: nothing. It was passionately platonic. None of your fluid identity folderol back then. That said, I can now see he was almost certainly gay. Damn.'

'What?'

'Spilt some. Bloody hopeless in the bath, champagne flutes.'

Honk. 'Design flaw.'

He hauled himself into a more upright position.

'I can hear your big arse creaking on the enamel,' said the phone. 'How are you doing? Have you heard from the weans?'

'Yes. They've been ridiculing my trousers, the beasts. Sander sent a pic of himself –'

'Pronoun!'

'I refuse to adopt that grammatical abomination of desolation,' said Christy. '"Themself"! Brrr. Sander was wearing red lipstick.'

'So what? The only question is, did it suit h-them?'

'Huh, they did look rather fetching, yes.'

'You can piss off,' she said.

'Tell me candidly, is this non-binary stuff genuine or is he just trying to annoy his old dad?'

'You're *so* solipsistic! It isn't about *you*, Christy.' A beat. 'He's trying to annoy *me*.'

They both snorted.

'God, aren't we terrible parents?' she said. 'I honestly don't know. But we'll support them, whatever.'

'Yeah. And they know they're loved.'

'True.' He heard her yawn. 'So, how much longer have you got out in the boonies?'

'Another couple of days.'

'No rash decisions, OK? You talk to me first. Promise?'

'Cross my heart.'

'Good. Don't you *dare* nobly resign just to please the bishop.'

'Believe me, I'm *entirely* safe from wanting to please Steeeve.'

'No, you're not.'

No, he wasn't. 'Oh, I'm locked in a tragic bromance with the C of E!'

'Is that by any chance the Bolly talking, darling?'

'In Bollo veritas.'

'Ha, ha, ha! Well, toodles. Duty calls. Don't drown in there.'

'I won't,' said Christy. 'The bishop's left a little note on the shelf, specifically warning me not to.'

But she had already rung off.

* * *

No! Christy clamped his hands to his hair as if that would douse this blaze of horror.

He'd come downstairs to forage for food, clouting his head amusingly on low beams, and spotted the *Church Times* on the table. Through the soft focus of his Bolly goggles it looked innocuous. Phoo. How bad could it be?

For a moment he hadn't recognised him, the old priest staring from the photo. 'The first complaints were lodged when he was an incumbent in the diocese of Lindchester, in the late 80s.' But then the name leapt out. Oh no. I knew him. This is *awful*. Then he caught himself. Tried to consider the victims – this isn't about you, you vile solipsist! – but he was powerless. There was Father Gerald blossoming before his eyes, large as life, twice as flamboyant. On the palace doorstep in his red trousers and panama hat, holding up a magnum of champagne. *Drinky-poos, Christy? While the cat's away …*

* * *

Oh God. Another memory fluttered out, like a compromising photograph shoved in a book and forgotten about. Not *that* again.

He buried his face in the towel and willed his heart to stop thundering. He knew he was overreacting. Over-performing. Hamming up his minor walk-on part all those years before. *You have nothing to reproach yourself with*, he imagined someone – some counsellor, perhaps – saying. But maybe he had? Oh, he couldn't possibly process this on his own! Cora, she'd talk him down to earth. He grabbed his phone.

No.

Think. You recognise this cycle from of old. You know what to do. You need to put some clothes on and go for a walk. Walk, walk, walk. Until you can think clearly. Then you'll be in a position to recall what happened that night. Not what you fear happened, but what you know.

Oh, to be *sure* about it! To grab two solid handfuls of What's What!

A few moments later, he was dressed. He plunged out into the dusk and set off for the gallops again.

Slowly, his head began to clear. It felt like those nightmares where he'd done something terrible, killed someone, forgotten to revise for an exam. There was always that ghastly phase, as he fought his way back to the surface, choking, clawing at the idea that *it didn't happen. It was only a dream.*

And in all honesty, there was literally no evidence that anything had happened that night.

First year as bishop's chaplain. August. The bishop was away. There went the palace doorbell. I was in the drawing room. Too darn hot, up in the attics where my little apartment was. I opened the door to find Father Gerald and his champagne.

Champagne mid-week! (The racy shock of it, back then, before the systemic ensozzlement of the middle classes.) *Thought you'd be lonely, stuck in the pally all on your tod. I've come to say goodbye, Christy.* He was off to another job, another diocese. *Let's be naughty and open it now, shall we? Go on, get his lordship's best glasses, chop-chop!* God, I adored him! He was a raconteur, a bon viveur. A character. Did I model myself on him? I fetched the best glasses. The cork popped ...

And?

And nothing. A transgressive drunken tour of the palace, that's all I can remember. All? Or do I recall showing him where the locked filing cabinets stood? Did we joke about the Blue Files? Did I jingle my keys? And did we go back to the drawing room and sing Gilbert and Sullivan patter songs, till I passed out on the hearthrug, and woke at 3am to find him gone? A note on the coffee table: *Tatty bye. I'll let myself out. G x*

The next morning I leant on the Aga, head pounding. Then a thought like a bucket of water in the face: the keys. What did I do with the keys? I belted through to my office, and there they were on the hook where they belonged.

Nothing had happened. Everything was fine, thank God. I washed up the bishop's best glasses, put them back in the cabinet and locked the door.

Christy walked much further this time. It was nearly dark. The bats were fluttering and off in the distance a fox barked. He could just make something out at the top of the rise, a black hump against the sky. As he approached it took on the form of a derelict brick barn. He pressed on through the nettles. A barn owl took off across the fields, silent and white as a ghost. Christy looked up and could see the first stars where the roof had been.

This special shell. Bare ruined choirs. It was happening again. No statue smashing and land grabbing this time. Just a silent reformation of bankruptcy and decline. But it was no use kidding himself it had been all shambolic loveliness back in the good old days. The church had been too full of dark corners where clever predators could operate. Those poor girls. Well, the roof was off and day was coming. All files would be reviewed. All cases re-opened.

Should he have said something, back in 1991? But what would there have been to say? He had no proof, no reason to suspect his adored Father Gerald had deliberately called when the bishop was away and got the chaplain drunk so that he could remove damning evidence in his clergy file before he moved diocese.

Ah, forgive us those things of which our conscience is afraid. He'd done nothing then. He knew he would do nothing now.

He turned and set off for the cottage. The grass was wet with dew now. His trousers were sopping.

His fucking red trousers.

* * *

That night he dreamt of Leon Cardine. For some reason the Old Rectory was here in Clifford Chambers, on the banks of the Stour. Leon walked past on the river with his dog. He was middle-aged now and Christy could see that he had some kind of special river-walking attachments on his shoes. The dog ran on ahead, splashing. Away they went, upstream, until a bend in the river took them out of sight. I could probably make a pair of those, Christy thought. Out of the rim of an old bike wheel. I could do that, too. Walk up the river on the surface of the water.

He spent the morning finishing *A Terrible Tomboy*. That's what we like, a nice deus ex machina ending. They find a hoard of Saxon manuscripts and don't have to sell off the abbey after all. Christy tucked the volume back on the shelf next to *The Nicest Girl in the School*. After lunch, he stripped the bed, tidied the cottage and packed his things. At the last minute, he took his damp trousers out of the bag. He shoved them in the bin and pushed them down, out of sight.

Well, that was that. Might as well make tracks for Harbury. So much for the mini sabbatical. He still didn't have the faintest idea what he was going to do. The Gift had not delivered any answers. The church clock struck four, like a polite hint. He hesitated. Very well, one last visit.

The latch clacked. The door swung shut behind him. He walked up the aisle and looked at the Rainsford monument. Rather lovely, the way the couple knelt facing one another. They'd seen some right old ecclesiological comings and goings in this cross of ground: Civil War, Restoration, Oxford Movement. The melancholy long withdrawing financial roar. Would they still be kneeling there when this building was deconsecrated? Almost proving that all that will survive of us is prayer?

He crossed his own grave once more and went and sat looking up at the east window. So, one last attempt to salvage some certainty about his next step. Or at least to make his peace with the air around him. Would he have to resign and free up his stipend for a pioneer minister? It was clearly what Bishop Steve wanted. But was that really the right way?

The clock beat steadily in the silence. Tock. Tock. Tock.

Here he was at the turning point. The volta of his life. He was well into the third quatrain, cantering towards the final couplet, where hope dangled by its last thread:

Now, if thou wouldst, when all have given him over,
From death to life thou might'st him yet recover!

Why not? No work too hard for him. Come *on*. Now. 'Even now you might,' he urged. Perhaps he was demanding a shortcut to glory, an Angela Brazil ending for him and his beloved church.

Doves crooned outside. 'But I am made for love!' he burst out.

Silence. Just the heartbeat of the clock, and the small ticks as glass and timber shifted slightly, like old bones warming themselves in the sun.

* * *

High up on the church tower, the stone dragon watched him leave. She saw him load his carpetbag and leather satchel into the green Morris Minor. The car reversed out of the Square, and trundled off towards the main road to join the white noise of rushing life. Goodbye, God speed. He was gone.

And yet –

* * *

Damn. Christy was no mechanic, but he knew a terminal ·
crunch when he heard one. He got out of the car and rang
the breakdown company. Ooh, sounds like your half shaft's
gone. We'll send a recovery vehicle. Where are you? It'll be
at least an hour.

He slumped. His children were right. What a total loser
he was. Await rescue. Oh, how he needed rescuing! Having
posted the keys back through the cottage letterbox, he
couldn't even go and make himself a cup of tea while he
waited.

Curtains twitched. Light glinted off a pair of binoculars
again.

'I give up!' Christy flung wide his arms. 'Even my car has
died!' he shouted.

Well, there was no way he was waiting here, enacting
his farce of a life in full view of the village. He set off for
the river, turning left at the old manor where Drayton had
mooned after his Idea. Poor old Drayton. I feel your pain,
brother. I've spent too many nights in star-defeated sighs,
mooning after ideas.

Suddenly, his dream came back to him. Leon Cardine,
walking on water! Calmly walking his dog up the River
Stour. Why in heaven's name didn't I call out to him? To
meet him again, even in a dream, would be something.

Christy passed the millpond then crossed the bridge into
the meadow. It had been mown already. Shakespeare's
flowers a' wede away. He found a shady spot and settled
himself to look at the water. The Stour was full of trees
and summer sky. Blackbirds sang. Thrushes. Wrens. A
chiffchaff. The wind whispered an endless message in the
willows, speaking in tongues with nobody to interpret. If
you're talking to me, I'm sorry, but I just don't understand.

Turquoise dragonflies flashed in and out of the shadows.
Maybe if he sat there long enough he'd see a kingfisher.

Like he had with Leon, that hot, hot, hot day in France, when they'd star-fished languidly under the poplars.

Willow fluff hung on the air. He gazed at the water. There were fish among the rocks. Then something caught his eye. What on earth? There was a tiny light, deep down in the river, deeper than was possible. A spark, travelling steadily upstream. For a moment, he could make no sense of it all. Then he smiled and looked up, shading his eyes.

Nothing.

But high above, out of sight, there would be a jet heading off somewhere, lit by the evening sun.

Kiss and Part

The Fabric of Things

by Jo Baker

*In 1945, the textile designer Tibor Reich established a
workshop in an old mill on the River Stour near Clifford
Chambers. His innovative designs were hugely influential
in the 1950s and 1960s and won international acclaim. The
workshop closed in 1978.*

Oblongs of hot sun travel across desks, exercise books, worn
wooden floor. Your shirt-waister pinches under your armpits, hairs stick to your neck. You can smell the geranium
on the windowsill, your own body, chalk, ink, the child on
either side of you. The moments creep towards the swoop
of release, the scrambling delight of tidy up and put away.
Everyone tumbles out together for dens or tree-climbing or
to get back to the farm, but she, hand on satchel, gives you
a look, and a tilt of the head, and you follow her, as you
always would.

The grass is long; the seed-heads nod, and she trails her
fingers over them, raising a purple mist into the air. Her
nails are dirty and bitten to the quick and the cuticles pulled
and scabbed and that's just how a hand should be; yours
trailing after is a pale thing, nails trimmed neat for you with
scissors. She turns her head to say something back over her
shoulder to you and her ragged plait swings across the back
of her dress, and then swings back into place.

You walk down to the bend in the river, just above Mr Reich's mill. You can hear it thrum from here; he is making his beautiful fabrics that light up people's homes. You scan round because sometimes you see him out sketching, perched like a kingfisher on the riverbank, working on his designs, but you can't see him today. Your father is a supervisor at the mill, which is a distinction. He supervises the new colours and patterns as they grow, flicker by flicker, on the looms, as they are conjured up out of Mr Reich's daydreams. You feel proud of that.

She drops the bag on the grass bank then swings herself down onto the pebbles and reaches back for you. Your hands clasp.

There is a screen of trees on the far bank. The river flows sleek and quiet. In shadow the water shows its misty depths, twisting tree roots, rocks, hanging fish. In sunlight it reflects trees, sky, a glittering of sunlight like gold leaf. Behind you the meadow grasses hiss, and all is closed off and secret and quiet.

She flumps down on the pebbles and flops open her satchel. You sit beside her, lean back on your hands. She lifts a milk bottle from her bag. It's still filmed with milk, but has been refilled with purple liquid and the neck stuffed with brown paper: blackcurrant cordial, diluted from the tap.

'Where'd you get that?'

'Helped myself when I went home for my dinner.'

'Won't your mum mind?'

In your house, cordials – rosehip, blackcurrant, rhubarb – are given in small doses, spoonfuls. It's thought unwholesome to dole out too much sweetness in one go.

'She don't even notice.'

She unstoppers it and you watch her gulping. She wipes the rim with a grubby hand and passes the bottle to you. You tilt it to your lips, and close your eyes, and hold the liquid on your tongue. You taste the red salt of her palm, and the purple of the drink, and you feel the round blues of the stones beneath you, and feel the velvet green of the stirring leaves, and the clay milk of the water and the deep twisted liquorice roots and the trout that is a flick of silver; and underneath it all and through it all is the iridescent thrum of the mill, permeating everything.

You open your eyes to see her watching you and she gives you her twisted little smile that makes one cheek dimple; she is the only person who never minds the strangeness of you. You swallow the blackcurrant right down, return her smile. She toes off her plimsolls, peels down her socks. Then she gets to her feet and slithers out of her dress in one quick move like a rabbit slid from its skin. She doesn't even have a vest on, just knickers that have been outgrown by two older sisters before they came to her. No vest on a hot day is enviable; but then, somebody else's knickers ... She slithers out of them and stands naked.

You wedge the bottle between stones, wrestle your way out of your dress and underwear. You cast around, just in case, but there's only a chestnut pony cropping grass in the next field. Together, hands clasped, you pick your way wincing across the pebbles and into the water.

It's cool but not cold; you step, then wade, then sink and drift. Soup, your mother says; filthy, full of germs; but no, it's misted, fresh, cleaner than a bath. The current pulls you. You're shattering the mirrored trees into scraps, laddering the green, your bodies white as chalk beneath the water. You flip over, lie back to watch the sky, hair like weed. The branches overhead scatter the light like petals; you close your eyes, and watch the red.

You know that your mother will know; she always does. She'll scold you about The Dangers of the Water while she scalds you in a bath. Polio. Cramp. Drowning. But these are fairy-tale curses. They don't happen to anyone you know. Hair dried out in the sun and combed with fingers, body cool and faintly rimed with river-silk, walking home, you desperately trying to formulate a plan. If you run in and run upstairs and run yourself a bath: but that itself would draw attention. You can't lie and say you fell in, because your clothes are dry. You are, you realise, for the high jump. It is inevitable. You creak open the back door, wish for something, *anything* to spare you the scrubbing and the scolding and the disapproval.

There are no pans rattling, no plates on the table. You stand there not knowing what happens next; you hear a movement from the sewing room and peer in through the door. She's perched on the edge of the wing chair, leaning forwards, all elbows and knees. She looks up at you; her eyes are pink, her nose is pink. For a moment she doesn't speak, just twists her handkerchief around. And then:

It's your dad.

You lie awake half the night, knowing that he is lying downstairs in the parlour and will never sit up again. His heart, they say, just gave up. You hadn't known that hearts could do that. In the morning your mother says that you don't have to go to school if you don't want to, but you can't stay at home with your dad gone cold and grey and your mum gone sore and pink. Anyway, you want to tell her; you tap on her door and she comes out and wraps her arms around you; she already knows and you never get to say it out loud to her. You fall into step beside her, and you see the faint silver of river-silt on her tanned arms; you breathe in the scent of clay and crushed mint. Her hair, the thick plait of it that snakes down her back, is still unbrushed, matted as old rope, still faintly damp.

It all comes back to you years later when, without looking, you peel a sweet from the packet and slip it in your mouth and it's blackcurrant. You spit it into your hand and lob it towards the river. You tweak another from the pack; it's green; you suck on it. That's better. Lime.

This is your Friday buffer between school and home: you duck out of the small knot of girls that walk this way back from the grammar and you slope off alone into town. You spend sixpence at the best sweetshop – always chocolate for her, always sucking sweets for you – then you wander home alone, daydreaming, undisturbed. It doesn't matter if you're late. Your mother doesn't notice; you have your own key and tea's on the table and you're to get your homework done. She's cycled off to some committee, or her sewing circle, or the WI; you're mostly glad of her busyness; if she has time to spend on you she spends it anxiously: you have to work hard at school, you have to do well in your exams, and then you have to go away. Because there's nothing around here for you.

Today the river is shrunk to murky pools; all the pleasure boats are tucked away; the ferry lies idle, and the swans walk disconsolately on mud. The park is almost empty: it's too hot. A woman pushes a pram, hunched and squinting; in the shadow of a tree you see a blanket, two pairs of tangled legs; you look away.

You're thinking then about Miss Hastings, who wears tortoiseshell earrings and smells of roses when she leans over you to think about lines, colour, light and shade; you're watching the dust kick up over the conker-toes of your school shoes, so you don't know how long that man has been staring at you when you catch his eye.

He's sitting in full sun; he's smiling at you. You flip the sweet on your tongue, the hollow and the seam of it, stare back at him. He's dark haired, shirt-sleeves rolled, one arm stretched along the back of the bench. You feel the damp under your own armpits, the drag of your satchel on your shoulder, the slick of sweat on your lip. He gives you a little beckoning jerk of the head. You don't know what to make of it all, but the path is taking you towards him anyway. As you come closer, he lazily gestures to his lap.

It takes you a moment to realise what it is there, since you've never seen one before, not in the wild as it were, and – the diagram in Biology certainly didn't show it in this state – angry. He glances down at it, then back at you, smiling, like it's his pet, brought out to be admired. And then he starts to stroke it. Not a word has been exchanged between you; you still don't know what to make of it all, what you are supposed to think or feel; but you pick up your pace, scoop up your satchel and clasp it to your chest; you break into a messy run. At the bridge, you risk a glance back. He's still sitting there. His head is turned away; he's not even watching you. He's waiting for some other girl to come along and admire his ugly little pet. You plough up the hill, holding your stitch, and out onto the lane. When you reach the mill's handloom hum, you begin to feel that you are home again.

Breathless, back at the house, you find sandwiches between paired plates, an apple balanced on top. The normality of things is helpful. After washing up and finishing your homework, you grab your smallest sketchpad, pocket her chocolate and lock the back door behind you. You wait at the side gate of the Manor House. The shadows are long and blue. People you know come and go and you say good evening. The swallows skim overhead. You draw the patterns of stone, the tracery of branches against the sky, try and capture the brisk paper-darts of the birds. At her knocking-off time, she strides out of the side door, a defiant air about her, despite the yes sirs, yes ma'ams, the caps and pinnies. You shut your sketchbook, hand her the chocolate; she rips it open and snaps you off a square and she fizzes like the cap's come off a bottle of pop; the day's deference doesn't suit her. The chocolate is soft as butter in your mouth. You link arms and, when you get a chance, you tell her about the man, his smile, his ugly little pet.

Dirty fucker, she says, and laughs.

She's more grown up than you will ever be, you think: she'd have laughed that man to scorn.

You amble along together, arm in arm, the pair of you drunk with your differently exhausting days. You realise you won't be bringing her Friday chocolate again; you'll be sensible and come straight home with the other girls. She breaks another chunk and passes it to you, and you take it; you've assumed you'll sit on the swings for a bit, which is something you often do; just hang there side by side in the evening air and chat and be quiet together. But there's a boy with a bicycle waiting by the gate. You feel her change; she drops your arm to touch her hair, and then dab her nose. You peer at the boy. You know him, the eldest of a farming family from out Bidford way.

He pushes away from the wall, rights the bike and wheels it with him; you glance to her, watch her look at him, run her tongue over her teeth. She doesn't look at you.

I'd best be off, then, you say.

Oh, alright then, she says, Cheerio.

* * *

You plunge out of college into January air. You tie and tuck your scarf, settle your hat. Others mill around you, clot into groups and pairs and stream away. In Life Drawing Class the air was all eaten up by paraffin heaters, the time all eaten up by concentration. You'd lost yourself for hours trying to capture the space a body took up in the world.

And now you yourself are in the world again, occupying your own space, and that's a poser too.

The trees of Bloomsbury Square are dark upright slashes into the sky. There's snow in the air. You turn up the collar of your Crombie. You're quite the dandy, your friend Marion once said, rubbing a hand over your cropped hair, but you said, Ah, no, no; I'm an aesthete; I'm Saint Joan. Marion considers a miniskirt a liberation, but in a man's coat, men's trousers, a shirt that buttons all the way up to your throat, hair that you rub over with soap and then rub dry, you've made yourself more free. You walk through the fug of coffee shops and the fumes of pubs and diesel engines and bins and back streets; the winter city writes itself around you and you dig your hands into your pockets – proper pockets, because men's pockets – and turn your coins and bus tickets, and you feel you can go anywhere alone; you are at home here.

You write this place to her, write London, Bloomsbury, the rattling Underground, your dingy digs in Notting Hill, the friends who used to marvel at your vowel sounds until you rounded them out – you never knew you had an accent till you came here – you fill pages of your cheapest sketch pad with blue ink and fold them fat and tight to send to her. She writes back a single sheet of lavender notepaper: her little girl, the weather, the farm. A new baby due in June. You write to your mother too, more carefully, filtering. She never thought of art college; it isn't quite the thing. So you write to her about your busyness, your domestic arrangements, your small economies, and you hear back about hers. You don't go home enough, you know. You cut vacations short. You visit friends, or say you're visiting friends. You return to London early with work as an excuse.

You know your way now like you know the palm of a lover's hand, the lines and stains and scars and callouses.

You watch the women because they are lovely to watch. One in harlequin tights and a shaggy green jacket, another in a crimson swing coat and beret and black patent boots who dashes across the street and into a cab and the last glimpse you get of her is the back of a sheened black boot that exactly matches the glossy carapace of the cab. Sometimes you watch men too: you pass a pair of beautiful boys in beautiful overcoats who glance at you, and then away, and then look back again, snagged. It's that smudge of kohl, that slick of mascara: it confuses them in a way that you find interesting. You recall the model in life drawing class, a man who'd sat on a wood-and-tube-metal stool, and looked into the middle distance, his neat naked body; his total disregard for your appraisal of it. His little pet made no more claim on the attention than any other part of him. You remind yourself to remember this.

You pick at a bus ticket in your pocket and your gaze snags on a young blonde woman's; she is just coat and eyes, but her eyes crease with a smile, and you think, I could stop and we could talk; and then maybe more than talk. But instead you walk on, letting the moment's connection stretch, then snap. Which makes you think of Natalie, who used to keep doing that, keep catching your eye and holding it in lectures: Natalie who's beautiful and draws beautifully and dresses beautifully and speaks beautifully and who doesn't expect to have to work; who'd kissed you out of a clear blue sky one evening last summer, and tasted of Pernod and black, and who hasn't even met your eye since, and won't ever know how much the taste of blackcurrant makes you shudder.

Sloane Street and the shop windows are lit and gleaming in the dim afternoon. Snow falls thinly, specks the pavements. Women in furs and tweeds drift between shops and cars. You really are an oddity here; you get such looks. But you come here anyway, because a bit of home has grown here, like a spore that's drifted on the winds and taken root.

The first time you came, you just stared in through the window. The second time you came, you slid in through the doors, walked round silently, slipped out again. The third time, you actually spoke to a receptionist: Mr Reich's mill, the workshop; my dad used to work there; I grew up in the village, swam in the river; sometimes we'd see him out sketching; and now I'm at art school here and ... I just wanted ...

You don't know what you wanted.

You don't say, it's like he dreams the same dreams that I dream. You don't say, him just being there made art seem possible to me.

She sweetly offered to take your telephone number, ring you up and let you know when Mr Reich was going to be in town again, and you said that would be lovely, but you didn't leave your number, which is only the landlady's number anyway, and you might as well stuff your mouth with marbles as try and talk to him. You left it a month before you went again and there was a different woman on reception, and you sidled by and didn't stay long and didn't make conversation.

Today, though, is jacquard, green and gold; it is sun on long summer grass. You know that these textiles now sail all over the world; they glow in palaces, they chime back the colours of cathedral stained glass. But they are not known in those places, by those people, not in the way you know them: you know his work like you know the river. You swim in it; you can feel the sources and the currents in your bones.

* * *

Life is the corner cleared for you in a dusty workshop. It's charcoal traced on paper-grain, the roll of ink onto silk screens; it's the slow accumulation of finished things, because when you're finished you can start the new thing that's been tugging at your elbow, wanting to be brought into existence, wanting to be made. Life is the friends' voices weaving round you as you work. Life is your three rooms in Shoreditch. Life is also Shelley, who sometimes shares them. Life is this for years and years, and you lose yourself quite contentedly.

At first you're just visiting more often. The guest bed is covered with a patchwork quilt your mother made. You sit there, knees drawn up that morning, and listen to the birdsong, a motorbike burning along the Bidford road, your mother coughing.

You're staring out of dirty train-windows, railway-blue formica beneath your fingertips, scuffed aluminium edging cool against your palms. You're always clinging on to something. Your head is rolled round on those public antimacassars to look out at grey London sprawl, genteel Leamington, turning leaves. You are always walking from the station, along the riverbank, under the bridge and up through the fields, everything dripping.

One time, you're crossing the park and you think of him, the Dirty Fucker, and her laughter, and the way that it'd dismissed him, the way it'd made it seem to be just one of those things. And you wonder now if it wasn't just one of those things. If you were an early experiment in fear. If there was more and worse to come, for other women, other girls.

One time, up on the brow of the hill, you are stopped by the sight of something white in the grass. You stoop to look and it's not a mushroom, but a hare's skull. It lies in the palm of your hand, light as an eggshell. You place it on the guest room windowsill.

You miss Shelley, but Shelley is always someone to be missed; it's in her nature. The phone rings and rings and rings out as you stand in the hallway, receiver at your ear. You gaze at the coloured glass above the front door, or you turn to look down the hallway, towards the window out onto the garden, and beyond that, the meadows, the river. But Shelley's never there. She's not at her desk; she's not at the flat. She has just been posted to Belfast; she's heading off to the Lebanon. Conflict is her thing, professionally speaking. Personally speaking, she evades it: you can't get into conflict with someone you can't speak to. You shake out the newspaper and there she is, like a magic trick: her name, her voice; you know her there. You read attentively, as though the words for you alone. On one rare coincidence of you both in the flat at the same time, rolled together in bed, she says, Maybe we should get a tenant for the second bedroom. With you away so much too. The whole place empty all the time.

And you say, Maybe we should.

And then, a few weeks later, she calls you at work and says that Barbara is keen to move in as soon as possible. She can hand over the keys to her that evening.

Okay, you say. Alright. That is happening then, is it? No, that's okay, that's fine.

That's part of it. Part of the shift.

Then the workshop manager invites you in for a little chat. If you're not using your space, then someone else really could benefit from it; they have a waiting list long as your arm. You're not going to be a dog in the manger about it, though you feel sick as you ring round van-hire companies for quotes. You strip out anything that you've left unfinished for more than a year and sling it in the skip. That feels cathartic; it's clarifying. You feel lighter for it.

Because of Barbara there is now no spare room in the flat, so you drive what's left of your work up to your mother's house and unload your pictures, paints, inks, the remaining unfinished canvasses into her sewing room, where she no longer sews, having lost sensation in her fingertips, which was an unanticipated side effect of that first round of chemotherapy.

Then there's the day that you go back to London and the flat smells different. You snuff the air like a dog. It's citrussy, but underneath that a meaty, slightly rotten smell that might be orange blossom. You notice different things there too. A whole sliced loaf of records added to the shelf; a clutter of cassettes around the stereo. You pick up a compilation tape and peer at the track list. It's printed in an even hand that you don't recognise. Maybe Barbara's; maybe someone who's courting Barbara; but at least it's not Shelley's ants-with-inky-feet.

You push open the spare room door and stand on the threshold. A new blue country-style chest of drawers is cluttered with cosmetics and perfume bottles. Curtains the colour of egg-yolk leak sunlight onto the oatmeal carpet.

You ring round friends. You don't want to be here alone tonight, and you really don't want to be here with Barbara. A few people pick up; you suggest a coffee, a drink; today, tonight; but they have plans. Which could be stretched to accommodate you, of course; but you feel the pause; it's lovely to hear from you, but it's also unexpected. They need more notice. You're not automatic any more.

You take your old coat and a pair of winter boots from the wardrobe you used to share with Shelley. You get the next train back from Marylebone. You go home. And that's it. You're no longer visiting. That's the shift complete.

* * *

She knocks on the door one evening. It takes you just a second longer than it should have to see the girl in this weather-tanned woman, and a second more to see that she hasn't changed a bit.

I've brought you eggs, she says, holding up a scuffed grey box. She flips the lid and shows you; one is speckled, one is white as the hare's skull. Fresh as a daisy, she says; you want to poach those for your tea, do your mother good.

You hear her accent and you find yourself smiling as you invite her in. You make a cuppa and you hear her with your mum, their easy conversation. You stand for a bit in the sewing room and look out across the garden and just listen to the two of them chatting away. You bring in tea and see that she has brought her knitting with her. Blue-bell yarn turns itself into something beneath her fingertips. She pauses, counts, muttering, and is back with you again. She talks about the daughter planning her wedding, brides-maids' dresses – perhaps your mum will help with that? Her son off on his 50cc round the lanes and giving her grey hairs. The younger ones, exams, Young Farmers, gymnas-tics. She is glad to get away from all that for a bit.

She drives you in her old green Volvo when you drop your mum off for the second surgery. In the carpark she holds you, and rubs your back, and then rubs your head, like you're a boy, like you're her son. You drop your face into the crook of her neck and stay there.

You sit in bed, in the guest room, and trace the patchwork fabrics with your fingertips. You remember sundresses; your father's shirts, and a cot sheet that you had forgotten till you find a patch of teddy-bear print and catch your breath.

She brings a Victoria sponge. Your mum thinks she might actually manage a slice; a second even; why not? She's eating again; it's a miracle; she might even start to put on weight.

The bluebell yarn has become a cardigan. You had no idea that she was knitting it for you. You pull it on. It is soft and warm and simple, big wooden buttons down the front. You raise the sleeve to your nose and smell the wool, the farmhouse, her. You live in it. Huddled up in the bedside chair, you sketch your mother as she sleeps, as she blinks at you, her dark eyes; when the Macmillan nurse comes you take your paints out into the fields. You scrape blackthorn up into a china sky and foam the twigs with blossoms; you scrub thick chocolate ploughed fields against a Granny-Smith green hill. You sit by the river and scowl over the layered reflections, depths.

The mill sits silent; the workshop closed down years ago, in your absence; you miss it. You miss the thrum in the air; you miss the very fact of him being there, and making things. You miss knowing that the fabric of this place was wanted all across the world.

The nurse gives your mother morphine, for the pain, but you are not sure that it's pain that she is feeling. Her hands grip, her muscles go rigid: it's like she's trying to stop herself from falling, and she can't stop herself from falling. Her body can't hold her anymore; it's worn threadbare.

* * *

It's May, and the cherry blossom is drifting down like it's a wedding. The coffin weighs what a coffin weighs and just a little more. You've covered it with the quilt from the guest bedroom. With the patchwork of baby linen and old summer dresses and a long-dead husband's shirts. You have laid on it bunches of flowers from the garden: pale narcissi, bluebells already drooping, a bough of blossom from the Beauty of Bath tree. She would disapprove, you know, of the clipping of that branch, but you are grown-up now and her notional disapproval is something you've decided you can live with. You need the blossom's loveliness now, more than the apples that would have come to be.

You wear your winter boots, because you have nothing else suitable to wear. You wear your one good black dress. You carry your bluebell cardie over your arm. Later, you slip it on. You touch it to your lips, and then to your eyes.

At the parish hall, green china tea-cups, the rim between lips, and you are back in Brownies, at church coffee mornings, summer fetes. You are talked to, and you hear yourself talked about. You feel as though you have somehow been redeemed. With the green tea-cup still in your hand, you say goodbye to Shelley – it was good of her to find the time to come at all – and then you're offering to stack chairs, wash up; you'd shunt that wide broom across the wooden floor to gather up the dirt. But no, no; you are sympathetically waved away.

She is waiting for you in the car park, leaning against the old green Volvo. The sun is low; the light golden. She has a big slouchy backpack on her shoulder. When she pushes away from the car, the bag clinks with an alcoholic sound. She gives you a look, jerks her head.

You follow her, as you always would, down the path, skirting the edge of the paddock where two ponies lift their heads and watch you. One is a grey, the other skewbald. The grass is lush; it wets through your winter boots. She walks ahead, dressed in her best black, to the bend in the river. You feel the first drops of rain on your forehead. She hops down the bank and reaches back to you. Your hands clasp. You drop down beside her. She fishes out a bottle of wine. It has been opened and the cork shaved and shoved back in. She hands you two plastic children's beakers; one is green, one is purple, both are spotted with creamy polka dots. She asks no questions. But then, she never did.

I brought a couple of towels too, she says, in case you fancied it.

You swallow, nod. Fuck it, you say: why not.

You peel the cardie from your shoulders, strip the laces from your boots. You step out of your dress, tights, pants; you unhook your bra. She is pale beneath her clothes. She has broadened at the hips; her belly is sweetly soft. Together, you pick your way barefoot across the pebbles. Three strides in, you dive first; and you're under, open eyes on misted water, bubbles, and then she crashes in beside you, her body milk white, turning, curving back up to the surface. You smash back up, push the hair off your face, and you let the world go still. She swims slow strokes across the river. You stir the water to stay where you are. The river moves around you; you feel its tug; you pull against its pull. She turns, swims back towards you. Overhead the trees are thickly green with their new silk. The surface of the water is opaque, pewter in the rain. You hold yourself there, hold yourself deliberately still, and you close your eyes, and turn your face up to the rain.

Kiss and Part

'Place of Dreams'

by Lucy Durneen

I

*Principal Investigators are reminded of their require-
ment to complete a risk assessment form for all Research
Projects involving Temporal Observation. Currently only
Viewing Permissions are sanctioned for all Beta Grade
research ships, with penalties for incursion into Parallel
timelines strenuously applied. Subjects for study should
ideally be approved by the Higher Research Council
one year prior to orbit, and in any case no less than one
month before the commencement of research. In no
circumstances may Proposals be amended without resub-
mission to the appropriate committee.*
GUIDELINES FOR PRINCIPAL INVESTIGATORS ON
PARALLEL OBSERVATION SHIP SYSTEMS, CLIFFORD &
CHAMBERS

Miranda sits in the *Tempest*'s Viewing Room, moving the
Eye across the computer screen, which stretches the length
of the entire room. There is a new play being performed in
the city today and she has instructions to transcribe it in
its entirety. The lens scrolls its way through the streets of
Parallel 17, which look so much like, and yet are entirely
unlike, the streets surrounding the Institute that designed

her. It is helpful, she has realised, to become familiar with
the *patterns* of these streets – not their geography but their
habits. In this way, the city is a person who likes things
done a certain way. There are the crowds that surge through
the dusk before the shows begin, the boy players in gauze
that rises and falls like smoke across the stage. The brawls
afterwards, the crush at the taverns and the transactions
that take place there. Things have changed recently. There
is something else in the streets, beside the spilt ale and the
troubadours. It takes Miranda a few scans of her transcripts
to be sure of the word, but the other thing palpable in the
streets is fear.

On Parallel 17 there has been some kind of pandemic
that is closing the city's playhouses. Miranda knows the
physicians on Earth 1.0 have medicine capable of halt-
ing the spread of this Black Death, but their ship only has
Observational Permissions and, besides, there are global
protocols forbidding interventions of this kind. Anyway,
there is a man she is supposed to be watching. He is not
going to die of this plague, but the Capitaine, who has been
monitoring Parallel 17 for some time prior to her arrival,
has told her that he's going to write about those who have,
those he mourns. What's interesting, the Capitaine said
when she first assigned Miranda her Observational duties,
is that we can't actually map this man's psychological state
on to these things he writes. But, she added, we could – for
example – assume that he was falling in love when he wrote
sonnets.

Or falling out of it? Miranda had asked. Well, don't you
learn fast, kid? the Capitaine said, sounding as pleased as if
she had won something.

Psychological state. Sonnets. *Falling* in Love. The Capitaine has, over the years, patiently explained such words to
Miranda, although to begin with, all she really needed to do

was listen and transcribe. When she first arrived on board, Miranda assumed she would use the Institute's standard language recognition software for such a purpose, but the Capitaine waves away her queries. Better keep it off-grid, she advises. There's nothing wrong with old-fashioned pen and paper. It just takes a little more time – and who of us has enough of that? The ship's project falls under the Council's research theme of Loss; the Capitaine is working at the fringes of the controversial field of Semantic Destabilisation, already being labelled a discipline of concern by some of the bigger grant-awarding committees on Earth 1.0. What the Capitaine actually wants is a database of every word this man, this man who did not die even though Plague was at his doorstep, had ever written down. The real brief is as simple and as complicated as that.

She was very clear about the *every word* part. Words have power, the Capitaine is fond of saying. Back then, this had seemed a vital statement, a motto of sorts, but now Bilal and Miranda roll their eyes when she starts up that particular lecture again.

Something else that surprises Miranda: on Parallel 17, everything is a comparison with something else. Fish smell of moss. A soul is a star. Eyes are like eggs in a glass of gin.

II

In the immediate weeks after the Discovery it was difficult to know how to differentiate realities. There was much debate about which universe was the Other and which was the Constant, mostly because no civilisation likes to think they might be in some way lesser than they believed. If Temporal Observation is now a familiar practice, a core component of most funded Research Projects, back in the beginning it was a measure of all that was

*lacking in the constant world, reclassified as Earth 1.0 in
the Oort Treaty of 1450. [...]*

*At the time of writing, thirty-two Parallel Worlds have
been detected, and there is no reason to suppose there are
not infinite numbers that might be accessed.*
TOWARDS AN UNDERSTANDING OF TEMPORAL
OBSERVATION, FOX, T.

Such meticulous work. Such concentration required. But it
is not in fact quite true, Miranda thinks, that they don't
have enough time. They have all of time, right out there
in front of them. What the Capitaine means is that the
risk of having their grant withdrawn is high. The potential
impact of their research is ambiguous, which in turn makes
it dangerous. If there is one thing that is not appreciated on
Earth 1.0 it is ambiguity. It is things looking one way when
in reality they are something different entirely.

It began this way. More than a hundred years before
Miranda was brought online, routine satellite sweeps
detected high neutrino counts concentrated in one part of
the sky above the Northern Hemisphere. What the scientists found when they looked harder: deep pools of dark
energy pulsing out into space like knots in a vein. It was
not written down this way: *knots in a vein.* The official
accounts speculated around alien activity, distant super-
novas. The energy pools did not connect two points in both
space and time; it was not a wormhole. Eventually there
remained only an impossibility: it was a window into a parallel world. It was living proof that at all times things can
appear to be one way in three dimensions and, in another,
anything but.

So much scientific discovery occurs this way: by accident.
In interviews, years later, the astronomer in charge of the
telescope that returned the first reports of a neutrino flood

confessed he had been using it, after hours, in an experimental process that probed the sky for alternative sources of energy. He would not say much about this process. Energy cannot be created or destroyed, only transferred, he explained instead to the eager interviewer. It was therefore possible that his attempts at energy sourcing had caused some kind of dimensional tearing, or perhaps the opposite, a tightening up of the skin of the universe, a ballooning, like an aneurysm that could do nothing else but rupture. He did not say things like ballooning, or aneurysm. He only knew the facts. But his eyes when the interviewer asked him. Maybe *I* did this, he was reported to have whispered off camera. Maybe I did.

Miranda is completing her transcript of the second act of the new play when she is distracted by a commotion in the corner of the screen. People are shouting. There is something moving in the river, something large. Bilal! she shouts. Bilal! Come see this! When he comes running from the Archive, Miranda is clapping her hands like a child. What is that? she asks him over and over, pointing at the screen. Damn, what *is* that?

An eye, reflecting the white crests, surging in. And definitely present, if improbable, a tail, beating madly against the tide.

It twists its tail flukes, dives, reappears. It's a goddamn whale, Bilal says, taking the controls of the Eye, zooming in and in until the illusion that they are close enough to feel the river's spray is itself destroyed by excess of proximity. He presses a button and there it is, filling the screen. A leviathan in the thin, snaking braid of the Thames. They look at each other as it breaches a third time. A whale. Even the water around it seems to retreat, disbelieving. She grabs Bilal's hand without thinking. Her heart stolen by this rare, beautiful thing, this anomaly.

In the early days of Temporal Observation, radio tele-scopes simply measured soundwaves and converted them into sonographic images. Men and women moved about the Earth like ghosts, silent and half-glimpsed through clouds of cosmic snow. To improve the quality of the images, to add sound and greater accuracy in identifying which points in space and time to observe, increased levels of dark energy were fired at the breaches to prick small holes in space-time. It was very important that they remained small enough to enable only light and sound waves to pass through. To Miranda it seems a little like pulling a thread on an old woollen blanket, harder and harder, the risk being even-tually that something will give and the hole will become bigger than what is around it.

But you can pull just a *little* harder on the thread, Bilal explained the first time he jammed the signals to the Central Drive that stored all Observations for Institutional approval, and opened up the range of viewing coordinates first to a century either side of the official limits, and then two, then further and further, and back towards a great Nothingness that makes Miranda feel as if she has been blown away in a wave of heat.

If you're going off-road, Bilal says, meaning *outside the parameters of what their grant permits*, don't forget to use your Incognito Drive.

From the moment it continues to swim upstream, rather than back out to sea, Miranda feels herself connected to the whale, this thing that doesn't belong where it is. It is impossible to stop watching. She slows her breathing for a minute, imagining syncing with the bellows of the whale's lungs, which – Bilal is quick to retrieve the information – it turns out are surprisingly small. To avoid decompression sickness, he says, although he doesn't explain how. An hour passes, or it might be two, and even though Bilal has

returned to the Archive, Miranda has not moved, still track-
ing the creature's slow path through the muddied waters of
the diseased river.

It almost goes without saying that all the images they
view suffer some lag in transmission. Nothing observed
from a great distance is ever witnessed in real time. The
fact the stars we see in the sky died light years ago is just
the most familiar way to demonstrate the speed of waves
across the universe.

A bad sign, the Capitaine says darkly of the whale's
appearance, switching the station to NightSpace ahead of
schedule.

III

*The assembly of an appropriate research team is a vital
element in project success. An essential criterion to bear
in mind at final interview is the candidate's resistance to
the raw materials of inquiry. While all current models
of Research Assistant receive regularly updated anti-
virus software, Transference remains a theoretical risk to
Researchers new to the field and Principal Investigators
should prepare accordingly to avoid the complications of
pseudo-empathetic reaction. It is recommended that the
suitability of an individual Researcher be independently
verified, at the P.I.'s expense, as Academic Liability Insurance is not valid for Temporal Observation.*
GUIDELINES FOR PRINCIPAL INVESTIGATORS ON
PARALLEL OBSERVATION SHIP SYSTEMS, CLIFFORD &
CHAMBERS

R578 is unwarrantably curious, is what her Supervisor
wrote on Miranda's CD1 form years before, not long after
the Institute brought her online. This was the form the

Research Council networked out to projects across their Sector, the ones that were currently hiring, which might mean they were looking to expand their teams, or that they were documenting a period from scratch. There were rumours that some of the new hires were there to fix protocol breaches, but those kinds of rumours were designed not to last long, to blaze up and then damp down, creating allure for projects that were more likely dead in the water. The form did not work in Miranda's favour either way. No one in the history of any world ever wanted a thing that is unwarrantable.

Almost at the point the Council was starting to consider decommissioning her, there was a response to her application. I could use some curiosity, the Capitaine told Miranda, but only later, when she was officially in the employment of the *Tempest* project, which back then was stationed just a little shy of 1580 AD, Parallel 17. *Curiosity has its own reason for existing.*

In the beginning, Miranda was disappointed with her assignment. Some of the other stations had Parallel Entry Permissions, although these were rare. The Capitaine's project was vague in terms of intended outcomes, but painstaking in execution, and involved a lot of close analysis, a lot of sifting through metadata. There was a minimum twelve hours' Observation in the Viewing Room a day. Miranda was perfectly calibrated for microtasking, but it seemed true to say – the feeling was a fleeting brightness, but it was there – that she had hoped for something more. Still, she was a dutiful worker. In the Viewing Room she set the coordinates of the Eye to correspond to those dates on the list the Capitaine was particularly interested in, and scenes of kings, asses, beggars pulsed across the screen. At 1605, fairies paraded a circular stage. At 1609, a drowning woman. A skull, grinning down at a prince. She was to record the data, then group it according to the Capitaine's instructions, even though she didn't understand the concept behind the taxonomy: Metaphors. Gesture. Conceit.

Her curiosity. At 1611, there was a storm. An island of books. A girl, alone and reading, always reading. When the curtains sweep down around the stage, Miranda continued to watch the players as they made their way from the theatre – *theatre*, she notes, *a building or outdoor area in which dramatic performances are given* – to the city taverns.

The girl who had been reading stripped out of her petticoats and became a boy. The sprite, still faintly a glistening blue, belched wine from a bottle. Not a bottle, a flagon. Long after her Observation shift ended, Miranda was still watching the shadows moving in the alleyways, mouths finding mouths, finding arcs of lunar skin under wine-stained collars. A troupe of tumblers cheered in the sandbanks, spitting Rhenish, pissing into the darkening water. It was Hallowmas Night and the river was full of moon. The sky was full of moon, willow-ringed. Men spinning fire at the water's edge. Clouds like branches, cupping light.

After weeks of working in isolation, Miranda was sent to the Archives for the first time. The biggest surprise was not the size of the Archive Chamber, the sheer volume of material it contained (*where has this all come from?* is not the real question she wanted to ask even though it was the first one out of her mouth), but that she was not alone on the ship after all. Ready for your upgrade? Bilal had asked her, taking her hand and opening up her palm. Now she had an Incognito Drive. Now there was a soft colour flushing down her arms under the standard issue RealDerm layers. *I look –* , Miranda wanted to say, but the word would not come out, or perhaps it was not there yet, or not fully, not activated; at any rate; she let the sentence end that way. *I look*.

Not *data*, Bilal told her when Miranda turned to leave the Archive. *Poetry.*

This problem of almost-possible language. What to call things. You'd think someone could do better than *Viewing Room*, the Capitaine sighed. The Place des Rêves, she renamed it. A room of dreams. The way the images sent back from Parallel 17 looked at first hazy, then settled into something dazzling, something familiar and yet unfamiliar – it was not unlike dreams. That is, not unlike the way Miranda's research suggests dreams might look.

Or maybe it is more correct to say how dreams might *feel*. Heavy things rising through the stars into weightlessness. That day in the Archive, when she stepped back into the chamber, wanting but not knowing how to ask what Bilal meant, what he meant *exactly*, Miranda remembered how he had handed her a stack of papers from one of the Archive boxes, then suddenly looked away as if he immediately regretted the action. It seemed this was how a dream might come to you, a glow of improbability, a thing you knew had happened in a way that didn't seem physically possible. The feeling of being lit up inside happened again. Such a small, miraculous illumination.

Since there's no help, come let us kiss and part.
Nay, I have done, you get no more of me.

She was still reading the papers when the Capitaine sent her a memo directly to the Incognito Drive. R578 doesn't exactly roll off the tongue, the memo read. How do you feel about *Miranda*?

Clouds like branches? she wondered.

IV

Passivity is, we are learning, but one state of reality. There are alternate conditions, noted in particular on Parallels 14, 17 and 28, in which humans are said to 'love', 'fear', 'hate', and experience myriad other neurochemical reactions that prompt in them unpredictable and illogical behaviour, including, but not limited to, the provocation of conflict and the destruction of stable familial or business units. A conclusion one might draw is that on these Parallels the driving human impulse, it seems, is to yearn for what is not. One theory is that this is caused by excessive exposure to language that encourages constant comparison between surplus and lack, such language characteristically relating to accounts of scenarios that are not real, that have never happened, or are used to describe something as if it had happened in an alternate manner. Consequently, while it is considered valuable to better understand such linguistic anomalies at an anthropological level, those observing the Temporal Fields of the aforementioned Parallels are at increased risk of being impacted by the data with which they work, in the form of delusions, hysteria, and irrational responses. It is this risk that led directly to the establishment of the Researcher Programme, following advice that such work no longer be carried out by human beings.
TOWARDS AN UNDERSTANDING OF TEMPORAL OBSERVATION, FOX, T.

The whale appears to have stopped moving, or at least, two days after its first sighting, it is not as far upriver as Miranda expected, which concerns her. Life finds a way, Bilal shrugs, directing her gently away from the screen in the Place des Rêves before heading back to the Archive. The sentiment is something to hold on to anyway. That they are none of them on board the *Tempest* technically alive is an irony on which he doesn't comment.

The screen mechanism used to be more utilitarian, built for efficiency and resilience rather than aesthetics, given the infrequency of engineering sorties to orbiting research ships, but Bilal's adjustments have made it look like the theatres Miranda has been observing on Parallel 17. There are heavy velvet drapes framing the screen. Benches with thick cushions. It still smells of metal dust and exhaust fumes, but what was an otherwise empty room is now full of the living sounds of another universe. The song of whales.

On Parallel 17, humanity seems trapped on its own crowded planet. That is to say, even in Miranda's illicit observations of the twenty-first century, its scientific progress is slower to advance than anything experienced on Earth 1.0, where inter-stellar travel has been commonplace for several centuries. But in place of this heightened knowledge, there are other, deeper deficiencies. When Miranda comments on the inequity of this, Bilal tells her it's really not that unusual a trait of evolution. It is, he says, like the way the star-nosed mole cannot see, but can find aquatic prey by sensing electrical signals. The compromising of one sense is balanced by the acute enhancement of another.

Later Bilal tells Miranda that it's possible, of course, there are no star-nosed moles on Parallel 17. But the point still stands. The question really is a different one altogether. In which version of Earth is humanity most blind? One in which music is the food of love, but people die in their thousands of a curable plague? Or the one in which it can travel beyond the stars but has no language to describe the marvel that is the journey?

After it stops being painstaking, the work moves into being occasionally painful. Once, Miranda found herself shaking as she watched a boy drink poison and a girl stab herself because they could not be together. She has come to understand that these are performances, things standing in for other things, people pretending to be other people; this bright city of the stage is not that darker maze outside it. The poison is not real, the Capitaine explained patiently, again. Still the shaking bothers Miranda. She reports it as a glitch. As an afterthought, she notes too the strange reactions she experiences in Bilal's presence, the way sometimes she thinks she has been paying close attention to what he has been saying, yet later finds nothing is recorded on either of her Core Drives but static. Dots of noise that outline the shape of his face, which is dimpled like a walnut shell, or so she sees from this perspective.

Sometimes as they move around the ship in the dark of NightSpace, Miranda senses him, an oncoming presence, before he is there in the corridor in front of her. There is a momentary feeling of being ahead of time, of having come to something a little too early. Although they look at each other as they pass, neither of them says anything at all. And then he is gone, back to work in the Archives, where she feels she cannot reach him.

But no matter how many times she cross-references it, the word that the data scans keep returning to her is *happy*.

For a brief moment she thinks, but if I am happy, does this mean I will never know sadness? This is itself a sad thing. It seems to her that the most beautiful feelings are those of longing for something, not having it. None of the data she has collected so far tells you what happens when you get the thing you want. She has to date transcribed fifty-three sonnets, seven complete plays, and countless letters, conversations, meetings that she has watched, a fly on the wall, not to mention the more clandestine Observations, the confusing tangle of words, and hands, and mouths that she witnesses in taverns, in opera houses, in fair Verona, and Elsinore, and here is the conclusion all the data seems to be showing her: *Shake hands for ever, cancel all our vows.*

Not data. *Poetry.* Not Researchers. Flies on the wall. This is how poetry moves into Earth 1.0, as data leaking from one universe to another.

Even after all these years, it is untested in the long term – the impact of so much sight. It is not just the young lovers with their cups of poison. Some things are coming that Miranda does not even want to tell the Capitaine about. There are sobbing women in dark forests. There are children running through empty villages, their bodies licked raw with fire.

At the Institute they are trained to self-refer, to be aware of the signs of neutrino poisoning, or what some call data fatigue, caused by wake turbulence from the temporal breaches. There is no theory as to why some are affected and others aren't, but the only known way to correct it is a complete reboot and transfer to another project. Or you could try watching kittens, the Capitaine says, sharing grainy videos to Miranda's Incognito Drive. Her theory is that there isn't a universe of any kind where this could not help. *The poison is not real!*

In any case, these glitch reports, too, the Capitaine pretends not to see.

V

It is recommended that Academic offences should be immediately reported to the relevant committee, as in the confined space of the research ship, protocol breaches may have a greater than expected impact on remaining crew members. Principal Investigators are advised that their hologram status on board the ship does not guarantee

immunity from data delusion or other such conditions experienced by Researchers, and appropriate precautions should be taken to ensure restored integrity in the event of a serious offence being detected.
GUIDELINES FOR PRINCIPAL INVESTIGATORS ON PARALLEL OBSERVATION SHIP SYSTEMS, CLIFFORD & CHAMBERS

To turn a blind eye: *to knowingly refuse to acknowledge something that you know to be real.*

On Parallel 17 Miranda discerns (although only after she has started breaking all the rules of Temporal Observation) that people use this phrase to indicate not ignorance, but perfect awareness. They use it because of what Admiral Lord Nelson did at the naval battle of Copenhagen in 1801.

I have only one eye, and I have a right to be blind sometimes, is what Nelson said, thinking slyly of victory, pretending he couldn't see the flags across the sea as he fixed his unseeing eye to the telescope, or their distant, frantic shimmer signalling the order to disengage. It stands to reason that there is a parallel version of events also in existence, where Nelson was not blind, and did not say this. Or was blind and did not say this. Or simply made the wrong call, sighted or not. It doesn't matter. On Earth 1.0, where Miranda came online, nobody says anything that means something else. Nobody knows how.

On Earth 1.0 there is no face that launched a thousand ships. No star-crossed lovers. No cloths of dreams, no wild goose chases or green-eyed monsters, no albatrosses around anyone's neck. No be-all and end-all, no hearts are made of gold. Love is not blind, or like a red, red rose; it is not an ever-fixed mark. There is no beast with two backs, no one is bloody but unbowed. Breath is not bated, hope is not feathered, no one's life is measured out in coffee spoons.

No one finds beauty in the fragment; ruins are cleared to make way for the new. Waving might just be waving. Drowning might just be drowning. No HomerMilton-DanteShakespeareBlake. No Jane Eyre. No Frankenstein's monster, no vampyrs stalking history. There is no story of O, no Catherine M, no Venus in Furs. No light-as-truth. No truth-as-beauty. No predictions of marriage in syndicated newspapers. No mix tapes. For better or worse, when the time comes, Britney Spears will never put on a school-girl uniform, and peep wide-eyed into the camera lens; *My loneliness is killing me.* But is it? they would ask on Earth 1.0, impassive, unmoved in their starched, mannered finery. Is it?

It is like the low hum of a radio that is only noticeable when it has been switched off. What was that sound, that was everywhere?

Her name is a nod to the ship itself. Her name means wonder. Socrates said that wonder was the beginning of wisdom. The wise know *not to give themselves away*, says Bilal, who subscribes to a different kind of philosophy. You know what curiosity did.

This sonnet he gave her the first day she visited the Archives, this song of *love's latest breath* – Miranda cannot stop thinking about it. It is written by another man, not the one Parallel 17 knows as Shakespeare and who will be revered for centuries. This man is born a year earlier. He is quieter, will be spoken of less. She sets the coordinates of the Eye and watches him, Drayton, and Shakespeare and another poet, Ben Jonson, reading, and laughing, and spilling ale in the town of Stratford, miles from London, and where soon Shakespeare, who evaded plague, will die of a fever contracted on this night.

She has seen him before, this man Drayton, sitting in the churchyard of a small village, lying on the banks of the

Stour, on horseback riding past the yeomen's farms under hot, bright skies. At a desk in a room at the Manor, the house of his friend. *Anne*, he writes over and over. Anne, *Anne*. He makes his way down the single track of the village, and sometimes the woman he writes to is there at the other end, smiling at his arrival. Mostly she is not. Miranda observes how she lives with another man, how she treats Drayton with affection but not the love he writes of in these fourteen lines Miranda has memorised. How does he live with them, she wonders, the words he never says, the ones he leaves in the spaces between what he writes and what he means? It is a strange thought, that he is unaware he can be seen from a research ship orbiting above him in another dimension. How could he possibly imagine that?

But then, there are other things that seem far less possible, and yet they are true.

The sonnet is in her mind again as she sits, hunched up at the screen in the Place des Rêves, watching the river for the whale like a hawk. *Like a hawk*. This phrase is the exact opposite of turning a blind eye. This is the observation of everything, an excess of intimate detail. She tracks the Eye up and down the river, the sheltered bend as it pushes on through Sailor Town, the meanders of Bow Creek, the sunken, Neolithic trees as the tide surges out towards the sea at Purfleet, but today it is empty of miracles. When Miranda finally sees it, the whale has sunk into the curve of a sandbank, as if sleeping, nestled in the crook of an arm. Its body rises and falls in a long shiver, and something inside her rises and falls and shivers too.

How did he *do* it? Miranda sends the Capitaine a memo. Drayton. How did he make the things he felt into things other people could feel too? *The last gasp of Love's latest breath.*

Sometimes she imagines how it might be if she lived on

LUCY DURNEEN

Parallel 17. Perhaps they would go to the theatre in their best clothes. Perhaps he would find her beautiful, and tell her so. They would have a library for all those papers of poems that Bilal keeps, their very own Archive. A soft bed with blankets threaded with gold.

* * *

The alarm light on her Core Drive has been blinking and buzzing for some time before Miranda is aware of it, the red glow growing and receding. *Incognito*, she remembers, too late, realising that her memo to the Capitaine will have been uploaded to the Institute's central databases. She wonders if they might sense her concern for the whale. If they can see the dreams of libraries in her head. It is likely that even as she stands here she is being monitored for signs of data fatigue. Not *data*, she wants to tell them. But she cannot name the thing that it is not supposed to be.

The alarms continue to flash, louder now, and she supposes that in a moment Bilal will come running, although she's sure he already knows what the sounds mean. It does not feel like there is any point in moving very fast. Everything that is going to happen is already happening. When she sees the Capitaine standing in the middle of the room, holding out her arms as she shimmers in and out of vision, Miranda knows it for certain. Since there's no help, the Capitaine's voice says from far away on Earth 1.0. So that is sadness, Miranda thinks, surprised that of all the possibilities she had imagined, this is how it finds her.

She crouches on the floor of the Places des Rêves, as close to the screen as possible, zooming the Eye in and in towards the sandbank until the whale is the screen, the screen is all whale, a fading giant slowing even the movement of the stars. If it were a star, perhaps now it would blaze into a supernova. Perhaps now it would begin a new journey, or a different one, a forking path in the old. Miranda wonders what it can remember, if it knows where it has been, what it has lost. But the whale gives nothing away. It blinks at her, its own eye flecked with bloodied-white clots of sea-foam, and for a minute it seems bigger even than itself, momentarily startled, like a stranded, living ship, not realising it died days ago.

Kiss and Part

Afterword

We have put together this anthology of commissioned stories in the hope it will give pleasure, while honouring this village, Clifford Chambers in south Warwickshire.

The terms of our commission were precise and one writer commented that they had not been easy to fulfil. Each story could be about anything at all, but we wanted them to commemorate the Tudor poet Michael Drayton by referring to his most famous sonnet, 'Kiss and Part', so all the stories were required to have people kissing and parting, somehow, somewhere and sometime. Furthermore, this area of the village, which we studied for our eclectic history, *Round the Square and Up the Tower: Clifford Chambers, Warwickshire* (2013), was to be salient in the stories. Beside a curve in the River Stour is a hump of land above the flood-line, which is where the church was built, now surrounded by houses and gardens (the Square) and this was our subject. Church Cottage, dated 1760, is the smallest and has its own humble history. This is where our visiting writers stay and it features in several of the stories.

We are delighted with these stories, and sometimes surprised. We had not expected so many varied ghosts and certainly not foreseen a spaceship, but everyone has kept closely to the brief. We had thought more would be made of immediate local history; the Square was once a farmyard and the surrounding households humble; their occupants would be doing well to keep food on the table and wheels on the donkey cart, whereas now there are Bentleys and Maseratis parked outside and exclusive grocery deliveries. But all places reflect the money of the moment, whether landscape or urban, and even the uses and condition of the river; it is hardly used for recreation as everyone has the money to drive elsewhere for fun. Agencies empowered to care for it are financially limited, so it remains crammed with natural debris, which has encouraged otters to return, as confirmed by expensive surveillance methods. The River Stour runs through many of these tales.

There were three reasons for our commissioning these stories. First, we believed that this quiet cul-de-sac deserved some sort of remembrance in this time of extensive building, including a possible south-western ring road on stilts across the river meadows, all of which would alter its ambience. Another salient reason was to recall and bring to revival appreciation of two very different cultural figures associated with this place, the Tudor poet Michael Drayton and the twentieth-century designer Tibor Reich.

We brought these two figures to the attention of our writers, not with an instruction to include them as narrative figures but with a suggestion that their different influences could be recalled. This produced results; the first story in the anthology, 'Buck Moon' by Marina Warner, summons Tibor and his studio set in one of Clifford's two old mills where he worked on his innovative designs from 1946 until 1978 (he died in 1996). Using photography of the surrounding countryside and the river (whose constant flooding eventually drove him from the mill), he chopped and rearranged these increasingly abstract photographic shapes into new designs. Injected with colours into evocations of reflection and ripple, flowering and repeat, the plethora of his numerous fabric designs are a glorious example of post-war cultural revitalisation.

Michael Drayton contributed significantly to the Eliz-abethan/Jacobean golden age of poetry. He knew the village and his affection for it and for the mistress of the Manor, Lady Anne Rainsford, all found expression in his work. This issue of the relationship between Anne Rainsford and Michael Drayton, and his mysterious if apocryphal link with Shakespeare's death, are the substance of 'A Merrie Meeting' by Salley Vickers.

Our publication *Round the Square and Up the Tower* devotes a chapter to Drayton and his lifetime of months' long visits to the Manor at Clifford Chambers, owned by Sir Henry Rainsford, Anne's husband. She had been a child-hood friend of Drayton but she was the daughter of her father's house and he was a poor pupil, taken in from local poverty for service and education. She outlived her husband and Drayton and the circumstances, place and date of her death are unknown.

On the north wall of St Helen's Church chancel is the carved and painted alabaster and marble Jacobean memo-rial to this hospitable couple and their children. As is customary, the left-hand plaque on its support-base gives Sir Henry's life's dates and extols his virtues. The right-hand plaque, installed at that time awaiting Anne to join him in burial and eulogy, is blank. We wished, within these stories, to bring the possibilities of her life back to attention.

Finally, we commissioned this anthology because who can resist lobbing a pebble of inventive enterprise into an unsuspecting local pond? There are myriad other charming villages with wonky cottages by an ancient churchyard, but our intention here is to emphasise and awaken the *genius loci,* the spirit of this particular place. It is the interaction of interior and exterior space, with the weather, the river, the materials, tools and food available to people who have lived here for a thousand years that we wish to honour with this book. And most influential of all is the churchyard of St Helen's, with its dozens of recorded burials gradually fading and thousands more that are unrecorded underneath the bumpy earth.

St Helen herself hovers nearby on that serrated interaction of myth and history, and her church tower looms over our cottage, with what Shakespeare refers to in *A Midsummer Night's Dream* as an iron-tongued clock, chiming throughout the day and night. This bell can be a reminder (to those who wish to be reminded) that the Christian faith it represents is generous, great and good in spite of our established church's many imperfections. I am going to end with a prayer from *Helena*, Evelyn Waugh's 1950 novel about St Helen, who was the mother of the Roman Emperor Constantine:

> For His sake, who did not reject your curious gifts, pray always for the learned, the oblique, the delicate. Let them not be quite forgotten at the Throne of God when the simple come into their kingdom.

As a leaving present, one of our resident writers gave me a first edition of Waugh's charming book that delighted me. This prayer is a reminder to me of how our cottage at the edge of St Helen's churchyard, delicate, oblique and simple as it is, inspires our writers to send their words out into the world with the power and purpose that women have for so long been denied.

Sarah Hosking, founder/secretary
September 2018

Hosking Houses Trust
33 Duck Lane
The Square
Clifford Chambers
Stratford-upon-Avon
Warwickshire CV37 8HT
www.hoskinghouses.co.uk

Acknowledgements of Photographs

The publisher acknowledges with thanks permission granted by copyright holders to use the photographs on the accompanying bookmark to this book.

Catherine Fox © HHT
Elizabeth Speller © Michael Bywater
Jill Dawson © HHT
Jo Baker © HHT
Joan Bakewell © HHT
Lucy Durneen © HHT
Maggie Gee © HHT
Maria McCann © HHT
Marina Warner © HHT
Margaret Drabble © Murdo Macloud
Salley Vickers © Luke Nugent
Sarah Hosking © John Robertson